# BLOW UP

# BLOW UP

## Ellen Crosby

**SEVERN
HOUSE**

First world edition published in Great Britain and the USA in 2023
by Severn House, an imprint of Canongate Books Ltd,
14 High Street, Edinburgh EH1 1TE.

Trade paperback edition first published in Great Britain and the USA in 2023
by Severn House, an imprint of Canongate Books Ltd.

severnhouse.com

*British Library Cataloguing-in-Publication Data*
A CIP catalogue record for this title is available from the British Library.

ISBN-13: 978-1-4483-0803-3 (cased)
ISBN-13: 978-1-4483-0805-7 (trade paper)
ISBN-13: 978-1-4483-0804-0 (e-book)

*All Severn House titles are printed on acid-free paper.*

Typeset by Palimpsest Book Production Ltd.,
Falkirk, Stirlingshire, Scotland.
Printed and bound in Great Britain by
TJ Books, Padstow, Cornwall.

To Donna Andrews, John Gilstrap, Alan Orloff, and Art Taylor –
my critique group friends and fellow writers, affectionately
known as the Rumpus Writers. Thanks for twelve
amazing years – and counting – of meeting every month
without fail during which we've collectively written
fifty-three books (eighty-five, in total) and more than
a hundred short stories, and won or been nominated for too
many awards to count.

'I am a kind of spy.'

'I mean, it's very subtle and a little embarrassing to me, but I really believe there are things which nobody would see unless I photographed them.'

# PROLOGUE

I was standing on a hilltop surrounded by twenty-two Corinthian columns that had once graced the US Capitol when Quill Russell finally told me the truth about my husband's death – or at least he told me part of the story. What I wasn't going to hear – and this I knew – was a detailed account of what exactly *did* happen. Especially when Quill said Nick's death could never be officially acknowledged because he had been working undercover for the CIA. Nick had left the Agency a few years ago, but *something*, some assignment, had lured him back one last time.

It had been three agonizing weeks since Nick's funeral. Quill and Vicki Russell had been there. Quill had seen the depth of my grief, my heartache, my numb disbelief. He also understood that I hadn't bought the made-up story the American Embassy in Vienna had put together: that Nick had been killed by a hit-and-run driver as he was leaving a bar in the Austrian capital late at night.

I knew Quill had picked this particular place to have our tough, unvarnished conversation partially for its panoramic view of the surrounding countryside but mostly because it was practically guaranteed that on a scorching August midweek afternoon no one else would be here.

The Capitol columns are arranged like a ruined Greek temple with a tumbling waterfall that leads down to a reflecting pool in a peaceful twenty-acre garden known as the National Arboretum. It is among Washington, DC's less well-known tourist attractions, but the Arboretum is a jewel. It is most popular in spring when anyone who knew just how breathtaking it would be made the pilgrimage through one of DC's more blighted, rundown areas to visit it; first for the cherry blossoms and later when the azaleas were flowering. Same thing in autumn when the foliage was at its loveliest. But now, on this late-August day, Quill and I literally had the place to ourselves – the kids were already back in school, summer vacation was over, folks had returned to work. The weather, however, was still hotter than the inside of hell, one of DC's notorious dog days when the hammering heat and withering humidity were so intense you worried that if you stayed outside too long, your insides would liquify.

Right off the bat, Quill told me no one at the CIA could ever admit Nick had been working for them – again – and that was how it had to be. The account the American Embassy had concocted was the official – and *only* – version of what happened. No one had seen the car that struck him. He had been pronounced dead at the scene.

'That's *not true*,' I said. 'You know it, Quill. Someone at the Agency should at least tell me what really happened. You could tell me. I'm his wife.'

'I know, sweetheart, I know. But other people are involved – other officers, people in the field. We can't afford to compromise them – you know that. Or the asset he was supposed to meet.'

'*Supposed* to meet,' I said. 'You mean they never met?'

A rare slip of the tongue for Quill. I caught the flash of surprise in his eyes when he realized he'd just said something I hadn't known. 'No,' he said. 'They didn't.'

'What happened?'

He compressed his lips into a thin line and shook his head. 'Nothing went according to plan. We figure Nick walked into a trap.'

I closed my eyes. I hadn't had a full night's sleep since Nick died, imagining what might have happened to him, especially after what I'd been through the last time. Three years ago, he had disappeared from our home in London – an apparent kidnapping after Crowne Energy, the British oil and gas exploration company he'd been working for, had unexpectedly discovered oil in a poor, remote part of Russia. Nick and his boss, Colin Crowne, were the only two people on the planet who knew the location and details of that reserve, and there were people who would – and did – kill for the information. It was months before I learned the kidnapping had been staged and that Nick was on the run. But in that awful interval, I had mourned my husband's death and it had taken a toll on me.

Now, here we were again, but this time it was for real. My grief cut new wounds over barely healed scar tissue.

A trap, Quill said. Had my husband suffered? Had his death been quick or prolonged?

'Where?'

'In one of the underground tunnels in the city. Those places have been there since the Cold War.'

'So he was murdered? My God, how? By whom?'

Quill took me by my shoulders. I thought he was going to shake me, but he just held me tight. His grip was painful. He looked into my eyes. 'Don't,' he said. 'Just *don't*.'

Which is when I knew.

'It was the Russians,' I said as the realization of what that meant swept over me like a rising panic attack. 'Who else would it be if Nick was involved? And it was Vienna? At least tell me that much.'

Nick spoke fluent Russian thanks to a Russian grandmother. And his former job in Russia with Crowne Energy had been the perfect post for an undercover CIA agent. Also, Vienna, where Nick had been killed, was, among other things, the headquarters of OPEC. The puzzle pieces were starting to fit together. *Of course* it was the Russians.

'I'm sorry,' Quill said.

*Sorry.*

The Russians were known for torture and brutal execution-style deaths. Quill wasn't going to say another word about how Nick died. *Sorry* was bad enough.

'He shouldn't have gone. He shouldn't have done it.'

'Sophie.'

'What?' I asked. But the look in his eyes told me everything. 'He volunteered, didn't he?'

'Yes.' He wrapped me in his arms then and let me cry it out. At one point, he pressed something into my hand. A linen handkerchief. Quill was an old-school gentleman.

I took it and wiped my eyes. After a few minutes, I hiccupped and said, 'There's mascara and eyeliner all over your handkerchief now. And snot.'

He chuckled. 'Keep it. I've got more.'

I hiccupped again and took another swipe at my eyes.

'Nick died a hero,' he added. 'He was a good man, trying to do a good thing.'

And no one could ever know about it. No posthumous award, no American flag folded into tight triangle points after being draped over his coffin and then handed ever so carefully and respectfully to the grieving widow, no nothing.

I wondered what the CIA definition of *a good thing* was.

'Are we going to retaliate for what they did to him?' I asked.

His smile was sad. He clamped an arm around my shoulder and guided me down the steps to the reflecting pool. It was so hot that even the birds had gone silent. Except for the burbling of the stream that ran through a channel in the middle of the steps and emptied into the pool, the silence felt oppressive and eerie. Plus, it was starting to creep me out that no one else was here and we were entirely alone in this huge park. Had the CIA orchestrated *that* as well?

'My need-to-know on this goes only so far,' Quill said to me. 'You know how it is.'

I did. Sensitive compartmented information. If you were supposed to know, you'd know. Nick had explained to me how it worked. No little chats among fellow CIA colleagues around the coffeepot and snack machine in the break room or the cafeteria because you didn't know who else was privy to whatever project you were working on.

But I also knew Quill, a former Secretary of State, hadn't lost his security clearance for a very good reason: he was part of a group of *éminences grises* – graybeards – comprised of individuals whose deep knowledge and decades of experience could help the President, the successors in their jobs, and others in the intelligence, military, or diplomatic world. In short, anyone who sought the advice and expertise of people like Quill when it was their turn to make the hard decisions, which could often mean choosing between bad and worse. So I *knew* Quill knew about Nick. He would have been talking to others in that sacred, secret, need-to-know-only elite circle.

What's more, Nick had been working for Quillen O. Russell & Associates, Quill's high-powered consulting firm, advisor to governments, companies, and nonprofits on global issues involving finance, security, and geopolitical strategic planning. QUORA, as it was known, also fixed 'problems' they couldn't really talk about – which was ostensibly what Nick was doing when he went to Vienna.

So, of course, Quill was the first person I went to – on my knees – and said, *Please. Tell me.* Nick was dead and buried, but I needed to know what had happened to him.

I needed some way to smooth the ragged edges of my grief. I needed closure. The CIA could at least give me that much, couldn't they, after what they had taken from me?

And here we were, the Arboretum in the middle of a sweltering August afternoon.

We had reached the Bonsai and Penjing Museum at the bottom of the hill. The grass was so dry it crackled under our feet.

'I'm going to stick around for a while, check out the bonsai and ikebana,' he said. 'See what's new since they rotate the displays.'

'I didn't know you were into Japanese flower arranging.'

He grinned. 'You'd be surprised.'

Our meeting was over. He didn't want our cars to be seen driving out of here at the same time. On the off chance that anybody was watching.

'Will you let me know if you learn anything new?' I asked.

'If I can.' He bussed me on the cheek and said, 'Take care of yourself. I'll call you soon. Let's have lunch, OK?'

I nodded and turned to go. A few steps down the path to the parking lot, I whirled around to ask him something I'd forgotten.

But he was gone.

As if he'd never been there.


It didn't take long for Quill to invite me to lunch. At the Cosmos Club, no less. Washington, DC's oldest and most erudite club, whose members were men and women who had done something amazing in science, literature, or the arts. During the rare times I'd been invited there, I always wanted to see the awards hall with its walls of photos of the many individuals who'd won Pulitzers, Nobel Prizes, or the Presidential Medal of Freedom.

The Cosmos Club sat on the edge of Embassy Row in a magnificent nineteenth-century Beaux Arts mansion – a relic of 'Old Washington,' with its sumptuous, almost over-the-top decor that could make you believe you were in a European palace in another century.

Over lunch – crab cakes (me) and rack of lamb (Quill) – Quill entertained me with amusing stories of some of the club's more memorable events and illustrious members – they were fiercely private – which I was pretty sure was a distraction until he got around to the real reason he had asked me here. Of course, I thought it had to do with Nick.

He waited until dessert – buttermilk panna cotta with preserved fruit, which we were sharing – before he told me.

'I want to hire you,' he said. 'I want to put together a coffee-table book of photographs of Fernway – the interior, the gardens, the greenhouse, the guesthouse, the pool, all of it – in every season. Aerial shots, too. There's no budget for this project.'

Fernway was his magnificent weekend retreat in Middleburg, a horsey, tweedy village in the heart of Virginia hunt country. Quill and his wife, Victoria, spent most weekends and every holiday there; they were neighbors of my mother and stepfather.

'I'll write the text,' he said and his cheeks unexpectedly turned pink. 'I was planning to include some of the poetry I've written Vicki over the years, excerpts of our love letters, the notes we've left each other.'

In other words, it would be an intensely personal book. I hadn't realized Quill wrote romantic poetry and love letters. I'd only known that he'd written several well-received historical biographies and two books on Russian history.

'I'm flattered you thought of me for this project, but you know I don't do that sort of photography,' I said. 'However, I know people who do and I'll find you someone – a really terrific photographer – who, I promise, will take exactly the kind of photos you want so you'll be thrilled with the final results.'

Because what he wanted were the photos you see in upscale shelter magazines with sweeping views of manicured gardens and sweet interior vignettes that made you feel wistful and a bit envious. Made you wish you lived in that beautiful home, where you just knew from the art on the walls, the antiques, the eclectic furniture, and the intriguing personal items the owners had collected that they lived fascinating fairytale lives.

I'm a photojournalist. Before Nick and I moved to Washington, DC three years ago, we lived in London where I worked for International Press Service, traveling at the drop of a hat to war zones, refugee camps, natural disaster sites, and remote at-the-end-of-the-world places that weren't on anybody's bucket list of must-visit-before-you-die. Before I went anywhere, though, my boss sent me to Scotland for a two-week intensive course in hostile environment training where a team of former British Special Forces operatives taught a bunch of inexperienced and naive journalists such useful skills as basic battlefield triage in case we accidentally ended up in the middle of a firefight or what to do if we were kidnapped. (Rule #1: Try not to find yourself in either of these situations.) I'd photographed the rubble and appalling poverty of post-war Afghanistan, the squalor of migrant camps on the Turkish–Syrian border, searched for the nearly extinct black rhino in Namibia. I'd taken pictures of presidents, prime ministers, dictators, royalty, Nobel Peace Prize winners, the Pope.

Since I'd returned home, I had worked briefly for a DC photo agency owned by a friend of my boss at IPS in London. After I left that job, I'd started freelancing and the work had trickled in slowly but steadily. Even though I was a bit at loose ends just now, photographing Quill and Vicki's home wasn't my idea of much of an assignment.

'You can't turn me down, Sophie,' he said. 'Please don't say no. There's no one else I want but you. The book is for Vicki. I was planning to give it to her next year on Christmas Eve, which is our silver wedding anniversary. So you'd have a whole year to take pictures – it's not a rush job or something you'd have to do over a couple of weeks. Obviously, you'll be very well compensated. You'll also have carte blanche to pick and choose what to photograph as long as the end result shows off Fernway in all four seasons. The only caveat is that this would have to be our secret. I want the book to be a total surprise.'

'What a lovely gift to celebrate twenty-five years of marriage,' I said. 'But I'm sorry, Quill. I'm really not the right person for this project.'

Our eyes met and he flinched when he saw the pain and loss in mine. Nick and I had only made it to twelve years.

'Oh, God, what an ass I am for not considering what you're going through.' He looked stricken. 'I'm so sorry. I was hoping that having a long-term project might keep your mind off things, help you get through a rough time.'

'It's okay. And that's very kind,' I said.

'Look,' he said, 'the real reason I want you is you're so damn good at what you do. I've known you since you were a teenager with your first camera. We're neighbors. Your mom and Harry are good friends of ours. And you know how much Vicki and I have always loved your work, admired it. Been so proud of all your successes.'

In his previous life, Quill had been a well-respected master of diplomacy in getting parties who hated each other's guts to sit down and negotiate over land or political grievances or whatever differences they had. To be honest, I didn't stand a chance with him. Eventually, he talked me into it, although it took until we were finishing our post-dessert espressos and the waiter had set down a small leather folder next to Quill.

'All right,' I said. 'I'll do it.'

'Thank you.' He smiled and pulled something out of his trouser pocket. A single key on a key chain with a jeweled Hamsa attached – the Hand of Fatima, Mohammed's daughter, the Muslim protection symbol meant to keep ghosts and spirits from inhabiting a house. A sign of good luck. He slid it across the table toward me.

'Your house key. And thank you. I'm thrilled you're taking this on. It's going to be a gorgeous book with your photographs.' He reached into the inside pocket of his suit jacket and pulled out two folded pieces of paper that he also handed to me. 'You'll need the code to the alarm; plus, I just so happened to have a check already written out, a down payment so you can start. I'll text you when Vicki's out of town or when I know she won't be at the house. We'll talk regularly and you can keep me updated.'

I put the check and the alarm code in my purse along with the key. That last statement was a complete giveaway. Yes, he wanted me to photograph Fernway because he liked my work, but now he had the perfect excuse for keeping an eye on me. Now he could make sure that I was OK during the first awful grief-stricken year without Nick, that I was holding up, maybe starting to live a little again. Because, truth be told, I think he felt some guilt and even a little responsibility for what had happened since Nick had been working for him.

'You were that certain I'd say yes, were you?' I said. 'I'm that predictable?'

He picked up a piece of chocolate-covered marzipan the waiter had left on a tiny plate next to the bill and popped it into his mouth, as if he were thinking about his answer.

'I wouldn't say you're predictable,' he said. 'But you're a good person with a good heart and I knew you'd do this favor for me. For *us*.'

It wasn't until much later that I wished I'd never said yes that day at lunch. I should have turned him down.

It would have been better for a lot of people – especially Quill – if I had.

# ONE

_October, thirteen months later_

I t was my next-to-last trip to Fernway, driving the fifty miles
from where I lived in Washington, DC to Middleburg to wrap
up taking photos for Quill's book. I had come on an early
Indian summer morning when the Japanese maple that grew near
their backyard patio was such a beautiful flaming shade of red
it almost hurt my eyes and the leaves of the ginkgo trees that
lined both sides of the driveway had turned a raucous, blazing
yellow. The very last pictures, if the weather cooperated, would
be when the ginkgoes dropped their leaves – shedding them all
at once as they always did, turning the dirt-and-gravel drive into
a golden path that looked like the yellow brick road to Oz.
I'd gotten some photos last October, but the light hadn't been
ideal, so I was hoping this year the weather might be more
cooperative.

I had arrived early enough – during what photographers call
'the golden hour' – to get photos of the ginkgoes when they
would be backlit by the early-morning sun, making their leathery
fan-shaped leaves an even deeper, richer shade of gold. Ginkgoes
have always fascinated me because they have been around for
so long – 180 million years, in fact, ever since the Jurassic period
– making them one of the oldest plants on earth and considered
by scientists to be living fossils because in all that time they
haven't changed.

It didn't take me long to get the shots I wanted of the _allée_
of ginkgoes. I pulled out Quill's house key and unlocked the
front door, letting myself in. The first thing that struck me when
I stepped inside was that the alarm wasn't on, though I heard a
beep acknowledging my entrance. Odd. Quill and Vicki were
always so careful about security since the house sat on twenty
acres at the end of a driveway that was at least half a mile long.
It was also surrounded by woods, isolated and extremely private,

which was the reason they'd bought it. Maybe the maids had come and gone and forgotten to reset it. There were no other cars in the driveway, so that was probably what had happened. I'd have to let Quill know, but for now he was in London on business and wouldn't be back until later in the week. I'd set it myself when I left and let him know when I saw him.

The house was Sunday quiet and welcoming as it always was, smelling faintly of lavender, Vicki's favorite fragrance. She grew it herself, a sweeping bank of hardy Provençal lavender that lined one side of the swimming pool and smelled heavenly. After it finished flowering, she dried it and put the pale purple buds in vintage Macao bowls that she scattered throughout the house.

I set down my camera bag on a high-backed chair upholstered in crushed persimmon velvet. The sun streaming in through the front door sidelights made long slanted stripes on the multicolored tribal Persian carpet Quill had brought back from a trip to Iran. I had taken hundreds of photos of every room in this house and by now knew it as intimately as its owners did. There would be a view of the maple and the patio from the library, which doubled as Quill's office when he was here on weekends. I wanted some interior photos looking out through the enormous bay window; I'd take the rest out by the pool.

The library was probably my favorite room, with its pleasant tang of wood smoke and the faint smell – mustiness mingled with a vague vanilla scent – of their many books. Two of the walls held floor-to-ceiling bookcases; there was even a library ladder that slid along a polished brass railing. I knew a lot of the titles by now – biographies, books on history, politics, art, sociology, science, nature, religion, even a few novels, reflecting Quill's and Vicki's wide-ranging interests. They were both bibliophiles, in part because of their careers: his as a diplomat and senior government official and hers as a smart, highly respected journalist who wrote about political campaigns, elections, and the now-unfortunately-controversial subject of voting rights for *The Atlantic*, *The New Yorker*, the *Times*, and the *Journal*. She was also a frequent guest on cable news talk shows. If the books filling the shelves – all of which I knew they'd read – weren't rare or vintage, they were signed by friends who had written them.

A mullioned bay window dominated another wall. Across from it was a large fireplace with a carved oak mantel and a pair of sad-faced greyhound art deco andirons Vicki had found at a flea market in the Cotswolds on their honeymoon.

What caught my attention just now, though, was the briefcase leaning against a paisley-print wing chair that faced the window. Scuffed, well used. Chocolate-brown leather, soft as butter. Expensive. Italian, maybe. An unusual gold-leaf emblem that looked like intricately worked initials in an elaborate design, although I couldn't tell for sure. Good Lord, was Vicki *here*? Was that why the alarm was turned off? I didn't recognize the briefcase as hers, but I knew she had more than one for the many facets of her busy life. Her work, her volunteer and community service projects, managing the finances and upkeep of Fernway and their Georgetown home.

I saw a flash of motion outside and scrambled to move out of view so I couldn't be seen through the window. All that hostile environment training years ago and you would have thought I would have known, or at least *sensed*, someone was here the moment I walked through the front door, especially when the alarm didn't go off. It had been a while since I'd been in a war zone, but this was exactly the kind of carelessness our trainers said got you killed.

I shifted again so I could peek outside to see who was there. It couldn't be Vicki. She was in New York City appearing on all the talk shows about the upcoming midterm elections; Quill, as I said, was in London. Maybe, after all, it was just the pool guy or the gardener, or a maid who had gone outside to tidy up, and I was spooked for no good reason. But where was a car or a truck with a logo on it? Besides, there was that briefcase.

They were in the pool, melded together as if they were one, wrapped around each other and locked in an intimate kiss that seemed to go on forever. And they were naked.

A man and a woman.

The woman was Vicki Russell. The man, whose body was turned at such an angle that I couldn't see his face, was not Quill. Taller, a mane of salt-and-pepper hair. Pale skin, not as muscular or athletically built as Quill. I pulled back, though I was fairly sure Vicki hadn't seen me. Frankly, a bomb probably could have gone off and she wouldn't have noticed. She was too engrossed in that kiss, her arms twined firmly around his neck, pulling him tight into her.

It was early to be going for a swim, although it was warm enough on this unseasonably balmy autumn day and, besides, the pool was heated. I doubted they'd just gotten here, so he'd probably spent the night.

No. He'd *definitely* spent the night.

Good thing I hadn't decided to take photos from the master bedroom, which had a balcony overlooking the patio and the pool. I wouldn't have wanted to walk in to find rumpled sheets and clothes that had been hastily shed and dropped on the floor. Not quite as bad as the yuck reflex of catching your parents having sex, but almost.

I went straight to the foyer, grabbed my gear, and let myself out. No taking photos of the Japanese maple today. I needed to get lost before they spotted me. And what if I hadn't seen *them* and had reset the alarm? Then what? The least of it was probably ruining the surprise Quill and I had kept for just over a year. Vicki would know someone had been here. She'd obviously parked in the garage; maybe he had, too. It was big enough for four cars.

So now I knew about an affair that – just taking a wild guess here – hadn't been going on since yesterday. Quill adored Vicki and I'd always thought she felt the same about him, that theirs was a marriage based on a love that had only grown deeper and stronger over the quarter century they'd been together, their twenty-year age difference notwithstanding. One of the rare Washington love-matches that endured, restored your faith that two people could still be happily married in a city known for playing hardball with relationships and often destroying them. People talked about the Russells, wrote about their obvious love and devotion to each other in the lifestyle section of the paper when a photo of them at a party or a gala or a big-ticket fundraiser popped up. Besides, you could see it in their eyes, the way they looked at each other.

I pulled out of the circular drive in front of the house, checking the rearview mirror just in case I'd see a man – or woman – in a bathrobe or wrapped in a beach towel, hands on hips, squinting at my car, wondering who the hell *that* was. Though Vicki, of course, would know. Fortunately, there was no one. By the time I reached the main road, Route 50, or Mosby's Highway as it was called out here, I didn't know if I felt more anger or revulsion or just sadness.

How could Vicki do that to Quill? What a sham, what a mockery this book project – Quill's labor of love – had just become. His tribute to their marriage that had lasted a quarter of a century: photos of the home they'd made together.

And now what was I supposed to do?

Tell Quill? Confront Vicki?

I was driving way too fast – nearly sixty – so I hit the brakes as I approached the village of Middleburg, where the speed limit slowed to twenty-five.

Vicki's affair was none of my business, though I wished I could unsee what I'd just seen.

What I needed to do – the only thing I *could* do – was keep my mouth shut and just finish the damn job.

# TWO

What I wanted to do was drive fifty miles back to DC, take a hot shower until I felt really clean, and gargle with bleach. Plus, practice my best poker face for when I saw Quill later this week and we talked about wrapping up the book project so he could get everything to the printer. As he had told me that day at lunch, he was sparing no expense, hiring an editor to proof the text and getting professional help with laying out the photos. Thick luxurious paper with a special fingerprint-resistant coating. Lay-flat binding, of course. Tooled leather cover – he'd chosen burgundy – with *Fernway* and the date of their twenty-fifth anniversary embossed in gold.

What I *didn't* want to do was contemplate whether Vicki's affair was so serious she might be considering asking Quill for a divorce. That scene in the pool didn't look like a casual hookup or a wanton fling – especially because I hadn't seen them leaving some no-tell motel together. She'd brought him to their *home*.

Fernway. Vicki and Quill chose the name when they bought the house, an anglicized version of a German word – *Fernweh* – that described an ache to get away and travel to a distant place, something even stronger than wanderlust. The two of them had done a lot of far-flung traveling during their marriage – together and separately for their respective careers. Quill once said that there were only a few countries on earth he hadn't visited and that he intended to rectify that situation when he eventually retired. One year for his birthday, Vicki bought him a beautiful and very expensive floor globe that also could be illuminated. I'd seen it in the library just this morning. A few months ago, I'd come by one evening and photographed it when it was lit from within, the continents and their countries glowing with a serene otherworldly light, the oceans dark and subdued.

I drove through Middleburg with its main street named for George Washington, who had been a friend of the town's founder. The only traffic light was at the intersection of Washington and

Madison (yes, named for James). If you didn't have to stop at that light, it took roughly forty-five seconds to drive from one end of town to the other. A minute and a half, give or take, if you moseyed so you could cast an eye at the charming shops, cafés, art galleries, and antique stores, many with horse-themed names. Half a mile west of town, I turned on to the winding country road where my mother and Harry lived.

I adore my stepfather who brought Mom and me to Virginia after he married my mother when I was fourteen, moving us from a cramped walkup in Queens to Mayfield, the two-hundred-acre horse farm that had been in the Wyatt family since colonial days. Harry made sure I knew he felt the same about me and that he loved me every bit as much as he loved Tommy and Lexie, my half-siblings, even though he and I weren't related by blood. I can't say the same about my relationship with my mother, which is – to put the best face on it – strained, because I am the in-her-face reminder of a mistake she made that changed the trajectory of her life forever. She was nineteen. I was *an accident.* All you have to do is look at me and my blonde, blue-eyed half-brother and half-sister who look like Ralph Lauren models and you wonder if I'm the Hispanic maid's kid or whether Mom and Harry adopted me. Dark, glossy chestnut-brown hair, dark-brown eyes flecked with black, skin the color of a caramel latte.

I was conceived during my mother's junior year abroad in Madrid on a reckless and, most likely, alcohol-fueled night when she got careless and went too far with Antonio Medina, a tall, dark, and dangerously handsome soccer player for Real Madrid. Later, when he became one of Spain's best-known and wildly popular athletes, there were posters and magazine covers and the usual gossip tabloids, often with some stunning creature on his arm who was not my mother. I devoured everything I could read about him, hungry to know who he was and what he was like. One look in his eyes – we had the *exact* same eyes – and I knew I was his daughter.

I came along seven and a half months after the hastily arranged Spanish wedding and Mom had left school. By the time I was two, she was sick of waiting for my father to come home from practice or a game, as well as dealing with the loneliness and isolation of his long road trips in a country that had become

increasingly alien to her. So one day, when he was out of town
on tour, she packed our things and moved us home to the US. I
never saw my father again, except on the Eurosport television
channels or the Internet when Mom wasn't around to catch me
watching. By the time we moved to Middleburg, I was certain
he had completely forgotten my existence.

After we left Spain, we turned up on my grandparents' doorstep
in Connecticut and my parents' marriage was over. Devout
Catholic that she was, Mom even got it annulled. I found out by
chance when I was looking among her papers for my Spanish
birth certificate and the document proving I was an American
citizen. For a long time, I just sat there on the floor of her clothes
closet, stunned and hurt – and angry. Her marriage to my father
was null and void – as if it had never happened – at least in the
eyes of the Catholic Church. So what did that make *me*?

When I was fourteen, Antonio Medina was killed in a motor-
cycle accident. The usual. Driving too fast on a narrow, twisting
road through the Sierra de Guadarrama mountains outside
Madrid, blood-alcohol high enough to be an IQ score. No guard-
rail. They found his body and that of his female companion – one
of Spain's top fashion models – at the bottom of a ravine. Mom
told me about it, nursing a very large Scotch.

Which wasn't her first.

We did not discuss my father ever again.


Ella, Harry and Mom's sweet black Labrador Retriever, greeted
me as I opened the front door to Mayfield, her tail thumping as
she put her nearly white muzzle in my hand and waited for me
to scratch her head. I leaned over and crooned in her ear that I
missed her all the time. More tail-thumping.

I love Mayfield. Although I didn't live here for very long, it
will always be home, the place where I feel as if I grew up.
Where I made my two closest friends-for-life, fell in love for the
first time, had my heart badly broken by the same boy, and
learned a few hard truths that knocked me around but also made
me stronger. Nick and I were married at Mayfield, a beautiful
spring outdoor wedding in the garden.

'Sophie? Is that you?' My mother's voice, light and high-
pitched, carried out to the foyer.

'Yes, it's me.'

'Oh.' The faintest note of disapproval. 'I'm in the kitchen.'

My mother liked her life to have neat, precise edges. She liked predictability, planning, and order. She disliked anything sprung on her at the last moment, or, God forbid, spontaneity.

We could not be more different.

'I didn't expect you for another hour,' she called.

Me neither, but I wasn't about to tell her that I'd just fled Fernway after catching Vicki and some stranger naked and practically having sex in the Russells' swimming pool.

'There wasn't much traffic driving out here.'

She was sitting at the oak trestle table where we always ate, her planner lying open in front of her and a dark-blue zippered leather folio, thick with papers, next to it. I knew what was in that folio: documents, correspondence, and bills pertaining to the estate of my grandfather, Charles Lord. Since Chappy died four months ago in June – eleven months to the day after Nick died – I'd watched that folder grow thicker and thicker.

Chappy had collapsed in his photography studio, an old barn my stepfather had renovated for him here at Mayfield after my mother finally persuaded her elderly father he shouldn't be living on his own in Connecticut anymore. I had been the one to find him that day, stopping by the house after another session at Fernway. I'd gone straight to the barn where I knew he'd be.

He was lying on the floor next to the desk where he did his photo editing, unconscious, his breathing shallow and thready. I had no idea how long he'd been there – he was just barely holding on. I called nine-one-one and moved him on to his side, tilting his head so he could continue to breathe. When I took his hand and leaned down to whisper in his ear that I loved him very much, I felt the faintest pressure on my fingers, so I knew he'd heard me. But by the time Mom and Harry arrived, followed almost immediately by the paramedics and firefighters, he was gone.

It was a shock. Except it wasn't – his health had been fragile for a while. Although he had been buried in Connecticut next to my grandmother, Nonna Gina, the funeral had been here in Virginia at St Michael the Archangel, the Catholic church in Middleburg, because my mother incorrectly and naively thought it would be more private further away from New York City.

Charles Lord had been one of the most sought-after celebrity and fashion photographers in his day, including a number of years during which he worked for Magnum, the legendary agency founded by Henri Cartier-Bresson and a group of his equally influential photographer friends after World War II. My grandfather's death made national and international news: we had been bombarded by press calls and requests for interviews until Harry finally got someone from the public relations department at Magnum to take care of the media and give us some privacy to grieve and mourn Chappy's death.

Eventually, the intense press interest faded. Now my mother, as executrix, was slogging through the paperwork and headaches that came with settling my grandfather's complex, substantial estate.

She looked up over a pair of bright-red reading half-glasses as I walked into the kitchen. 'Hello, darling. I just ground some beans and made another pot of coffee. Hazelnut and French roast. Help yourself.'

She tilted her face and leaned toward me so I could kiss her cheek.

'Thanks, Mom, it smells great.' I got a mug out of a cabinet and poured myself a cup of coffee.

'Sweetie, could you refill mine, too, while you're there? Please?' She held out her mug without looking at me, preoccupied with something in her planner.

'Sure.' I did and set it next to her on the table.

She still looked impossibly young with her shoulder-length blonde hair done up in a messy bun and a few tendrils framing her face. Her makeup just right, simple gold hoop earrings, the enormous diamond rock Harry had given her glittering on her left hand along with her diamond eternity ring. Faded jeans, perfectly pressed white Oxford blouse, unbuttoned so I could see the heavy gold chain she always wore, barefoot, perfect pedicure to go with the perfect manicure. She was beautiful.

I sat down and flicked a glance at the leather folio. 'What are you working on?'

She looked pained. 'I'm still trying to close some of your grandfather's accounts. And there's so much correspondence to take care of, writing to people he worked with all over the world.'

'At least Isabella is making good progress with the photo inventory,' I said. 'The last time I was out here, she thought she might finish by the end of this week or early next week at the latest.'

'You're an angel to help her out. You didn't need to, you know. It's Knox's project. We're out of it completely.'

'I don't mind. It helped Isabella speed up the process of going through everything. Besides, I know more about Chap's work than she does.'

'I know you do. That's why I don't understand the reason your grandfather did what he did. We're his *family*.'

'Mom. Come on. We have to let it go. It's what Chap wanted.'

'He might have told us.'

What she meant was that he might have told *her*. His daughter.

When Chappy moved down here a year ago, Mom and Harry had his entire collection of photos, negatives, slides, contact sheets, and all his files brought to Mayfield. The prints and contact sheets were stored in archival boxes on rows of metal shelves in the barn, the negatives were in sleeves in zippered binders, also on shelves, and the entire barn was now carefully climate-controlled, thanks to Harry. He'd also installed a back-up generator. Chap's digital photos – the ones he hadn't printed out – were on hard drives in the guest cottage where he'd been living.

After he died, Mom had contacted his lawyer in Connecticut to ask about her father's will. To which he had replied, 'What will?'

Eventually, we found it – or *a* will – in the top drawer of the bedside table in his bedroom in the guest house, tucked into the front of Nonna Gina's well-worn *Daily Missal*.

Handwritten. No notary, no legalese, no nothing that looked official.

Sam Constantine, our family lawyer, told us that holographic wills – handwritten wills – were valid in the Commonwealth of Virginia as long as the document was in one person's handwriting and it had been signed and witnessed by two people who were not beneficiaries or related to the decedent.

It was and it had. So Chappy's will was legal.

If the will had been a surprise, his bequests – or bequest – had been an even bigger shock. Charles Lord had left his entire estate to the Connecticut Institute of Fine Arts, a small, relatively new, and mostly unknown school with an enrollment of just over 400 students. He also laid out conditions that any money from the sale of his photographs was to be used to establish what he intended would turn CIFA into the premier school in the country offering undergraduate and graduate degrees in photography, photojournalism, and digital media. What was not sold of his vast collection of photographs Chappy wanted kept in his home in West Redding, Connecticut, which he directed should be turned into a combination study center and art gallery managed by CIFA. There, photos taken by its students as well as exhibitions by other photographers were to be displayed on a regular basis. Last but not least, he wanted every CIFA student to attend school on a full scholarship. The complete package, all expenses paid, no debt hanging over your head once you graduated.

The only other stipulation in his will had been that all of his camera equipment would go to me. Hasselblads. Nikons. Prime lenses with really good glass that I couldn't possibly afford. His lighting equipment. All of it.

I met Dr Knox Porter, the young, hip-looking director of the Connecticut Institute of Fine Arts, in the paneled book-lined conference room of Sam Constantine's law firm two weeks after Chappy died. Since I was the only other beneficiary of the will, Sam, Mom, and Harry had wanted me there when it was read to Knox.

Although he had acted appropriately surprised, humbled, and grateful when Sam read the will aloud to all of us, I've photo-graphed enough people in my life to know when someone's faking it. Knox's tell had been a very slight twitch in one corner of his mouth.

He already knew.

My mother had smiled her most engaging smile at Knox and congratulated him, but I knew she was still getting over the shock and disappointment of Chappy's decision: that someone other than his family would inherit her father's estate. *All of it.*

'I promise you, Mrs Wyatt,' Knox had said to her, 'that we will be good stewards of Charles's generous gift and that we are incredibly grateful to him for entrusting us to carry out his wishes in a way that will honor his legacy. It goes without saying that we fully intend to keep you informed of our plans.'

The penny dropped and I'd said, 'Wait a minute. Are you saying you already *have* plans?'

There had been the tiniest hesitation before he'd nodded. '*Preliminary* plans.'

Sam had jumped right in. 'In other words, you knew about the will, Doctor Porter. Before today.'

Knox hadn't flinched. 'Yes. Charles made me aware of it before he moved to Virginia. I'm grateful that he did because it allowed me to express how honored we were by his incredible generosity . . . and also to ask him for as much guidance and input as he could offer about how he envisioned the future of CIFA.'

'Doctor Porter,' Sam had said, 'as Caroline Wyatt's attorney, I have to ask if you were aware of Charles Lord being influenced or perhaps coerced into drawing up a handwritten will without benefit of counsel? Especially because your school is the sole beneficiary of that will, with the exception of Mr Lord's camera equipment.'

'That did not happen, Mr Constantine. I assure you.'

'And you know this, perhaps, because you were present when Mr Lord wrote that will?' Sam had asked.

'I was.'

My mother's gasp was audible. Harry reached for her hand and squeezed it. She pressed her lips together and I knew she was trying not to blurt out something she'd regret saying. But if she'd been upset before, she was angry now.

Sam wasn't too happy, either, and he still had the floor.

'So not only did Charles Lord tell you about the will, but he showed it to you. Correct? Meaning, as you stated, that today is not the first time you've seen it. Also correct?' He had shifted to his courtroom witness-questioning voice. When the witness was representing the other side.

'Yes. Correct on both counts.'

'Did you pressure Charles Lord – directly or indirectly – to leave his entire estate to your school?'

'I did *not*. Charles *wanted* me to be there when he wrote out his will. It was entirely his decision and a huge surprise to me when he told me what his intention was.'

'Who were the two witnesses?' Sam had tapped the paper with the end of his pen.

'We were in a restaurant,' Knox had said. 'A waiter and a manager acted as witnesses.'

A restaurant. I'd caught Harry's eye. That sounded *exactly* like Chappy. At least he hadn't written the will on a cocktail napkin.

Knox had reached down, picking up a worn backpack that looked as if he might have circumnavigated the globe with it, and pulled out a fat legal folder, which he turned so we could read the writing on the ledger. *Charles T. Lord School of Photography and Photojournalism* in thick black marker. He'd slid it over to Harry, Mom, and me.

The four-page document on top outlined general plans for the new school. But what Knox had wanted us to see was immediately obvious: not only had Chappy read the paper, but there were extensive margin notes and comments throughout in his familiar angular handwriting. Lots of exclamation marks. Yep, Chappy definitely was on board with this project – his legacy.

No one had put a gun to his head and made him do it.

'All right; now, what's next?' Harry had asked Knox.

Knox clearly had thought this through. He most definitely had a plan.

'Charles's collection of photographs – by his own estimation – numbered around a hundred and sixty thousand photos, slides, negatives, and digital images,' he'd said. 'It will take years to catalog all of them, as I'm sure you can imagine. And as Mr Constantine will confirm, we don't have that kind of time before we're required by law to settle the estate. What we've decided is to have someone come to Virginia to do a rough inventory of his collection. Pull out the photos that are obviously valuable, some of which we'll need to sell in order to finance setting up the school and, honestly, just to pay for maintaining his extremely large collection. Storage. Paying whoever will go through every picture, slide, negative, and computer image and curate these images. The gallery costs of exhibiting them. It's a wonderful bequest, but since there's no endowment to pay for these expenses, we need to finance the costs somehow.'

My mother had looked dazed and Harry had said, 'When is this person coming to Mayfield to do your inventory?'

'We were hoping next week,' he'd said. 'Her name is Isabella Filippova. *Doctor* Isabella Filippova. She's very good and I promise she'll work quickly. But she'll need unrestricted access to Charles's photo collection as well as his notes, diaries, and papers.'

'We'll arrange that,' Sam told him in a tight voice.

'What about the exhibition?' I'd asked.

Knox had given me a blank look and said, 'What exhibition?'

Which was when he found out that Chap had already committed to loaning a collection of his photos to the Dupont Underground, an avant-garde arts center in downtown Washington, for an exhibition of edgy never-seen-before photos of celebrities and fashion models. The exhibition would be called *Out of the Public Eye: Exposing the Unknown Side of Charles Lord*. The word 'eye' was shaped like a startled wide-awake eye, the expression of someone who looked shocked and a bit scandalized because of the content of the photos. Sensuous, sexy – a bit erotic. It had been scheduled to open in September, but after Chappy died, the date had been pushed back to just before Thanksgiving.

We had worked it out then and there that I would be the liaison between Darius Zahiri, the director of the Dupont Underground, and Isabella Filippova to make sure the photos were delivered in time for the exhibition. The arrangement hadn't set too well with Isabella when she arrived and discovered that I intended to remove thirty-five of Chappy's photos – all originals because the negatives and any copies had been destroyed – so the Underground could have them for two months. Also that I needed them fairly quickly. So the quid pro quo to make things go more smoothly was that I had begun coming out to Mayfield to help her on weekends. After my visit with my mother today, I planned to drop by the barn to check in with her and remind her that I needed the photos for Darius by the end of the week whether she was finished with the inventory or not.

'Are you here to pick up the photos for the Underground exhibition today?' my mother asked me now as we sat together drinking coffee.

'Not today. Isabella asked if she can have them for a few more days before she surrenders them. She wants to make digital copies of everything I'm taking, and she hasn't gotten around to it yet because she's been so busy with everything else. I figured I'd give her another nudge, though. Darius is impatient because he's agreed to have them framed since Chap didn't manage to get that done. And he needs time for that.'

'You drove all the way from DC to Middleburg just to nudge Isabella?' My mother glanced at her watch. 'You could have called or texted her.'

'I had to drop something off for a client who lives out here,' I said. 'Plus, it gave me a chance to see you and Harry. I know it's been tough since Chap died, Mom. I wanted to see how you're doing.'

Well, most of that was true. I'd kept my word to Quill: no one knew about the book project and how often I was really out here, not even Harry and my mother.

She looked me over with a critical eye and I knew what was coming next. 'This early in the morning?' She clicked her tongue against her teeth. 'You're *always* working these days, Sophie. You never stop. And you've lost weight.'

'Mom.'

'What? Don't give me that look.'

'I'm fine.'

'You're *not*. It's been over a year now. You ought to start getting out again. You can't work all the time; it's not good for you.'

'*Mom*. Please.'

She set down her coffee cup, folded her hands, and leaned across the table so she was looking me in the eye. 'When was the last time you went out somewhere? I mean with another person. Dinner. A movie. A drink. Anything.'

Grocery shopping evenings at the Safeway at 17th and Corcoran with Max Katzer, my downstairs neighbor who was in his sixties, probably didn't count.

'I'm going out tonight,' I said.

She sat up, surprised. 'Oh? Really?'

'Yes. I'm meeting Jack and we're going for a run since he's training for the Marine Corps Marathon. Then we're going out for dinner.'

'Sophie, he's a *priest*. It's not the same thing.'

'It's dinner and I'm going out in the evening with another person.'

She gave me the 'nice try' look. 'It's like a date with your brother. Look, Jack's a good person. But he is already rather committed, you know? To the *Church*. Though I did always think you two were so good together when you were dating.' She paused and added, 'I'd even hoped . . .'

I cut her off. 'Don't. It wasn't meant to be. Besides, I met Nick.'

'I know that, sweetie. I'm sorry. I just want you to be happy again.'

'I was happy with Nick.'

'Sophie. I know. Look, you're young and you have so much of your life ahead of you. You'll meet someone, I'm sure of it. Look at Harry and me. Just give it time.'

I got up and rinsed out my coffee cup. My mother's voice, what she was saying, sounded like fingernails on a blackboard, setting every one of my nerves on fire. 'I should go. I heard a car drive by, so I think Isabella just got here.'

'She'll be at the barn. She's finished with everything at the cottage.'

'Thanks.'

'And give Jack my love,' she called when I was scratching Ella behind the ears on my way out the door. 'Tell him not to be a stranger. I haven't seen him in ages. Why don't you bring him to dinner one of these days?'

'I'll ask him,' I said.

But I wouldn't. Because my mother didn't just want to see Jack for dinner. She wanted to find out if there was still any chemistry between the two of us. We had dated for years until he told me he'd decided to become a priest and was leaving to study in Rome with the Jesuits. I'd been devastated, caught completely off guard. Getting over him had been rough.

I drove over to the barn and had a quick conversation with Isabella, who told me she planned to be finished with inventorying Chappy's photo collection by the end of the week and that she'd call or text when I could come by and get the Dupont Underground photographs. On the trip home, I thought again about Vicki and Quill Russell and wondered what was going to happen to them – to their marriage – if Quill found out about her affair.

I also thought about Jack O'Hara and wished my mother hadn't stirred up old memories.

They say you don't die from a broken heart. You only wish you did. Nick had filled the void in my life after Jack left, and I had loved him more than anything in the world. Now Nick was gone, too.

My mother said more than a year had passed since Nick died, but it had been the longest year of my life. I wasn't ready to 'get out there again' as she wanted me to do.

Queen Elizabeth II once famously said that grief is the price you pay for love.

She was right.

# THREE

The story about Jack and me is complicated.

We dated in high school and we'd been in love, but it was high school and neither one of us talked about forever and ever. When we left for college – Fordham, him, George Washington University, me – I knew he saw other girls just as he knew I went out with other guys. But the summer between our junior and senior years of college, when we were both back home again, something clicked. Suddenly, we were inseparable, and it was *serious*.

Or at least I thought it was until he came home after graduation a year later and told me he'd decided to become a priest. A Jesuit. And that he was leaving for Rome in two weeks. It felt like the bottom had just dropped out of my life.

The first person I told was Grace Lowe, my best friend who had gone to St Michael the Archangel High School in Middleburg with Jack and me. She'd been as stunned as I was.

'I'm so sorry, Soph,' she said. 'I thought you two might . . . I mean, you were . . . especially after last summer.'

'Yeah, me, too.'

'Oh, honey.' She'd hugged me and let me cry it out. 'I don't get it. He's so gorgeous and so damned good-looking in that dreamy dark-Irish way. The two of you were so *good* together. When he becomes a priest, he's got to take a vow of *celibacy*. He's going to be another Father What-a-Waste.'

Which is what we'd called all the good-looking young priests who taught at St Mike's.

I didn't tell Grace that Jack might have to become celibate but he wasn't a virgin. I knew that for a fact because that last white-hot summer we'd been together, we'd spent a night together and we'd had sex.

What had happened that night hung in the air between us thick as smoke after he told me he was leaving for Rome. So, on his last day home, he had taken me out to Sky Meadow Park where we walked and talked until the light faded. When we finally stopped to sit down, the trees and bushes had morphed into dark silhouettes against a pale blue-white sky and the substantial darker outline of the low-slung Blue Ridge Mountains.

We sat side by side on an old log, shoulders touching, watching the sun set the sky on fire as it started to drop behind the mountains. And we still hadn't had the conversation we needed to have.

He started it. Leaning forward, forearms resting on his lap, hands clasped as though he were praying, eyes fixed firmly on the view. I glanced at his handsome profile and felt that my heart was going to break in two.

'Look, me becoming a priest doesn't change the fact that I still love you, Sophie. You know that, right?' he'd said. 'It's just a different kind of love now.'

I rested my head on his shoulder. A platonic relationship. That was what he was offering, all we could have. Telling me now that it would be enough for him.

He had to know that I was still in love with him, realize how hard it was for me to let him go.

'I know.' I hated that my voice sounded as though I was fighting for control. 'And I love you, too. I just wish you didn't have to leave.'

'I don't *have* to. But I *want* to. I've been thinking about this – discerning it – most of this last year. I really believe I've been called to serve God and that's my vocation. What my life should be about.'

I finally said it. 'What about that night?'

He had prepared his answer. 'I'll never forget it. I mean, how could I? Especially because by choosing the priesthood I *know* what I'm giving up. *Understand* what I won't have. Marriage. A wife. Children. A family.'

After a moment, I said, 'Do you regret it?'

He knew I was talking about having sex, not giving up having a family. 'No, I don't. Do you?'

'No.'

When he didn't say anything else and I didn't think I could bear any longer the aching silence between us, except for the sound of my heart breaking into hundreds of tiny shards, I stood and pulled him up with me.

'It's going to be dark soon. We ought to be getting home.'

On the way back to the car, he said, 'I'm going to miss you – you know that, don't you? We'll stay in touch, OK? Once I'm settled, come visit me in Rome. I'll know my way around so I can show you the sites. We'll have fun.'

'Sure,' I said, 'that sounds great.'

He draped an arm around my shoulder and pulled me to him. 'Come on. This isn't a funeral. We'll still be close, Soph; we've known each other too long, too well. This isn't going to change our friendship.'

'I understand,' I said and made sure I sounded chipper and upbeat this time, even though I didn't understand at all. Because he was wrong. What he was doing changed everything.

I never did go to Rome.

And then I met Nick and fell in love again. Before long, we got married and moved to London just as Jack came home from Rome. His ordination was one year later at Holy Trinity Church in Georgetown. I was on assignment in Afghanistan for International Press Service and, well, *Afghanistan*, so it was out of the question that I could leave and fly home to be there. I hoped he'd understand.

He wrote and told me he did.

Grace sent photos, of course. She also sent pictures of Jack vested for his first Mass. Green cassock because it was Ordinary Time in the Catholic Church, but also green, the color of hope. If Hollywood ever wanted the most perfect-looking, devastatingly handsome priest since Richard Chamberlain played the heart-breaking Father Ralph de Bricassart in *The Thorn Birds*, they needed to look no further than Father John Patrick O'Hara.

Grace was also the one who pushed me to get back in touch with him after I moved home from London three years ago. When Nick died, Jack said his funeral Mass at St Michael the Archangel. Don't ask me how I got through it because I still don't know.

Full circle. Life and death. Alpha and omega. Back then, a couple of teenagers who fell in love until one of them ended it. Now, a priest and a widow.

Maybe because we were nearly twenty years older, maybe because of everything we'd each been through during those two decades, we grew close again. Figured out how our relationship from long ago could evolve into a friendship that worked for who we were now.

After the funeral, Jack began checking on me regularly. We started seeing each other more often. Occasionally, I wondered if I wasn't leaning on him too much, relying on him more now that Nick was gone. Then I'd forget about it – our dinners, the occasional movie, going for a run together. It was all harmless stuff, two old friends hanging out.

We'd figured out how to make it work and that was enough for me.

My photography studio, a sweet ivy-covered red-brick carriage house in the alley behind my home, has become my sanctuary, my refuge ever since Nick died. It is a few paces from the row house where I live on the 1800 block of S Street, Northwest, a pretty tree-lined street of Victorians and Greek Revival homes built in the late 1800s and early 1900s. The neighborhood sits nicely on the fringe of Dupont Circle in downtown DC, near enough that I can walk to restaurants, a grocery store, a dry cleaner, and a Metro stop, but quiet enough that I don't feel as if I'm living in the middle of a city. There are at least half a dozen embassies of countries that would probably have to spend their entire gross national product if they wanted one of the opulent palaces uptown on Embassy Row; instead, they are ensconced in our little neighborhood. It also means we have excellent security with so many diplomats close by. As a result, I've always felt safe here despite DC's post-pandemic newly revived reputation as a city of out-of-control violent crime.

When I got home from Middleburg, I went, as I usually do, straight to my studio to make a cup of peppermint tea and download my photos. I spent an hour or so editing the ginkgo pictures and then turned to the project that had been occupying much of my time for more than a year: documenting the lives of DC's homeless population – especially the city's ongoing efforts to literally bulldoze out of existence the many tent camps that had sprung up under bridges and in out-of-the-way places. Some of them were on public land, which meant that property fell under the jurisdiction of the National Park Service rather than the DC government. Although there were eviction notices posted everywhere warning of what was to come, every single time a group of DHS or Park Service employees in white hazmat suits and gloves showed up with bulldozers and garbage trucks, there were always holdouts who had remained behind because they had no place else to go. The clearing-out was swift, ruthless, and harsh, and no one whose tent or cardboard lean-to had been bull-dozed out of existence ever ended up moving into a shelter, which was what the mayor promised would happen. Instead, the homeless – who were homeless all over again – would disappear, scattering like a flock of startled birds until they alighted somewhere else: another camp, leaving town, or just vanishing altogether.

After an hour of editing those photos, I got up to walk around, clear my head, and wonder for the millionth time how in such a wealthy country as America so many people could be so marginalized and living in such poverty. I never had any answers, but I was done with editing. If I continued, I'd just want to throw something or else cry.

There was one more project, though, before I left to meet Jack – something no one knew about, and it involved Nick. Even though no one had told me what he had been doing in Vienna, I hadn't stopped trying to find out. For the last year, I'd been trawling the Internet, setting up a search for any information that contained the keywords *Vienna*, *oil*, and *Russia*, which seemed like a good place to start given his native-speaking fluency in Russian and his previous job with Crowne Energy. I was nearly one hundred percent certain that his trip had something to do with Russia *and* oil – especially because Vienna was OPEC headquarters. But that was all I had to go on and it was just a guess.

That's when I played a mind game I call *if only* – even though I knew better because it didn't do me one bit of good.

If only I'd asked Nick more questions, probed more. What was so urgent that all of a sudden he had to dash off to Vienna? And, more importantly, why hadn't I asked if this trip had some-thing to do with the Agency? Had he agreed to work for them again? Not full-time, mind you – he promised me he was out – but maybe this had been a special request. I doubted he would have told me the truth – which is when I stop my little game and try not to beat myself up about things I can never know. I knock off playing *if only*. Covert is covert. You keep your mouth shut about what you're really doing. You've signed papers swearing you'll do so. Plus, they tell you that if you blab, you could be looking at time in Leavenworth, and they're not kidding.

Still, he'd gone to Vienna. Nicknamed the City of Dreams, a place of magnificent castles and palaces with sumptuous gardens, charming cafés, the beautiful blue Danube, Strauss waltzes, and Lipizzaner horses that performed their dazzling airs above the ground. But it was also a city of spies. A place of shadows and whispers, a favorite meeting spot between the Americans and the Soviets during the Cold War. Some of the subterfuge took place in the catacomb-like warren of underground tunnels and hideouts that crisscrossed the city where Quill told me Nick's body had been discovered.

For the hell of it, I added *CIA* to a second search, though I figured that would go nowhere. Every so often, I got a hit, but nothing that seemed promising. Just lots of dead ends. But now as I checked my email and scrolled through the cascade of unsolicited ads, bills, professional mailing lists, and the rare note from someone I wanted to hear from, I found an 'as it happens' alert, a news update for something that contained my search words – that is, all but *CIA*. I clicked on the link, which took me to a story in yesterday's *Washington Tribune* that I'd missed when I'd read the paper. No wonder. What I was looking for was buried – a couple of lines – in a much longer piece about cybersecurity and American efforts to track down hackers who were increasingly making inroads into computer systems connected to our power grid, the water supply, and the nine-one-one emergency network.

> . . . *the US government has also been investigating a group of hackers who call themselves Möbius Strip and have been attempting to breach the security wall of the computer systems of major oil companies including ExxonMobil, Chevron, and ConocoPhillips. It has long been suspected that the Russian government is funding Möbius Strip and that the real target is OPEC. The other efforts are merely 'training exercises.' Last year the US came close to learning*

*the identity of Möbius Strip at a prearranged meeting in Vienna; however, the encounter was ultimately sabotaged and the group remains elusive and at large.*

I'd skimmed the first few paragraphs of the story yesterday, but I hadn't read the whole article. Nick wasn't an expert in cybersecurity: he was a geophysicist. And even though no one expected Crowne Energy to find oil in the poor and politically unstable Russian province of Abadistan – also a thoroughfare for drugs entering the country from Afghanistan and Pakistan – they *did* find a rich oil reserve.

Meaning Colin Crowne, owner of Crowne Energy, and Nick suddenly had a secret worth millions, if not billions, of dollars that was worth killing for. Of course, the Russian mafia learned of it instantly, and soon after that Colin's body was found floating in the Danube River. In Vienna. So Nick, who had the only copy of well logs that spelled out exactly where the discovery had been made, went on the run. Eventually, his CIA cover was blown, his covert days were over, and he'd been PNG'd from Russia for good.

Declared *persona non grata.*

During those awful months when he was gone, I decided to move home from London to Washington, where I was given the name of a contact I could reach out to if I needed someone: Napoleon Duval. Conversely, if I heard from Nick – since everyone was looking for him, from the CIA to MI6 to the Russians – I was supposed to report that information to Duval. Not surprisingly, I didn't hear from Duval when Nick died – more of the 'we can't acknowledge this ever happened' family-friendly way of conducting the spy business – but I'd kept his number, which I hoped he hadn't changed.

I'd gotten as much information out of Quill as he was willing to share; maybe Duval knew another piece of the puzzle since he was Deputy Director of the National Counterterrorism Task Force and probably knew a different constellation of people in the intelligence world. In fact, as near as I could tell, Duval's reach was extensive and he could stick his finger into any pie that interested him.

I still had his contact information in my phone. Text or phone call?

Phone call.

I left a voicemail and kept it as bland and generic as possible. 'Hi, it's Sophie Medina. I know it's been a while, but I'd like to talk to you. Please give me a call when you get this. You know how to reach me.' I hesitated and then added, 'I really hope you'll be in touch.'

He'd know why I was calling. But he was also a by-the-book kind of guy, and no one needed to tell him, *Don't talk to the wife.*

Either I'd hear from him or I wouldn't.

Right now, I figured it could go either way.

# FOUR

Father John Patrick O'Hara, S.J., lived at Gloria House, which overlooked Stanton Park on the edge of Capitol Hill. The house had gotten its name from the Jesuit motto: *Ad majorem Dei gloriam.* For the greater glory of God. Once upon a time, it had been someone's grand nineteenth-century mansion, but it had been added on to and updated so many times over the years that it now had a kludgy architectural style all its own that was vaguely Victorian. The Jesuits bought the four-story red-brick building after they built Georgetown Law School over by Union Station, and it was home to eight seminarians and a few professors like Jack who were on the law school faculty. Jack taught ethics.

He met me at the door after I parked around back in their small parking lot, already dressed for our run, wearing navy shorts and a faded gray Georgetown Law tee-shirt.

He pulled me into his arms in a bearhug and planted a brotherly kiss on my forehead.

'Good, you're already dressed. Give me your bag. I'll dump it in my room. Both guest rooms are taken, so you'll have to shower there before we go out to dinner.'

I hugged him back. His tee-shirt smelled of the laundry detergent the housekeeper used for washing their clothes. Clean, wholesome, comforting.

'I'm already hungry. I'll be famished by the time we're through,' I said.

When he came back downstairs, he said, 'You did eat something today, didn't you? I don't want you passing out on me, Medina. I'm not carrying you piggyback if you poop out.'

'*Father. Please.* I would *never* poop out on you. And of course I ate.' A couple of crackers and some cheese a few hours ago. 'We're doing our usual loop today, right? You didn't decide to tack on another five miles for training reasons, did you?'

'Nope. Our usual loop. You get off easy. Come on.' He grabbed

my hand as we dodged a car and jogged across the street to
Stanton Park.

Our usual loop was a ragged ring around Capitol Hill, although
if you looked on a map, it looked more like a parallelogram, of
sorts, with a spout: across Stanton Park and up Mass Avenue to
Eighth Street, over to Eastern Market and down to Barracks Row,
then backtracking a few blocks and down Pennsylvania Avenue
to First Street, where the Capitol would be on one side of the
street and the Library of Congress and the Supreme Court would
be on the other. The last leg was short: up East Capital to Fourth
and back to Stanton Park. Every so often, if it was the right time
of day, we'd stop and either sit on the steps of the Library of
Congress or a bench by one of the fountains in front of the
Supreme Court to watch the sun start to set in the west behind
the Capitol. It was a view I could watch every day and never tire
of seeing. By the time we'd get back to Gloria House, it would
be twilight and the streetlights would be just coming on. We'd
have a beer in Jack's suite and then take showers. As for our jog,
we always began by keeping the pace slow enough so we could
talk, and then, after a while, we'd pick it up and concentrate on
the run.

We jaywalked, dodging a couple of cars on Massachusetts
Avenue. Then we settled in once we reached the sidewalk and
found our stride, warming up. Jack glanced over at me and said,
as he always did, 'So what's up? Anything new?'

There was nothing I couldn't tell him. Because, as he always
reminded me, he was in the secret-keeping business. Besides, if
I was really going to bare my soul, tell him something in strictest
confidence, he always seemed to know. As if he had a laser that
saw straight into my brain where he could read my mind. If I
hesitated, he'd say, 'Do you want stole time?'

It was a shortcut we'd devised to mean that whatever I told
him, our conversation would be as sacred and secret as if he had
put on the violet stole he wore when he heard confessions in
church. He would take whatever I told him to his grave.

I wondered, sometimes, how he could deal with the horrific
stories he heard during confession, how he processed what people
told him and buried those awful things somewhere deep inside.
The confessions of murderers, abusers, drug dealers, rapists,

embezzlers, arsonists, thieves – he must have heard it all. The worst, I suspected, involved children: pedophiles and those who committed incest or sodomy. And then, at the end of each confession, he would ask God to give pardon and peace to whoever it was, before saying, 'I absolve you from your sins in the name of the Father, and of the Son, and of the Holy Spirit. Amen.'

That's it. *Forgiven.* Clean slate, though you did have to say you were sorry. And mean it.

I knew he was going to ask me now if I wanted stole time. I also knew that, for reasons I wasn't certain about myself, I didn't want to tell him yet about finding Vicki and her lover in the Russells' swimming pool this morning. Naked. Practically making love. Jack knew the Russells, though not as well as I did, since he'd grown up nearby in Leesburg. But I also hadn't told him about Quill hiring me to photograph Fernway over the last year.

I can keep secrets, too.

'I was out in Middleburg this morning,' I said. 'I saw Mom and stopped by to talk to Isabella since I need to get the photographs for Chap's exhibition at the Dupont Underground from her by the end of the week. They're waiting for them because they need to get them to a framer.'

'Oh, yeah? Everything OK?'

He dropped behind me to let someone pass us on the sidewalk, then caught up again.

'Fine. She said she's on track to finish in the next few days. I think Knox Porter is supposed to come down from Connecticut after she's done.'

'How's Caroline taking all this?' he asked. 'How's she doing?'

'I think she's still processing what happened. That Chappy bypassed his family – bypassed *her* – and left everything to a school in Connecticut. I mean, she gets it – that he wants to help young people who want a career in photography – but still. She has no say, no role, in anything.'

'I'm sure it hurt.'

'It did. It does.'

'I get why Chap did what he did. And it's not like your mother needs the money, being married to Harry. But a will is someone's legacy. It's how they want to be remembered by those they left

behind. It would have been better – easier – if he'd told her his
plans before he died. At least she would have heard it from him
rather than learning about it when she found his will after he
was gone.'

'Maybe he was going to tell her,' I said, 'and he just didn't
get around to it.'

'People keep secrets for all kinds of reasons. Just when I
think I've heard it all, someone manages to surprise me with
something I never saw coming. After all this time.'

'I'm surprised you're surprised,' I said, and he grinned. 'People
tell you everything.'

'So what else is it *you're* not telling me?'

I gave him an indignant look. 'I don't know what you're talking
about.'

'Like hell you don't.'

'Father. Don't be vulgar.'

He laughed. 'Are you going to tell me or not?'

When I didn't reply, he said, 'It's about Nick.'

I slowed our pace to a trot. 'How did you know?'

'I didn't. I guessed. And you just told me.'

The oldest trick in the book.

'Did you find out anything new about what happened to him?'
He wasn't going to let this go.

'I don't know.'

He waited until I gave in and told him about getting a hit on
my search words and the article in yesterday's *Washington
Tribune*. If he was surprised I'd been looking for Nick all this
time, he didn't say anything.

'You think that article was referring to Nick?' he asked.

'I do.'

'So what are you going to do about it?'

Jack didn't know Napoleon Duval, but he knew of him.

In for a penny.

I told him about leaving the voicemail. Contacting Duval for
the first time since Nick died.

'Are you really sure you want to do this, Soph?' he asked. 'Are
you sure it's such a good idea?'

I knew he'd say that. Which was exactly why I hadn't
breathed a word while I'd spent the last year looking for

anything I could find out about Nick. Because Jack would have tried to persuade me not to keep searching. And I didn't want to be talked out of doing that.

'Yes, I'm really sure,' I said. 'On both counts.'

'What if you find out something you wish you didn't know?' His voice grew gentle. 'Haven't you been through enough? Whatever you learn – if you do hear from this guy Duval – it isn't going to change anything.'

'I know that.'

'Then *why*?'

'Because I still want . . . closure.'

'Don't you think you have that already?'

'No.'

We'd reached the intersection of North Carolina Avenue and Eighth Street. The traffic light was in our favor, and so was the *walk* sign, so we kept jogging.

'Closure,' he said. 'What does that look like?'

'I don't know.'

'Then how are you going to know if you get it? And what are you going to do if you don't?'

'Hey,' I said, 'what's going on up there? The sidewalk's blocked off.'

'You're ignoring me.'

'I'm not. It *is* blocked off.' Orange traffic cones were set out across the sidewalk. Behind them, a pile of dirt and a mound of broken asphalt spilled on to the street. A bulldozer swiveled back and forth, excavating more dirt. From somewhere behind it came the metallic drilling sound of a jackhammer. I had to raise my voice so Jack could hear me. 'Why don't we cross the street and go over to the other side?'

'Let's take the alley instead,' he said. 'It'll be quieter and less dirty.'

We turned left into a narrow alley that ran alongside an elegant Victorian gingerbread and then made a sharp right so we were jogging behind the row of homes. In most places, the alley was only wide enough for one car, so I imagined the residents probably regularly played chicken with each other to see who would back up first to let the other one pass. A few cars were parallel-parked next to locked gates that led to postage-stamp-sized backyards behind the owners' homes. Except for the now-dull noise of the jackhammer and the bulldozer on Eighth Street, the alley was quiet and we were alone.

We were running single file with me in front, so I saw the man before Jack did. He lay on his side on the ground next to a silver BMW. The car door was open as if he had been about to climb inside and drive off. He wasn't moving.

I turned around. '*Jack.*'

He caught up with me and we ran. When we reached him, we both knelt down and Jack shook him gently. 'Hey,' he said, 'can you hear me? Wake up. Please wake up.'

I touched his carotid artery. 'I can't feel a pulse, but that doesn't mean he doesn't have one. We need to get him on his back.'

We rolled him over and I checked to see if he was bleeding. He wasn't. In DC, a gunshot wound would not have been a surprise.

'Oh my God,' Jack said in a faint voice.

'What?'

'Do you know who this is? Call nine-one-one.'

'I'm calling them. Who is it?'

'Everett Townsend.' Jack put his ear to the man's chest. 'He's breathing, but it's really shallow. He's still alive.'

'The Supreme Court justice?'

'That's right.'

A woman answered my call. I told her who we'd found and that he was unconscious but breathing. I also told her where we were.

She had a few more questions and then said, 'Please remain on the scene. Someone will be there as soon as possible.'

She disconnected and I wondered if 'as soon as possible' would be soon enough. This was a city with enough crime to keep fleets of emergency vehicles and the Metropolitan Police Department on their toes full-time.

'They're coming,' I said to Jack.

'They'd better hurry. He's barely hanging on.' He made the sign of the cross above Townsend's face and began murmuring. I heard him quietly absolve Justice Townsend of his sins.

I had seen photos and videos of Everett Townsend in the news, of course, but I wouldn't have recognized the ashen-faced man crumpled in front of me as quickly as Jack had done, maybe because I'd been out of the country for so long. Or maybe because he was one of the more circumspect justices who seemed to shun the limelight. Still, it was obvious he was *somebody*. Impeccably dressed in a dark-gray suit that looked bespoke. Cream-colored shirt, black-and-gray striped tie. Conservative. Well-polished black Oxford tie shoes. A thick gold wedding band and a Rolex on his right wrist. I reached for his right hand and turned it over, touching his wrist to see once again if I could find a pulse.

Still nothing.

I gave his hand a gentle squeeze. No response, but it was unexpectedly rough and calloused. There was also an unusual dark cigar-shaped birthmark on the back of his hand.

'I think I hear sirens,' I said. 'Though it's hard to tell with the construction noise.'

Jack cocked his head. 'It *is* sirens. Hopefully, they're for us.'

'That was fast, if it is.'

Jack pointed to the sky. 'I have connections.'

A firetruck screamed down the alley toward us; we could hear other vehicles behind it, all single file in the narrow, tight space. Jack got up, waving his arms like a semaphore, and then the place was swarming with firefighters and equipment and flashing lights and people in blue EMT jumpsuits. Someone lifted me up and moved me gently but firmly out of the way. 'Thanks,' he said. 'We've got him from here.'

A moment later, one of the EMTs who had knelt next to the man said, 'His blood sugar is ten. No medic alert bracelet.'

So Townsend was a diabetic. Even I knew enough to realize that number should have been around one hundred. Your body shuts down when your blood sugar is that low. No wonder he'd passed out.

Someone who appeared to be in charge of the EMTs put an oxygen mask over the man's face and said, 'Get me D50 while I start the IV. Also, his breathing is shallow. Get the bag valve mask so we're ready to assist his ventilation. After that, put him on the heart monitor.'

There were now three of them working on the man with concentrated efficiency. One cut through the fabric of the man's expensive suit and the cream-colored shirt, exposing his chest and arm. The paramedic who appeared to be in charge inserted an IV in the man's arm and hung an IV bag from a hook. His colleague injected fluid from a huge syringe into the IV line near the bag. I moved back to get out of their way and my right foot landed on something hard and twisted under me. I looked down. It was a briefcase handle; the briefcase itself was mostly hidden under the car. I bent and pulled it out – and froze. The embossed gold emblem and unusual design of intertwined letters looked *exactly* like the one I'd seen at Fernway this morning. Two-toned brown leather as soft as butter. Well worn, stuffed with papers or files, maybe a laptop.

The same, the same, the same.

How many of those could there be?

I heard someone say, 'He's not responding. We've gotta give him a second dose of D50.'

I clutched Everett Townsend's briefcase to my chest and watched one of the EMTs administer more fluid into the IV line. And wait.

Finally, the paramedic in charge checked his watch and said in a tight, tense voice, 'Three minutes. This isn't doing anything for him either and his blood sugar is reading two forty-six. Something else is going on. Let's get him out of here. *Now.*'

They were fast, shifting him on to a gurney so they could get him into the ambulance waiting behind the firetruck. A mask covered Townsend's face to assist him with breathing, a heart monitor was attached to his chest, and the IV was still attached to his arm. He hadn't stirred, hadn't reacted as they moved him.

My God, this was the same man who had been naked and locked in an embrace with Vicki Russell in her swimming pool this morning. One of the nine United States Supreme Court justices.

I looked up to see Jack reading something off his phone to a female EMT who was making notes on a clipboard.

'Thank you, Father,' she was saying. 'And thanks for the next-of-kin contact information. We'll get in touch with his wife right away.'

I joined the two of them, clutching the briefcase. 'I think this is Justice Townsend's. It was under the car.'

The EMT took it and said, 'Thanks. One of the guys found a wallet and a phone on him. Hopefully, he's got his personal physician on speed dial.' She opened the briefcase and looked inside. 'Damn. Here's his insulin kit.' She looked over her shoulder. 'I gotta go. We're taking off.'

She ran back to the ambulance as the firetruck started to move toward us through the alley, lights flashing and sirens beginning to wail. The ambulance followed and a Battalion Chief's SUV brought up the rear.

This morning, Everett Townsend had been alive and well, naked and making out in a swimming pool with a woman who was not his wife. Now he was in the back of an ambulance after Jack and I found him lying in an alley. Barely breathing and hanging on to life by a thread.

I hoped Jack and I hadn't gotten to him too late. Because if we hadn't found him when we did, I was pretty sure by now Supreme Court Justice Everett Townsend would be dead.

# FIVE

The crowd that had gathered in the alley to find out what was happening still hung around, a tight little group of neighbors talking among themselves. One of the women detached herself and came over to Jack and me.

'Was that Justice Townsend?' she asked.

'It was,' Jack said. 'How did you know?'

She pointed to the house and car. 'That's his house. That's his car. Is he going to be OK?'

'I hope so,' he said, and I knew he had no intention of divulging that Townsend was barely breathing when he'd been lifted into the ambulance.

'Do you have any idea how long he might have been lying there?' I asked.

The woman shook her head. 'I'm afraid not. It's pretty quiet around here. That's why he likes it. He stays at this place instead of his Georgetown home when the Court's in session. It's closer and he says he can get more work done when he's by himself.'

'I knew he had a place on the Hill, but I didn't realize it was here,' Jack said.

'He likes it because of the privacy. And the alley is especially useful when he's entertaining guests who want to be discreet about coming and going.' She winked at us, a coy smile on her lips as if we were sharing an inside joke. 'If you know what I mean.'

'His . . . guests?' I said.

She winked again, this time even more lascivious and exaggerated. 'Honey, you work it out.'

'Right.' Jack sounded sharp. 'We get it.'

He pulled out his phone and started scrolling, discouraging any further crude gossip the woman might want to share.

'Sure.' She got the message and drifted back to the group of neighbors. The chattering grew in volume as she presumably relayed what she'd learned to the others.

So Townsend brought women here for trysts, as well as making house calls. I wondered how long it would be before that little coffee klatch put the word out on social media about what had just happened. Probably a couple of nanoseconds.

'I didn't realize you knew Everett Townsend,' I said to Jack.

'I do know him, but I know his wife better.'

'Is that who you're calling?'

He hit a button on his phone and nodded. It rang and after a moment a disembodied voice said, 'You have reached . . .'

'Damn. Voicemail.' He waited until the beep sounded and said, 'Diana, it's Jack. Give me a call when you get this, please. It's urgent.'

He disconnected. He hadn't bothered to leave his last name.

'You must know her quite well.'

'I've known Diana Townsend for years,' he said.

We had started to walk back toward Eighth Street.

'How did you meet?' I asked.

'Everybody in Catholic-Land knows Diana,' he said. 'She's the executive director of the Catholic Alliance. Actually, she's the founder. She thought there ought to be a coordinated response, a network, that would connect the smaller US Catholic charities any time there's a natural disaster or a war, some unexpected tragedy where there's an ad hoc need for an infusion of money. The kind of national or international event where parishes take up special collections and organizations tap generous donors for extra contributions. Diana especially does a lot of work with immigrant communities, people displaced by war, and the homeless.'

'She sounds like a good person.'

'Diana is a living saint.'

*Whose husband was cheating on her.*

'How well do you know him?'

'Rhett? I've met him socially a few times. At Diana's parties.'

*Diana's* parties. Not *their* parties. 'What's he like? Besides, um, apparently being a womanizer.'

'Yeah, he does have that reputation.' He sounded curt, disapproving. 'He's also brilliant, a scholar. You must have read about him. He's the justice who writes the most erudite opinions of the whole Court. A bit of a lone wolf. Not that he cares.'

'What do you think of him?'

'I respect his intellect.'

'You don't like him, though.'

'I didn't say I didn't like him.'

'You avoided saying you *did*. Is it because he cheats on Diana?'

He didn't answer right away. Finally, he said, 'He's also arrogant, ambitious, occasionally condescending. Holier than thou. Associate Justice is an OK title for Rhett, but the story is he's hoping the current Chief Justice retires soon and he gets named to take his place.'

'Would he be a good Chief Justice?'

'He'd be brilliant, but he's not the most popular judge on the bench among his colleagues, and he's not without baggage. That reputation of his as a skirt chaser has hounded him for years.'

'That must be hard on his wife.'

'It is, but I think they've worked things out. She loves him, so she turns a blind eye.'

'That's sad.'

He shrugged. 'Every marriage is different, Soph.'

We had begun jogging at a leisurely pace, retracing our route to Gloria House. Neither of us spoke, both of us lost in our thoughts.

'I hope they took him to the ER at George Washington,' I finally said as we reached Stanton Park. 'It's not the closest hospital, but they're the best for handling that kind of trauma. And he's a VIP.'

'If they've got an Associate Justice of the Supreme Court unconscious in the back of an ambulance, I bet that's exactly where they're taking him. I'm sure they've picked up a police escort by now,' Jack said. 'Is Tommy working tonight?'

My half-brother, Dr Thomas Wyatt, worked as an ER doctor at George Washington University Hospital.

'I don't know.' I pulled out my phone and texted him. 'I'll find out.'

We had just walked through the front door of Gloria House when my phone pinged.

'He is,' I said after a moment. 'Evening shift.'

I could hear male voices in the dining room, quiet chatter and laughter mingled with the clinking sounds of china and silverware as the residents ate dinner together. The rector had hired a terrific chef who came in to prepare the evening meal each weekday afternoon before leaving for her regular job at one of DC's hard-to-get-a-reservation restaurants. On weekends, the seminarians and the law school teaching staff were on their own for meals. Tonight's dinner smelled amazing, the mingled odors of cumin, cinnamon, cardamom, and cloves – fragrant spices that reminded me of Mediterranean cooking and meals I'd eaten in Morocco, Lebanon, or Tunisia.

*Is Everett Townsend in the ER?* I texted Tommy.

A moment later, he replied with hasty shorthand: *how do u no???*

'Townsend's at GW,' I said to Jack. 'Tommy wants to know how I know.'

I typed: *Jack O'Hara & I found him. How is he?*

No reply to that. Either he couldn't say or didn't know.

As soon as we got upstairs to Jack's suite, we went straight for the hard stuff, bypassing our usual beers. Jack made gin and tonics, light on the tonic. We sat outside on his plant- and flower-filled balcony overlooking Stanton Park as the evening rush hour wound down below us and the sky grew dark. The city noises receded except for the occasional wail of a siren or a car driving by. It had grown cooler now that the sun was down. I shivered, so Jack went inside and got a Georgetown hoodie, which he handed me.

'Thanks.' I put it on and zipped it up. 'Still nothing from Tommy. I wonder what's going on.'

'Nothing on the Internet about Townsend having taken ill or being at GW, either.' Jack scrolled on his phone.

'I would have thought those neighbors might have put the word out instantly on social media, but if they did, it didn't get around much.' I set my drink on a small glass-topped table between our two patio chairs. 'I'm going to take my shower now. OK?'

'Sure,' he said. 'Do you still feel like going out for dinner?'

'Not really, after what happened earlier. Do you?'

'No.'

'Any chance there are leftovers from that amazing-smelling dinner?' I asked. 'I'd be all in for that.'

He stood. 'While you're in the shower, I'll find out. If there is, we can heat them up and have that. If not, we could always order a pizza. Or Chinese.'

'You choose. But my first choice is leftovers.'

I showered quickly and changed into the long flowing skirt and white blouse I'd planned to wear to the restaurant. Jack loaned me his hairdryer and I dried my hair in his bedroom while he took his shower. I didn't see Tommy's text until after I turned off the dryer.

Jack walked out of the bathroom barefoot and in jeans and an untucked dark-green short-sleeved polo shirt. His longish dark hair was mussed and still wet.

'Tommy just texted me,' I said.

He saw the look in my eyes. Blinked once and said in a flat, matter-of-fact voice, 'Townsend didn't make it.'

'No.'

He made the sign of the cross, blessing himself. 'God rest his soul. Come on. Let's turn on the television. What do you bet the news is out now?'

It was. We turned on CNN, which was showing and re-showing the same video of a black Mercedes driving up to the entrance to the George Washington University Hospital Emergency Room and a tall, willowy blonde wearing oversized sunglasses being helped out of the back seat of the car before being whisked inside the hospital by a couple of men who looked like security guards.

'That's Diana,' Jack said in a grim voice.

'I figured. She's beautiful.'

'She is.'

'Do you think you'll hear from her?' I asked.

'When she gets my message, she'll know why I called,' he said. 'That paramedic took down our names, so she'll probably find out we were the ones who called nine-one-one and stayed with Rhett until the ambulance got there. I'm sure she'll want to know what happened, how we found him, all the details.'

The picture on the television changed and now showed a correspondent at the hospital who said that the head of GW Hospital and the doctors who took care of Justice Townsend would be making a statement and answering questions from the press soon. The President, who had apparently already called

Diana Townsend, would also be making a statement once Marine One landed at the White House later this evening. Finally, there was a statement from the Chief Justice on behalf of the entire Court expressing their shock and sadness, and sending condolences to Diana Townsend.

The story then moved back to the newsroom anchor who said they were going live to the Supreme Court where their legal correspondent also spoke of the shock, grief, and disbelief felt by Townsend's colleagues. A small crowd had gathered behind him. Townsend wasn't that old – in his mid-sixties – and was in excellent health except that he was a diabetic. He was fiercely competitive on the tennis court and loved to sail. His colleagues referred to him as the brains of the Supreme Court because of his erudition and knowledge, as well as his photographic memory for arcane facts and details that anyone presenting a case before him learned not to challenge.

Back to the newsroom where the anchor had already rounded up a couple of analysts who ran through a list of names of possible candidates that had come up under the current administration should there happen to be a vacancy on the Supreme Court. Along with an assessment of the uphill battle the President faced to get a new justice confirmed before the midterm elections in a few weeks.

'Jesus,' Jack said. 'His body's not even cold and the vultures are already circling.'

'Are you surprised?' I asked. 'It's Washington.'

'No. More like offended. For Diana.'

I wondered then if Vicki Russell happened to be watching the evening news tonight – and if so, how she was handling the death of the man she'd most likely slept with last night. Vicki was attractive, but Diana Townsend was stunning. A living saint, Jack said. Why would Rhett Townsend want to cheat on someone like her?

And if Townsend had spent last night with Vicki, then what had Diana Townsend been doing – presumably alone? Had she known her husband was with another woman? Or guessed? Maybe she'd assumed he was at the Capitol Hill condo working on Supreme Court business since the Court was, after all, in session.

'. . . go downstairs and heat up dinner,' Jack was saying. 'OK?'

'Sure . . . what?'

'I just said, I don't think I can bear to watch this sideshow anymore, so let's go downstairs and heat up dinner.'

When we were getting out pots and pans in the very large institutional-sized kitchen, Jack said, 'What's bugging you, Soph?'

I set a saucepan down on an island that was in the middle of the room. It was as big as my entire kitchen at home.

'I don't know. I guess I'm still processing what happened. Did you think Everett Townsend was going to make it when they put him in the ambulance?'

'I prayed he would.' Jack took a long-handled wooden spoon and a metal spatula out of a drawer. 'But to tell you honestly: no. At least God took him quickly; there's some mercy there.'

We ended up eating dinner – chicken tagine with basmati rice infused with saffron, cinnamon, cloves, and cardamom – at one of the long refectory tables in the dark-paneled dining room, opting not to go back upstairs to Jack's suite since we had the place to ourselves. Jack found an open bottle of Oregon Pinot Noir on the sideboard and poured some into our wine glasses after he said grace.

When we finished dinner, we loaded the dishwasher and did the few dishes that needed to be washed by hand. Jack washed; I dried.

His phone, which was on the counter next to mine, rang while he had his hands in the soapy water, scrubbing the rice pot. I glanced at the display. One word: *Diana.*

'You'd better take this.' I gave him my dishtowel.

He dried his hands and scooped up the phone. 'Thanks.'

He walked toward the dining room, his back to me, voice muted. I stayed in the kitchen and finished the dishes. Gloria House's kitchen dated from the days when the seminary was bursting at the seams, filled with young men who believed, like Jack, that God had called them to a life of serving Him. Their numbers had gradually dwindled as the Church was rocked by scandal, but the kitchen was still equipped to serve meals to multitudes. The oversized cooking utensils and appliances – a huge mixer that sat on the floor and looked like an amusement park ride that whirled you around as an octopus arm raised and lowered you, pots and pans big enough to take a bath in, a walk-in and walk-*around* refrigerator, two massive stoves and a wall of ovens – always made me feel I'd shrunk to toy-size like Alice did after she went down the rabbit hole.

Jack was gone for a good five minutes. When he returned, sober-eyed and subdued, I was checking my phone to see if there were any new developments concerning Everett Townsend's death or speculation about possible successors. There wasn't – just a rehash, and a rehash of the rehash, of what had already happened. There would be no further news tonight. As for the circumstances surrounding Justice Townsend's death, one of the paramedics who had shown up in the alley had been located by an intrepid journalist. Fortunately, he left Jack and me out of the story, commenting only that two Good Samaritans out for a run on Capitol Hill had found Townsend and called nine-one-one, staying with him until medical assistance arrived. Justice Townsend died shortly after he arrived at the ER. The official cause of death was complications due to a hypoglycemic event.

'How is Diana?' I asked Jack.

'In shock. But she's strong and she'll lean into her faith to get her through this.' He gave me an apologetic smile. 'Look, I, uh, need to go see her.'

'Now?'

He nodded. 'Sorry to cut our evening short, but she asked me to come.'

'To the hospital?'

'No, she's still there, but she's leaving now. I'll meet her at the house in Georgetown.'

'You're not cutting anything short. Don't give it another thought – you need to be with Diana Townsend. Let me get my stuff from your room and we can leave together.'

'If you can wait a minute,' he said, 'I need to change into my work clothes since this is an official visit.'

He got dressed in the bedroom while I watched his television on mute in the living room. The news had moved on to other stories, but the *Breaking News* crawl along the bottom was all about the sudden tragic death of Associate Supreme Court Justice Everett Townsend.

My heart gave the little tug it always did when I saw Jack

dressed in his blacks. He was carrying his prayer book in one hand and car keys in the other.

'Ready?' he said.

'Yes, Father,' I said. 'I'm ready.'

We took the stairs down two flights to the basement where the recreation room, laundry room, furnace, and storage room were all located, along with a door to the parking lot. He walked me to my car, hugged me, and kissed me on the forehead.

'Take care,' he said. 'I'm there for you, too, if you need me. Don't think I haven't thought about how what happened this afternoon must be affecting you with everything you've gone through.'

'Thank you,' I said. 'Diana Townsend won't know me, but please give her my condolences.'

'I will,' he said.

He watched me drive off. I wondered how he'd comfort Diana Townsend, whose husband had probably spent his last night on earth in the bed of another woman.

Did she know or at least suspect?

And would she grieve his death?

# SIX

Once a week, Grace Lowe and I met for breakfast in the light-filled solarium at Kramer's Bookstore on Dupont Circle in their friendly, laid-back restaurant known as All Day – as in you can get breakfast *all day* – before she had to be at her desk downtown at the offices of *The Washington Tribune.* We had decided that Mondays and Fridays were out because they bookended the weekend – I have no idea why that mattered, but it did – so we settled on Tuesday, Wednesday, or Thursday, depending on Grace's schedule, which was far more constrained than mine. We walked to the restaurant from our respective homes; for me, it was practically like falling out of bed and tumbling down the street, whereas Grace, who lived in Adams Morgan, had a jaunt of about a mile and a half from her house. It was, however, all downhill. Once we finished breakfast, she'd hop on the Metro at Dupont Circle for the one-stop trip to Farragut Square where the *Trib* building was located. Usually, I walked home to do some work in my studio.

The regular breakfast get-together had been Grace's idea and we'd been doing it for more than a year. The ostensible reason was that her teenage son and daughter were now old enough to get ready for school by themselves, especially since they were *driving.* And her husband, who was the Majority Staff Director of the Senate Foreign Relations Committee, often ate breakfast in his car on the way to work or else picked up something at one of the restaurants in the Capitol. So, once a week, Grace splurged and let someone else make *her* breakfast for a change. The real reason – this I knew – was that Grace, like Jack and Quill, was worried about me after Nick died and she, too, wanted to keep an eye on me.

She was already sitting at the table we'd claimed as ours when I arrived a couple of minutes after seven. I'd slept badly and knew it showed. She looked gorgeous, as she always did – blonde, blue-eyed, ivory skin, patrician features, reed slim. A head turner. Named for Grace Kelly whose acting career and fairytale life as

Princess Grace of Monaco were subjects of endless fascination to her mother. As it turned out, her namesake daughter was practically a double for the real Grace Kelly. Stunning.

I slid into my chair as Jolene, our favorite waitress, brought me a latte before I'd even asked for it.

'Here you go, baby.' She set down the cup. 'Two usuals?'

'We're so predictable,' I said. 'And thank you for the latte.'

'One of these days we should order something different,' Grace said. 'Just to surprise you, Jolene.'

Jolene grinned. 'Don't mess with a good thing, Sugar. You like what you like. I'll be right back with your food.'

After she left, Grace gave me the once over. 'Jeez, Soph, you look like something they forgot to shoot. Is everything all right? Are *you* all right?'

I knew she expected me to tell her that whatever it was had something to do with Nick. I also knew she'd be totally bowled over by my answer.

Not to mention – she was a journalist, after all – annoyed.

'Jack and I went for a run yesterday afternoon on the Hill. We're the ones who found Everett Townsend in that alley. I haven't been able to stop thinking about it, so I didn't get much sleep last night.'

'Wait a minute – *what?* How come you didn't let me know?' Yup. Annoyed. We had witnessed A Major News Event before anyone else knew about it. And hadn't called to inform her.

'Gracie, come on.'

'You and Jack *found* Everett Townsend? *You're* the Good Samaritans I heard about on CNN?' Not just annoyed. Seriously pissed off. We could have given her a scoop.

A few heads turned in our direction when she almost screeched Townsend's name. I put my finger to my lips.

'Sorry.' She lowered her voice. 'Tell me *everything*.'

'There's nothing to tell you that you don't already know, except that Jack and I planned to go for a run, then we were going out for a pizza.'

'That's not what I meant. I'm talking about Townsend.'

'I *know* what you meant. Hold on, OK? So we started to do our usual loop, until we got to Eighth Street near Eastern Market and there was construction blocking the sidewalk. Jack suggested we take the alley. Townsend was on the ground, unconscious, lying next to his car. We couldn't rouse him. No pulse that we could detect, but at least he was breathing – though just barely. I called nine-one-one while Jack said some prayers for him, gave him absolution. The paramedics came and discovered he was a diabetic and that his glucose had sunk like a stone. It was ten instead of something like one hundred. They gave him a shot and put an IV in him. Then they blasted off with him in the ambulance because he still wasn't responding. You probably heard the same thing I heard. He died at GW not long after he got there of complications due to a hypoglycemic event. That's it. The end.'

'Obviously you recognized him. You knew who he was.'

'Actually, I didn't. Not right away. I just thought he looked familiar. Jack knew him, though.'

'I really wish you had called me. Or at least texted me.'

'You mean, in between Jack giving him a final blessing and me calling nine-one-one?'

'No, and you know it.'

'I love you,' I said, 'but informing the press wasn't our first thought. Even you. Did you know that Jack and Diana Townsend are friends? *Close* friends?'

Her eyebrows went up. She didn't know. 'I'm not surprised, considering who she is.'

'You should have heard him last night when CNN brought on a panel of experts discussing possible candidates to take Townsend's place on the Court. I think they waited all of about fifteen minutes after it was announced he was dead before they rounded up the usual suspects to opine on his successor. Jack was livid. He said it was like vultures circling a still-warm corpse. He would not – and I mean *not* – have called to give you a blow-by-blow we-were-at-the-scene-exclusive, Grace.'

'OK, I'm sorry. I know I sound crass and exploitative. But it *is* news. And it *is* a big deal,' she said as Jolene set our breakfast plates – Soho omelet for me, no meat; Smoked Salmon Benedict without the champagne salad for Grace – in front of us. We thanked her and then Grace added, 'How do *you* know Jack and Diana Townsend are good friends?'

'Because he called her as soon as the ambulance left. Didn't even have to leave his last name. He just said, "Hi, Diana, it's

Jack. Call me." She returned his call just after we finished dinner when she was still at the hospital. We never did go out; we ate leftovers at Gloria House. Anyway, she asked him to come by her house in Georgetown and see her. As in, right then and there. I left when he did.' I picked up my fork and dug into spinach, eggs, and Swiss cheese.

'Diana Townsend knows anybody who is anybody in Catholic-Land, as Jack likes to call it. She's so well-connected it wouldn't surprise me if she had the Cardinal and the Papal Nuncio on speed dial. Plus, she speaks perfect Italian and knows all the right people in Rome. So of course Jack knows her.'

'He said he knows her because of her philanthropy. Working with immigrant groups, refugees, and the homeless.'

Grace raised one eyebrow. 'He also knows her because she is *connected.* And he's ambitious. Diana is a good person to know if you want a purple beanie someday – which he most definitely does. Frankly, I think he wants a red zucchetto, too. He doesn't only want to be a bishop. If you ask me, he wants the whole megillah. He wants to be a cardinal.' She gave me a critical look and said, 'You look surprised. Didn't you know that? Or at least suspect it?'

'No,' I said. 'It's not something we've talked about. He told you that's what he wants?'

She set her fork down and pointed her two index fingers directly at her eyes. 'I use these, honey. And I listen.'

'What about Diana Townsend? How do you know so much about her?'

'The *Trib* did a profile on her when her husband was nominated for the Supreme Court. I helped write it.'

'I was in England then.'

'Lucky you. It was one of the uglier confirmation hearings. Not as bad as Kavanaugh or Thomas – those take the cake. But not pleasant.'

'Refresh my memory.'

'Townsend's a skirt chaser.'

'I've heard about that.'

'Yeah, well, nobody could ever pin anything on him – nobody said he had nonconsensual sex with them or groped them or talked dirty to them. At least no woman who would testify.

Everyone learned their lesson from what happened after Anita Hill and Christine Blasey Ford talked. *Nothing*. Of course, Diana stuck by his side through the whole thing, pooh-poohing the idea that he was anything but a model husband.' Grace shrugged. 'What else is she going to do? Just like every other loyal political wife who's had to stand there while you're imagining the thought bubble above her head filled with what she *really* wants to say as her man denies he was diddling where he shouldn't have diddled. But where there's smoke . . . you know?'

I *did* know. I knew it for a fact. I hadn't told Jack about Vicki Russell. And I wasn't ready to say anything to Grace just now, either.

'One of his gossipy neighbors who came outside when the ambulance showed up decided she needed to inform Jack and me that Townsend used his Capitol Hill pied-à-terre as a place to work while the Court was in session. And as a little love nest where he entertained guests who used the alley to slip in and out so they could be discreet.'

Grace skewered a piece of salmon with her fork. 'I'm not surprised. He was quite the party boy. Straight-laced by day. Blew off steam at night.'

'I don't understand why Diana Townsend would stay with someone like that.'

'Beats me. Apparently, she didn't like some of the friends he socialized with, and he didn't share her love for the Church, which is her whole life. I mean, she goes to daily Mass at the cathedral. He wasn't exactly a C&E Catholic, but he wasn't anywhere near as devout as she is.'

C&E. Christmas and Easter.

'So he had girlfriends on the side and he partied hard,' I said. 'That could describe half of official Washington. It didn't stop Thomas and Kavanaugh from being confirmed.'

'True, but there's more,' Grace said. 'A few Senators on the Judiciary Committee who opposed his nomination wanted to bust his chops, so they went over his cases when he was a judge for the DC District Court with a fine-tooth comb *and* a magnifying glass. There was one case where Townsend gave a lenient sentence to a guy charged with conspiracy to launder drug money through his real estate company because he said the prosecution did a lousy job of proving their case. People were furious – those drugs ended up on the street, people died, *kids* died – but he's a by-the-book judge. The other side didn't do their homework, and they left the door open a crack, enough for there to be reasonable doubt. There were a couple of other cases like that, but Townsend was unrepentant. He hates sloppy lawyers, sloppy lawyering. If you don't do your due diligence, he's not going to cut you any slack.'

'You know a lot about him.'

Grace shrugged. 'One of Ben's friends from law school who's the General Counsel for the Senate Judiciary Committee clerked for Townsend when he was a District judge. We've had her over to dinner a few times, and she, shall we say, shared a few highly personal insights about him after a couple of glasses of wine.'

'Such as?'

'That he was brilliant and she learned heaps from him professionally. She also learned heaps *about* him personally, though he was discreet and kept his trysts under the radar. She called clerking for him "a once-in-a-lifetime experience." And once in her lifetime working for him was enough.'

'Did he ever try anything with her?'

'She's the kind of person who doesn't take crap from anybody. She would have bitten off his hand if he did.'

'I guess that's a no.'

Jolene laid the check down exactly in the middle of the table. 'No rush, y'all. But I know it's gettin' on near eight fifteen.'

Which was when breakfast had to be over for Grace to get to work on time.

'Thanks, Jolene.' Grace set her credit card down on top of the bill. 'My turn.'

We traded who paid every week. The other one left the tip, always a generous one. Always cash so it went straight into Jolene's pocket, after I discovered she was a single mother who worked two jobs – waitressing here during the day and overnights as a supervisor at a homeless shelter – to help pay the tuition for her only, much-beloved son who was now a senior across town at Howard University. When Jolene came back with Grace's credit card and the receipt, I slipped a twenty into the leather folder and closed it. As usual, Jolene pretended not to see my sleight of hand, but she winked and smiled and said in her sassy way, 'See you next week, Sugars. Y'all have a good one.'

We stepped outside into cool morning sunshine. During the pandemic, the street behind Kramer's had been blocked off to traffic and the restaurant had installed a large tent for outdoor seating. It was still pedestrian-only, and I hoped the city would keep it that way, even though DC's rush hour was gradually returning to what it had been before everyone started working from home.

'I'm heading into town,' I said to Grace as we walked toward Dupont Circle. 'I'll take the Metro with you.'

'Great,' she said. 'Where are you going?'

'Streetwise.'

'Taking more photos for your homeless project?'

'No, just a quick visit to talk to Finn,' I said.

Streetwise was a multi-media nonprofit located in downtown Washington that helped the city's homeless population and also put out a weekly newspaper about – and, in part, written by – homeless individuals. Finn Hathaway was its editor-in-chief.

'Finn is a sweetheart,' Grace said. 'You know very well he makes peanuts working there, even though he could make twice as much if he worked for us – and it's not like we pay a fortune. He's a good writer. But he won't budge from Streetwise.'

'He does a lot more than just managing the newspaper,' I said. 'He showed up with me in front of Union Station last week when the National Park Service cleared out the tent city that had been there for a while.'

Grace groaned. 'You were there when they cleared out the encampment at Columbus Circle? It's not humane what they're doing. The *way* they're doing it.'

'I took pictures,' I said. 'I promised Finn he could have them for the next issue of the paper.'

'Good,' she said. 'We had a guy there, too – you probably noticed him. I saw the pictures he brought back. That removal squad was ruthless. They didn't mess around.'

'The eviction notices were posted for weeks, so the crew that showed up said it wasn't a surprise raid. But plenty of people didn't want to leave and were still there with all their belongings.'

'That's because they're *homeless*,' she said. 'Where exactly would they go?'

But the mayor had made a campaign promise to clean up the

tent camps as well as to find somewhere for everyone to sleep at night so they'd have a roof over their heads. Plus, there were plenty of complaints from local residents who claimed the camps, which were scattered throughout the city, were public nuisances. My brother Tommy told me stories about St Elizabeth's Hospital – DC's hospital where individuals with severe mental health issues were sent – releasing some of the less severely ill patients when they became too overcrowded. *Dumping them on the street*, he said. With no support system and no place to go, guess where those people ended up? With their homeless brothers and sisters. And with no medication to stabilize their mental health anymore, it wasn't long before some of them started making threatening statements or exhibiting bizarre or even hostile behavior that terrified the locals.

Grace and I reached the escalator at the entrance to the Dupont Circle Metro. Although it wasn't the deepest Metro stop, it was still plenty deep since it ran directly under the traffic circle. Grace stood behind me on the escalator for the long, slow trip underground.

She leaned down and said in my ear, 'Speaking of Streetwise, you can't say anything yet, but I might have managed to get Javi a six-week internship working with me on the Metro Desk. It would begin just before Christmas and last through the holidays until the end of January when everyone wants to take off and we're short-staffed.'

Javier Aguilera had been living on the streets after he aged out of foster care six years ago when he turned eighteen. His father, who was Black, was doing a life sentence in the Florence Supermax prison in Colorado – in part for his crime of brutally murdering a restaurant owner and his wife, but also for the simple reason that there were no prisons in DC. His mother, who was from Thailand and a drug addict, died of an overdose of bad drugs when Javi was ten.

He'd done all right on his own – better than a lot of people – because he was smart and savvy and charming. During the day, he hung out in the Martin Luther King Library at 9th and G, where an astute librarian hooked him up with the library's adult literacy program. He also started showing up at Streetwise's writing work-shops, where Grace had met him. Then Streetwise hired him to help with distributing newspapers to their vendors – homeless individuals who sold copies of the newspaper on the street – as well as reimbursing them later for the papers they sold to people who bought them via Streetwise's cashless phone app. A few months ago a Streetwise caseworker helped him find a small basement apartment in northeast DC and Javi was off the street for good.

I swiveled around and looked up at Grace. 'Are you serious? Javi might have an internship at the *Trib*? That's *fantastic.*'

Her smile was strained. 'Well, yes, except I had to promise I'd do a month on the overnight shift in return, since Javi's not coming in through the system. Our paid internship program is always in the summer when everyone is off school, so he's definitely not doing this through channels. But I did manage to get a small grant, so he'll get paid.'

'I'd like to add to your grant,' I said. Knowing Grace, she and Ben had funded it themselves.

She gave me a knowing look. 'Thanks. We're keeping this on the down-low since he's not going through our application process and the usual vetting we do.'

Because if he did have to go through the usual process, Javi wouldn't have a prayer.

Those who were accepted were studying journalism or photography or digital media in a top program at a good J-school. Occasionally, Daddy knew somebody, which, of course, helped because, well, *connections* – after all, this was Washington, the Land-of-Who-Do-You-Know. Applicants were top-of-their-class brilliant, almost certainly future Pulitzer Prize winners because their writing was so good, so polished, so *stellar*. They would gladly gnaw off an arm if an editor asked them to do so on day one, and although they got their chance to write stories, take photos, or work on the Internet desk so that they left with some by-God actual experience, they also did the Starbucks run and the other sundry tasks every intern did.

'I still haven't said anything to Ben or the kids about the overnight thing,' Grace said. 'Don't tell my boss, but for Javi, I'd do two months of overnights.'

'When are you going to know for sure if he got the internship?'

'Hopefully, in the next week or so. At least before Halloween. Then I've got to talk to Finn and tell him I'm going to steal Javi for six weeks.'

'Finn will be over the moon,' I said. 'You won't have a problem with him.'

The rush-hour train that pulled into our station was standing-room-only crowded. Grace got in and I joined her as the chime rang that the doors were closing. I held on to a pole in the middle of the car. Grace held on to my arm.

'What story are you working on today?' I asked.

'What do you think?' she said. 'Everett Townsend.'

'His obit?'

'It was already written. Someone just had to update it.'

We had done that, too, at IPS when I used to work for them – all news organizations did. Obituaries of famous people were written long before the person died so you didn't have to start from square one when they *did* pass away. You already had something in the can.

'Then what are you writing about him?' I asked.

She leaned close to me, so her mouth was practically against my ear. 'That boy was complicated. There was more to him than meets the eye, and I'm not just talking about his reputation with women . . . whoops, here's my stop.' The door opened and she stepped on to the platform. She blew me a kiss as the door closed.

With a jerk, we started again, picking up speed toward Metro Center.

Grace hadn't meant what she said in a good way. Maybe I needed to bone up on the Senate confirmation hearing of Associate Supreme Court Justice Everett Townsend and find out what she was referring to. Now that he was dead, there would be plenty of information about him out there.

The train pulled into Metro Center, my stop, and I got off. Twenty-four hours ago, I'd seen Vicki Russell and Everett Townsend making out in her swimming pool.

I wondered if anyone else knew about it. If not, that just left Vicki and me. They say three can keep a secret if two are dead. Townsend was dead and Vicki had much more invested in keeping their relationship a secret than I did, although I would never do anything that would hurt Quill. So maybe Vicki and I were an exception to the rule: two people could keep a secret.

Because if Quill found out, it would kill *him*.

# SEVEN

The offices of Streetwise were located in an annex attached to the Church of the Epiphany, a beautiful Gothic Revival Episcopal church that was nearly dwarfed in the middle of a block of modern office buildings and shops on G Street between 12th and 13th Streets. Founded in 1842, the little stone church with its intricate stained-glass windows and dark-red arched doors was now on the National Register of Historic Places. It had been a hospital for Union soldiers during the Civil War, but the church – located on the edge of the geographical divide between north and south – had seen its congregation split into deeply divided factions during the war.

Before becoming President of the Confederacy, then-Senator Jefferson Davis had rented a pew in the church; three of his children had been confirmed there. After he moved to Richmond, his pew, ironically, was rented by Abraham Lincoln's Secretary of War. Lincoln himself had attended services at Epiphany Church, as had Franklin Delano Roosevelt. In 1901, the church held memorial services for President McKinley and Queen Victoria. Its bells – which chimed every quarter hour – had rung for the inauguration of every President since Calvin Coolidge.

A small tent city of homeless people occupied part of the sidewalk in front of the church and its leafy green courtyard. This part of downtown DC had nothing whatsoever to do with federal Washington's marble and granite Greek temple-like buildings, museums, and monuments to the Founding Fathers.

Washington is a complicated, complex place that I occasionally believe is dealing with an existential identity crisis because it can't quite figure out what it ought to be, beyond the government buildings and tourist sites. Federal Washington empties out at night; to take a drive after hours down those wide streets lined with their enormous hulking buildings is like driving through a ghost town. Federal Washington also, in my opinion, doesn't coexist easily – or really even at all – with the rest of the city, in large part because it doesn't want to. Or need to. Non-federal DC is predominantly Black, poor, and not well educated, which is not surprising because one in three kids ends up dropping out of a crappy public school system that ranks forty-ninth out of fifty-one in the country. There is also the city's nasty reputation as a place of violent crime fueled by drugs and gangs, especially in the poorer neighborhoods in Northeast and Southeast DC.

For all intents and purposes, Washington is a one-trick-pony that revolves completely around the government – even if you don't work for Uncle Sam, you very likely have a navel-gazing job that feeds the beast. Lobbyist, journalist, diplomat, contractor, or another kind of ancillary support. The city is also not America's cultural center the way so many other capital cities like London or Paris or Rome are. We have New York for that. Nor is it the financial center of the country. And no one would ever accuse Washington of being a fashion center.

DC residents aren't represented in Congress, either, except for a non-voting member of the House of Representatives, and, let me tell you, its citizens, who pay their fair share of taxes, resent being left out. So much so that year after year, they and their non-voting member of the House raise holy hell and lobby Congress to become the fifty-first state. Not to mention that their outrage has morphed into the motto on the city's red, white, and blue license plates, a slogan first used by American colonists against the British during the prelude to the Revolutionary War: *Taxation Without Representation.* To be strictly correct, though, DC was never meant to be a state. It was established as a federal district, with the now remarkably naive presumption that governing our country would only be a part-time duty and no one would need to stay here year-round.

It took me less than two minutes to walk from the Metro Center station to the Church of the Epiphany. I texted Finn that I was on my way so he could come downstairs and let me in to the Streetwise offices. The wrought-iron gate creaked as I pushed it open and entered the courtyard. An arched red door leading to the annex opened a moment later and Finn bounded out.

Finn Hathaway could easily be mistaken for James Taylor – though a much younger version – with the same tall, slender build, tonsure of hair that was just beginning to go gray, and intense blue-gray eyes that looked deep into yours and read you like a book. He had an easy smile and a kind face. Today he wore faded jeans and a navy hoodie with the Streetwise logo on it that often meant he'd been out in the homeless community that day, checking on folks and offering help.

He and I had gotten to know each other well enough over the last year that we now exchanged hugs, so I got a bear hug and he said, 'Let's sit outside for a few minutes. I hate being cooped up when the weather is as beautiful as it is today. Last night was a late one and today, of course, the place is humming.'

'That's partially why I came by,' I said. 'To buy my newspaper.'

We sat on a semicircular bench in an adjacent courtyard. Finn rubbed his eyes, tilting his face to catch a ray of sunshine that had filtered between the buildings. The Streetwise newspaper came out every Tuesday, so Mondays were always busy, as he'd said, putting it to bed and getting it to the printer. It had started as a monthly, but became a weekly as Streetwise grew and expanded. Now it was one of only five street newspapers in the US to be published every week.

'Your photos,' Finn said, 'were outstanding. Thanks so much for taking them. For *giving* them to us.'

'You're welcome,' I said. 'I was glad to do it – I mean, glad to *document* what happened. Not glad to be there. What they did to those people was awful. Have you found everyone who was evicted yet?'

He yawned, shooting me an apologetic look, and shook his head. 'We're still trying to track a lot of them down. The mayor's office swears they're going to get these camps cleared out and the people who lived in them into a place so they have a roof over their heads. But you know what? I can't think of a single individual – so far – who had their tent and all their belongings swept up by those bulldozers and then spent the night in an actual shelter.'

'So where do they *go*?'

He shrugged. 'Wherever they can find a new place to live. Maybe they move to another camp or go off the grid, or they leave town. Our caseworkers are sometimes out in the middle of the night looking for folks because a lot of them – even though they have no home – have a day job.'

The DC Department of Human Services had a center where homeless families could go to apply for emergency shelter in buildings they had been able to procure as temporary housing. Mostly, these were places that had been publicly owned and were no longer used, like schools and hospitals. Some were older apartment buildings the city had managed to purchase. But there were plenty of folks who either didn't *want* to live in a place run by the local government – too many restrictions, you got sick there, your things got stolen, fear of abuse – or else they couldn't get in for one reason or another.

Finn had explained to me that people became homeless for a lot of reasons: they aged out of foster care like Javi Aguilera, or they left prison or a nursing home. Some needed to escape domestic violence or they were veterans with no place to go. Those who fared the worst were the substance abusers and those with mental health issues. Then there were the cases that broke your heart. A catastrophic illness with medical bills piling up, which led to losing your job due to your prolonged absence, which led to foreclosure on your home because you could no longer make the payments – a terrifyingly quick downward spiral. The next thing you knew, you and your family were living in your car with no street smarts, no idea how to survive and cope.

'You look exhausted,' I said to Finn. 'And you keep yawning. Have you been out looking for people as well?'

His smile was rueful. 'I'm a little low on sleep. I'll catch up over the weekend. I hope.'

The wrought-iron gate creaked as someone opened and closed it. Two men wearing reflective orange-and-green vests with the Streetwise logo on them had come inside and were heading toward the entrance to Streetwise. When they saw us, they walked over to our courtyard.

'Jimmy. Ranger. Morning.' Finn nodded at them.

I knew them, too. 'Good morning, guys.'

Ranger raised his hands to his face pretending he was holding a camera. He pushed an imaginary shutter button. 'Hey, Finn, hey, Click. You coming to the photo workshop next week, Click?'

One of the things I loved about Streetwise was that it had been able to evolve from not only putting out a newspaper but also into a multi-media organization that offered workshops on writing, poetry, art, and photography to anyone in the homeless community who wanted to attend. The Streetwise staff led the workshops when they could, but they had also recruited a group of volunteers to back them up – including Grace and me. Ranger called me Click the first week I showed up at a photography workshop and the nickname stuck. Now that's what everyone here called me.

'I'll be there. Will you?'

'You bet.'

'Picking up your newspapers, gentlemen?' Finn asked.

'And our *mo-neh*.' Jimmy flashed a toothy grin. 'I got over two hundred dollars coming to me.'

Streetwise had a small army of vendors, many of whom were homeless – or *unhoused*, as Finn had taught me to say. Every Tuesday, they came by to purchase newspapers from Streetwise for fifty cents a copy, which they then sold on the street for two bucks plus tip. There was a phone app for buyers who didn't have cash so they could still purchase a paper. Streetwise staff collected the app money which they held at – of course – the App Desk until the vendor came in to pick it up in cash. Full payment, no commission. Vendors could also 'earn' free newspapers by attending a workshop.

'We discourage begging,' Finn told me the first time we met. 'These folks may not make a living wage selling newspapers, but at least they're earning *something*. We make it easy, too. You can buy papers, but an easier way to do it is to just show up for a workshop, sign in, and then you get a couple of papers for free. Plus, you might learn something as well.'

'Tessa's waiting for you at the App Desk,' Finn said to Jimmy and Ranger. 'With your money.'

After they left, he turned to me. 'So what's up? You said you wanted to talk about something.'

'I did. I also want to buy my newspaper.'

'That's easily done. What else?'

'Would you be interested in taking me on as one of your staff photographers?'

His eyes widened. 'Wow. I didn't see that coming. Of course I would. But I couldn't possibly afford you. I couldn't even pay you a fraction of what you're worth.'

'I'd like to do it pro bono.'

'You're not serious,' he said. '*Are* you?'

'I am.'

He stuck out his right hand. 'Then you've got yourself a deal.'

I shook it. 'OK. You've got yourself a photographer.'

He stood up. 'Come on. Let's go get your newspaper before I tell the staff that we've got a ringer on board now. I mean it, Sophie. I can't thank you enough for this.'

'You don't need to.'

'Then why?'

'Why what?'

'Why are you doing this?'

We started walking toward the arched red door.

'Since my husband died, I've been doing a lot of thinking about what I want to do with my life and my work. And the answer is that I can do whatever I want. I've got Nick's pension, the money from a life insurance policy I didn't know he had, and our savings,' I said. 'What I've decided is that I'd like to use my photography for good causes. Take pictures of people and events that might be overlooked or forgotten. Get them published where they'll be *seen*.'

Finn had been studying me, watching me, so I finally said, feeling self-conscious, 'That's it. I hope I don't sound arrogant or egotistical.'

He opened the door and held it to let me go first. 'No,' he said. 'You don't. Not at all.'

There was no one in the small lobby when we entered, except the white-haired grandmotherly woman who checked everyone in. I said hello, signed in, and she said, 'Good to see you, Click.'

Muted organ music came through the other side of the wall and filled the room: the church organist rehearsing for Sunday services. 'O God Beyond All Praising.' One of my favorite hymns.

Finn grinned, watching me cock my head to better listen to the music. 'It's one of the many benefits of working here,' he said. 'Some days, this place feels like God's waiting room when that music floats through our offices.'

'It's beautiful,' I said.

He badged us into another corridor. A large, high-ceilinged

room the church used as a fellowship hall and Streetwise used for some of their larger workshops was directly in front of us.

'Tessa's got newspapers,' Finn said as we bypassed the elevator and took the stairs to the second floor. 'Do you want to buy one from her?'

'Please.'

Tessa Janko was one of Streetwise's newest employees, a former vendor who was now working at the App Desk, where people came not only to get their money but also to pick up their mail since Streetwise let their clients and the vendors use their address. Tessa was in her late twenties, but she could easily pass as a high school teenager. Long dark hair, soulful brown eyes, a dusting of freckles across her nose, a gap-tooth smile, almost painfully thin. All I knew about her was that she was a runaway – from where, I had no clue. She'd made a comment once when we were chatting that made me wonder if she had been a victim of sodomy or even incest. She never said and I never asked. But for someone who had been through so much so young, she had a good, caring heart – mothering the vendors, checking up on everyone, making sure they were fine.

She flashed a smile when she saw Finn and me. 'Hey, Click. Good to see you.'

'You, too, Tessa. Finn says you might sell me a paper.'

'You bet.' She took a newspaper from a pile that was on a table behind the App Desk, folded it in half, and handed it to me.

I gave her a ten.

'Let me get your change,' she said.

'No change.'

'Thanks.' She grinned again, folding the ten and putting it in an over-stuffed worn-looking fabric purse that was hanging off the back of her chair.

'How's everything?' I asked.

'Goin' good.'

Tessa and Javi both worked at the App Desk and were friends. 'Is Javi coming in later?' I asked. 'Grace Lowe asked me to say hi for her.'

She didn't look up as she straightened a stack of papers on her desk that didn't need straightening. 'No,' she said. 'He's not.'

'Is he sick? Javi always works on Tuesdays when the paper comes out,' Finn said.

'I don't know,' she said. 'All I know is I got called when he didn't come in.'

Finn's eyebrows went up. 'That's not like him. Have you talked to him?'

She shook her head, eyes still downcast. 'No.'

I caught Finn's look of dismay. She was lying. Of course she had checked up on him.

'Tessa,' he said, 'if there's something going on, you know we only want to help.'

She looked up and jutted out her chin. 'There's nothing going on. Just that I heard his landlady was sick.'

I wanted to ask where she'd heard that – like maybe directly from Javi – but instead I said, 'Is Javi taking care of her?'

'He might be. I think he is.' Her eyes darted between Finn and me. 'Yeah, he's taking care of her.'

The elevator door opened outside in the hallway and someone stepped out. Another vendor coming for newspaper money, an elderly lady with a walker, sunglasses, and long cornrows tinted purple. As Finn and I greeted her, Tessa got busy pulling up the woman's information on the computer.

We stepped into the hall so she could enter the room.

'Thanks for coming by,' Tessa said to me. 'And thanks for buying the paper.'

'Of course,' I said. 'Good to see you.'

Finn took my elbow and steered me down the hall into a large room with three plain vanilla IKEA desks with computers on them and an entire wall of shelves lined with boxes labeled with the names of items that anyone who stopped by was encouraged to pick up. Disposable toothbrushes, hand- and foot-warmers, gloves, scarves, tampons, sanitary napkins, tissues, lip balm, wet wipes – things you might need if you lived on the street. It was also the room where Streetwise caseworkers met their clients. At the moment, it was empty.

'Where is everyone?' I asked.

'Still out checking the camps, looking for the people who got displaced when they cleared Union Station. Plus we have to do a PIT headcount.'

Any organization that got money from the government needed to do a point-in-time count of the number of people who were unsheltered or sleeping on the street. It had been required by the Department of Housing and Urban Development for the past fifteen years, ever since they realized they had no clue how many homeless individuals were out there. *In the entire country.* Finn said the PIT numbers still grossly underrepresented the actual number of homeless, which in turn led to not enough resources being allocated for programs that could help folks get off the street. He told me once in a moment of despair that he thought homelessness was an unsolvable problem, no matter how much we tried to 'fix' it. The biggest obstacle was that there weren't enough homes for everyone who wanted or needed one. As for those lucky enough to find housing after being homeless, often they couldn't hang on to the place because they didn't know what they needed to do to keep it. Before long, the rent would be overdue or utility bills wouldn't be paid – and then came the inexorable slide back into homelessness.

'Tessa knows something about Javi,' Finn said to me now.

'I know she does.'

'Javi didn't tell anyone in the office he wasn't coming in. He just didn't show. That's not like him. Something's going on.'

'I was planning to take some supplies to the NoMa camp on L Street this afternoon. Javi lives on Lincoln Road, which isn't far away. Why don't I stop by and check in on him?'

'Would you mind?'

'Of course not.'

'That would be great. Let me know?'

'I'll call you.'

Tessa didn't look up when we walked by the App Room. Instead, she seemed engrossed in something on her computer screen.

Whatever she knew about Javi and why he hadn't come in today, she wasn't going to say a word. I wondered whom she was protecting – Javi or herself?

Because whatever it was, she was scared.

# EIGHT

When I got home from Streetwise, I got out the supplies I'd bought to make packages to leave at the tent camps under the L Street railroad bridge in NoMA, a DC neighborhood located north and east of Union Station. The neighborhood wasn't new, but the name was; the initials stood for 'North of Massachusetts Avenue.' As with other parts of the city, it had been a beatdown area that had undergone a renaissance, suddenly becoming trendy, hip, and expensive. On one level, the revitalization was good, but it had the added consequence of pushing out the Black community that had lived there for generations because they could no longer afford the prices. So where were *they* going to go?

My supply packages were similar to what was in the boxes at Streetwise, except I included a thick pair of athletic socks instead of gloves and a scarf and added a granola bar plus a Starbucks gift card with ten dollars on it that I stuffed into a quart-sized plastic bag and then sealed shut. Indian summer wasn't going to last forever; the colder weather would be here soon. And then it would be winter: hypothermia season if you lived on the street. You could nurse a hot coffee in Starbucks on a frigid morning for a few hours and warm yourself up.

I laid out everything on the mid-century teak dining-room table Max Katzer, my downstairs neighbor and one of DC's most sought-after interior designers, had helped me buy when I moved back from London after selling all our furniture in England except an antique grandfather clock I would never part with.

'You're not paying retail for anything, Sophie darling,' he had said to me. 'I know people.'

He wasn't kidding. Within a few months of highly organized and efficient shopping with Max, the duplex was filled with a wonderful, eclectic, homey mix of furniture he'd helped me acquire, from his own gallery in upper Georgetown, from his friends' shops, or from consignment shops he frequented. After

Nick died, I couldn't imagine moving out of this place and living anywhere else, especially with Max downstairs.

I turned cable news on the television in the living room since I could see it from where I was working. More stories about Everett Townsend, many of them focusing on a list of possible Supreme Court successors. I picked up the remote and hit *mute*. Tommy had been in the GW Emergency Room last night when the ambulance brought Townsend in. Even if he hadn't been one of the doctors who attended him – and I doubted he would have been since he was so new and junior – he'd know about Townsend's condition when he arrived. He would also know what happened *after* he got there, including details that might not have been revealed in the news. Tommy told me once that it's an unwritten rule that no one 'dies' in an ambulance. You aren't pronounced dead until a doctor does so at the hospital. Had Townsend made it to the ER or not?

I got my phone and texted my brother, inviting him for dinner. He'd know the answer to what had happened to Everett Townsend.

It was his day off and, Tommy being Tommy, he'd sleep for a good part of it because he would be so dog-tired. When he woke up, he'd probably eat whatever he could find in his refrigerator, which generally amounted to condiments and beer. I also texted Lexie, who worked in the office of the White House Press Secretary, and invited her.

Tommy wrote back first, all caps: *YES WHAT CAN I BRING?*

I wrote back: *An appetite. Come at 6.*

A moment later, his reply: *Bringing appetite & booze.*

Lexie called. The caller ID on my phone said *private number* so I knew she was calling on her office phone.

'I wish I could come,' she said, 'but I'm working late tonight. I'll eat here.'

'How late is late?'

She yawned. 'For the past few weeks, it's been around ten or eleven. With the midterms coming up, every day is like drinking out of a fire hose. Actually, most days are like drinking out of a fire hose. Now it's like trying to drink out of two of them.'

'Do you get weekends off?'

'What's a weekend? I used to know.'

'Jeez, Lex. Can you take a break *sometime*?'

'At the midterms. No one will be around – everyone from the Hill will be in their home states, so it will be quiet around here. Quiet*er*.'

'Doing anything special?'

'Yup. Going to Jamaica for a week.'

'Nice.'

'I can't wait.'

'Solo trip?'

She hesitated.

'Sorry,' I said. 'I wasn't trying to pry.'

'Of course you were. You wouldn't be my sister if you weren't prying. And no, not solo, but he's nobody you know. He's a bit older than me and just got divorced. Do. Not. Tell. Mom. She'll have a coronary.'

'Oh, don't worry. I'll leave that conversation for you.'

'Yeah, I can't wait. You're the only one who knows, by the way. I haven't said a word to Dad or Tommy, either.'

'My lips are sealed.' Harry would want to know if 'a bit older' meant he and Lexie's new boyfriend were the same age. Mom would freak out about the 'just got divorced' part. If Nick had been alive, he would have checked out Lexie's new man in the CIA database.

'I appreciate that,' she said. 'And speaking of not saying anything, I heard you and Jack O'Hara found Justice Townsend last night and stayed with him until the EMTs showed up.'

'How do you know?'

'Really? Where do I work?'

'Oh. Of course.' The White House.

'I got asked to write the President's statement expressing condolences to Diana Townsend and the other justices,' she said. 'Which was interesting since everyone knows Townsend and the President, uh, didn't like one another.'

A total understatement. They had despised each other.

'I'd forgotten about that since we were living in London during Townsend's confirmation hearings. Grace reminded me that your boss was the Ranking Minority Member of the Judiciary Committee back then.'

'Yup. He sure was. No exchange of Christmas cards between Townsend and the President, I can tell you. However, he has ordered all flags to be flown at half mast for a week,' Lexie said, 'though Townsend's not going to lie in state in the Capitol.'

'Why not?'

'He's going to be cremated. There won't be a casket. At all.'

'Are you serious? I'm surprised his wife didn't want a full-blown funeral. Jack says she's holier than the Pope.'

'Beats me. I heard she wants Townsend's body released from the GW morgue ASAP. She wants the medical examiner to sign off that it's OK to cremate him, so the funeral home can come by and get him. The funeral's already planned.'

'He died *last night*.'

'Hey, don't ask me. It's going to be Friday morning at St Matthew's. Well, it won't be a funeral, just a memorial since there won't be a body. The Cardinal is going to say the Mass. The President and First Lady are going out of respect, of course, and . . . oops, Soph, I gotta go. My boss is on the other line. Love you. Bye.'

She was gone.

How odd. A memorial Mass instead of a funeral because Everett Townsend was being cremated. The Catholic Church preferred a body in a casket at the Mass. The cremation could take place afterwards at something called a committal ceremony. You would think Diana Townsend being the *ne plus ultra* Catholic would want to follow those preferences. Plus, she seemed in quite the rush to bury her husband. I wondered if Jack had been with her when she made those decisions and if he had also helped her plan her husband's funeral.

My guess was probably yes.

When I moved back to Washington three years ago, I bought a mint-green Vespa, which I'd used for getting around town unless the weather was really bad. I'd owned one in London because it had been the ideal way to zip around without worrying about dealing with the two biggest headaches of driving in any city: traffic and parking. On the rare occasions when I had needed a car here in DC, my landlady loaned me her late husband's racing-green Rolls Royce, which was like docking the *Queen Mary* every time I had to parallel park. Eventually, I bought a red-and-white Mini Cooper so I had my own car. But for traveling to photo shoots or running errands, nothing beat the Vespa – even though these days I had to share my coveted sidewalk parking spots with all the bicycles and electric scooters that suddenly seemed to be everywhere.

The weather was as perfect as it had been yesterday, and the trip across town to NoMA through neighborhood streets lined with brilliantly colored trees was quick and easy. Last year, the DC government commissioned me to take photographs of some of the city's more unusual species of trees for a brochure called 'Trees in the District.' Before I did anything, I sought out a naturalist who worked at the Smithsonian and asked her to tell me what I needed to be looking for. Which is when I learned that ever since the city was founded in the early 1800s, more than three hundred species of trees had been brought to Washington from Europe, Africa, and Asia, as well as all over America. I also discovered that DC's nickname was – who knew? – 'the City of Trees.'

The brochure would be part of a public relations campaign to make Washington's citizens aware of a program to plant more than 11,000 trees in the District *every year* until the early 2030s, resulting in a tree canopy that covered at least forty percent of the city. The benefits were obvious: more shade, reduced energy bills, less stormwater runoff, a more diverse ecosystem for wild-life, to name a few. But the tree campaign also gave me hope every time I saw more blockades, barricades, and chain-link fences go up around federal Washington, turning it into an ugly concrete fortress to protect our legislators and leaders from . . . we the people.

I chained the Vespa to a street sign when I got to the underpass at L Street. The camp wasn't crowded since a lot of people took off to work or do other things during the day. I went around quickly and left my supply packages, saying hello to folks I saw, some of whom I knew by name. I also took photos of anyone who gave me permission and then took another photo on my phone which I printed on a small handheld printer to give as a thank-you gift. The gift photos were always a huge success – everyone wanted one.

Fifteen minutes later, I was on my way to Javi Aguilera's place off North Capitol Street. This time, I chained the Vespa to the wrought-iron fence in front of the red-brick row house where his basement apartment was located. The painted brick was peeling like a bad sunburn and the house looked old and forlorn, though it once must have been a Grand Dame, someone's elegant home. The grass in the front yard was nothing but weeds and hard-packed dirt, and the concrete steps down to Javi's apartment were chipped and spalling.

The entrance gate was unlatched and ajar.

Blue, the ex-British Special Forces ranger who had been my favorite instructor in the hostile environment training course, taught us never to walk into a situation or a place where we weren't in control if we could help it.

I wasn't, so I stopped.

Javi wasn't inside. I already knew that, but I called his name anyway.

No answer.

If someone was inside waiting – which was doubtful – I needed something to defend myself. I went back to the Vespa and unstrapped my tripod. Better than nothing.

I opened the front door. In the dim, washed-out light that filtered in through dirty casement windows, it was even more apparent that no one was here.

I went inside, holding my tripod like a club.

Someone, or more than one person, *had* been here, though, and there had been a struggle. A chair was overturned and a lamp had fallen to the floor, the ceramic base and the bulb smashed to pieces around it. I found the blood in the kitchen. A trail of drops on the linoleum floor that led to the back door, which was open. So was the gate in the scruffy, weedy back garden that led to the alley. There was an empty slot in the knife holder by the kitchen stove. One of the large butcher knives.

What I didn't know was whether the blood was Javi's or if it belonged to whoever had come after him. And now he was gone, more than likely disappearing into one of the homeless camps where he still had friends, where it was easy to get lost in that mercurial, fluid world if you wanted to. Where others would close ranks around him, protect him from whoever was after him.

But what I really didn't understand was *why*. If this were a random burglary, he would have stuck around and cleaned up.

He might even have called the police, though I doubted it because of the blood. Especially if he had wounded the intruder. He wouldn't want to go down that road, figuring he might be accused of being the aggressor instead of the one who had been attacked.

Instead, he was gone and possibly wounded.

I wondered who had come after him.

And what he had done to provoke his attacker.

# NINE

Tessa Janko said she thought Javi was taking care of his sick landlady. Javi lived in the basement; the landlady lived upstairs in the rest of the house. Maybe she was home. Maybe he was with her. But when I climbed the sagging stairs to her wide front porch and knocked on the door, no one answered there, either. I peered through the windows into the living room. The house was dark and quiet, not a single light or flickering screen anywhere inside.

So where was Javi's landlady, especially if she was ill? With him? Somewhere else?

But what I really wanted to know: *where was Javi?*

I walked back to the Vespa and called Finn as I'd promised. The call went to voicemail, so I said I was getting ready to leave Javi's apartment and to call me as soon as he got my message. He returned the call when I was home making pesto – Tommy's favorite. I told Finn about Javi's apartment and what I'd seen. He didn't say anything, which made me wonder whether he was surprised by my news. Then I told him about the bloody trail to the back gate.

He swore, something I'd never heard him do.

'Was Javi in trouble with anyone?' I asked him. 'Maybe the vandalism was just a random break-in, though I doubt it. And if it wasn't, then someone came looking for him.'

'If he was in trouble, I didn't know about it.' Finn said and now he sounded really concerned. 'You're sure what you found was blood?'

Like what, maybe, it was ketchup? 'Do you know how many war zones I've been in during my past life?'

'OK,' he said. 'Sorry.'

'Where do you think he is now?' I asked.

'Probably one of the tent camps.'

'That's what I figured. With all the vendors that work with Streetwise, you've got a small army of people who could be out looking for him. Right?'

'I hope so. I'll get the word out.' He paused. 'And then we'll see.'

It was my turn to say, 'You'll let me know?'

'Of course.' But his tone of voice wasn't upbeat or even confident. *If Javi wanted to be found.*

I disconnected and tried to decide whether I should call Grace and tell her what had happened. I ground more pepper into the mixture of basil, walnuts, parmesan and romano cheese, and garlic. Then I turned on the food processor and slowly added olive oil until the pesto was the right consistency.

Maybe it would be better to wait and see if Finn learned anything from anyone in the tent camps before I called Grace.

No sense in both of us being beside ourselves with worry.

Tommy brought a six-pack assortment of craft beer he'd carefully selected and spent ten minutes explaining the subtleties of taste, flavor, and brewing method for each one. He also brought an expensive bottle of Châteauneuf-du-Pape. I'm mostly a wine girl, but after living in England for as long as I did, I like a beer now and again. He opened our beers – a pale lager for me, an ale for him – and leaned against the counter in my kitchen while I heated up the water for our homemade fettuccine. He'd given me an electric pasta maker as a Christmas gift to replace the manual one I'd brought home from England, joking that it was a gift for both of us. Especially any time he came over for dinner and I made pasta – which, to please him, was most of the time. I gave him a corkscrew so he could open the wine and let it breathe.

'Tell me about finding Everett Townsend,' he said as he pulled the cork out of the bottle with a soft pop.

'There's nothing to tell that you don't know already,' I said. 'Jack and I found him in an alley behind Eighth Street near Eastern Market when we were out for a run. We happened to take the alley to avoid some construction. If we hadn't done that, who knows how long he would have been lying there. If only we'd gotten to him sooner, he might still be . . .'

'Don't. You did what you could.'

I dropped the pasta into boiling water. 'OK, now you tell *me* what happened when he got to the hospital.'

Tommy took a swig of his beer. 'Off the record, right?'

'You know better. Of course it's off the record.'

'You still have a bunch of journo friends.'

'Never burn a source, Tom. *Never.*'

'OK.' He leaned against the door jamb and watched me stir the fettuccine with a pair of tongs. 'We knew Townsend was coming to GW, of course. Then we get word that while they're in transit, his EMTs noticed there's swelling starting to show up next to his right temple.'

Fresh pasta cooks in just a few minutes. I stirred it and checked my timer. Two more to go. 'Swelling from what?'

'They didn't know. Maybe he coshed his head when he collapsed. He was still unconscious, so there was no way to find out.'

'Was he still alive when he got to the ER?' I had wondered if Everett Townsend had made it to the hospital. If he'd died in the ambulance en route, no one would have said anything. Time of death is always declared when you're at a hospital.

Tommy nodded. 'Yes, but just barely. When they were wheeling him into the ER and transferring him to us, Townsend started to posture. It's a bad sign because it meant he definitely had a head injury. He was breathing with the bag valve mask, so he needed help to breathe – that's already not good. Then one of the nurses who was admitting him noticed a blown pupil.'

I turned off the burner and dumped the pasta into a colander after pouring a small amount of the water into a glass measuring cup in case I needed it for the pesto.

'What is that?'

'You know how doctors always check your pupils to see if they react to light? They shine a bright light in your eye and your pupil is supposed to constrict, right?'

'Right.'

'When nothing happens, it means your brain is no longer functioning. It means you're dead.'

I put the fettuccine into a bowl with the pesto and added some of the cooking water. 'Oh my God. Did the blown pupil have anything to do with his head injury?'

'Everything. That first dose of D50 the EMTs gave him should have revived him instantly. I mean like Lazarus rising from the dead,' he said. 'But because they didn't see any sign of head trauma at that point, they gave him a second dose – which was the logical thing to do. If they'd known about the brain bleed, they never even would have given him the first dose.'

I stopped stirring the pasta. 'Brain bleed?'

'It's exactly what you think it is. They found it when they did an X-ray and a CT scan at the hospital. It was pretty bad, Soph. He'd gone downhill fast. If you really want the details . . .'

'I do. Jack and I found him. Tell me.'

He took a long pull of his beer. 'OK, since you asked, the brain bleed was causing intracranial pressure on his brain stem. The X-ray also found a fracture near C3 in his spine, so there was a second bleed, also near his brain stem. Now his docs are saying this is dangerous because part of the spinal column close to his neck is sheared off, which probably happened when they were trying to move and stabilize him in order to intubate him. So the guy's got two brain bleeds putting pressure on his brain stem, plus the added complication of the D50 leaking into the brain tissue and possibly causing necrosis. In short,' he said, 'to use the proper medical term, he's fucked. Official cause of death: complications from a hypoglycemic event.'

'Jesus.'

'By the time his wife got to the hospital, she found him hooked up to tubes and machines that were keeping him alive. She had to make the decision to pull the plug, turn the equipment off.'

I closed my eyes and thought of Nick. I would have done it – turned the machines off – if the doctors told me he was gone, but it would have been the hardest thing I ever did in my life.

Tommy put his hand on my shoulder. 'He'd left instructions. No extraordinary measures. He wasn't even supposed to be kept on life support, but no one knew until Mrs Townsend got there. She also wanted his body moved as soon as possible and taken to a funeral home, so she kicked up a fuss to get a doctor to sign the death certificate right away.'

'Lexie told me about that.'

'*She* knew?'

'Well, look where she works. She knew Diana Townsend wanted him out of the hospital ASAP. And that she planned the funeral the next day.'

'I heard that.'

'Did you see him when he got to the ER?'

'Briefly, when they brought him in. Usually, Monday nights aren't that busy unless it's raining. Fridays and Saturdays are when all hell breaks loose. But for some reason we had ambulances lined up like it was a parade outside the ER entrance, so everyone was scrambling, doing triage, getting patients inside as fast as we could,' he said.

I handed him his plate.

'He never woke up, never knew a thing once he collapsed in that alley,' he said. 'It was quick.'

'I suppose that's a blessing.'

'That's how I want to go.' He stopped talking and looked aghast. 'Oh, God, sorry. I know this must be hard for you to talk about. Maybe we should change the subject and, uh, dinner smells amazing.'

I smiled. 'Thanks, sweetie. Everything's ready. The table is set in the dining area and the wine glasses are there. So if you bring the wine I'll bring the salad after I dress it.'

He picked up the bottle. 'What's for dessert?'

Typical male question. 'Some of the peaches I canned last summer, cooked in white wine with mascarpone and caramelized pistachios.'

He moaned. 'Oh my God. That sounds fantastic.'

After I lit the candles and he said grace – the economical one: 'God's neat, let's eat' – I said, 'One more question. Did you see Diana Townsend when she was at the hospital?'

'No, but I heard she was pretty composed and stoic after she got over the shock of seeing her husband. No waterworks, no nothing. Made a couple of phone calls and said she wanted his body released as soon as possible once they turned off the machines.'

When Nick's body came home, I was a mess. I couldn't imagine being by his side in a hospital, watching him die and being emotionless. And making the hard decision to end his life. Diana Townsend must have been an incredibly strong woman to be so self-possessed and calm after dealing with what she had just been through.

'She's good friends with Jack,' I said. 'She called him as she was leaving the hospital and asked him to come over to her house in Georgetown. Probably to ask him what happened when we found her husband in the alley.'

Tommy spooled pasta on to his fork and shrugged. 'Like I said, Diana Townsend wasn't exactly a grief-stricken widow. Every time I see someone show that kind of stoicism, either they're in shock or they're not exactly sorry their loved one is gone. In her case, my money's on door number two. I don't think she was that broken up about her husband's death.'

After Tommy was gone – he stayed to help do the dishes – I texted Finn Hathaway and asked if there was any news about Javi. No reply.

I finally gave in and called Grace. She was as upset as I was. Actually, more upset.

'Oh my God. *Where is he?*' she asked.

'Finn and I figure he disappeared into one of the tent camps, but who knows? Finn promised to put the word out on the street, ask the vendors to check around and see if anyone knows where he is. If I hear from him, I'll let you know.'

'I don't care what time it is, just call me,' she said. 'And, Soph, I'm heartsick. I don't have a good feeling about this.'

She hung up.

I didn't have a good feeling about what had happened to Javi, either.

I took the last glass of Tommy's wine upstairs to my bedroom and sat in the darkness in bed with my laptop, searching until I found YouTube videos of Everett Townsend's confirmation hearing – both days. As Grace had said and Lexie confirmed, he and the President – who had then been the Ranking Minority Member of the Senate Judiciary Committee – hadn't gotten along. They had sparred mostly over Townsend's time as a District judge for Washington, DC, specifically over Townsend's lenient sentence for a real estate mogul who had been accused of laundering drug money through his company. Townsend had been surprisingly arrogant and not at all repentant about his sentence, claiming he hadn't found that the prosecution produced evidence that left no margin for doubt. Was the real estate mogul guilty of the charges? It looked as if he might have been. But Townsend let the guy off easy because the lawyers for the other side did a less than stellar job of presenting their case.

Townsend then delivered a scathing, masterful statement directed almost entirely to the Ranking Minority Senator citing the Founding Fathers as well as Cicero, Homer, and Plato, whose ideas had been integral in contributing to the founding of our republic. A republic based on *laws*. He ended by reminding the committee that the statue of Justice outside the Supreme Court was blind because the law should be based on facts and evidence, not innuendo, unsubstantiated assertions, or prejudicial beliefs. When he was finished, the room erupted in applause and cheering, effectively shutting down any further discussion of his record as a lower court judge, and that was that.

The committee vote had ultimately been six-six, with everyone falling into step and voting along party lines, but it was a known fact that Townsend would be confirmed because there were enough votes in the Senate to make him the 117th justice appointed.

At least now I understood the animosity between him and the President of the United States. Who would soon be nominating Everett Townsend's successor to the Supreme Court.

Tonight at dinner, Tommy said that Townsend had sustained a blow to his head, presumably when he fell. But wasn't it possible someone could have hit him over the head with something instead? Nothing that caused any external bleeding, which was why the EMTs hadn't realized he had a brain bleed or a head injury until the swelling started showing up when he was in the ambulance.

Maybe a jealous lover struck him after a quarrel? A jealous lover like Vicki Russell? Jesus, I hoped not. But what if she'd shown up after their romantic tryst earlier that morning only to find another woman leaving Townsend's little love nest? The gossipy neighbor in the alley had implied that Townsend did *a lot* of entertaining. Or what if Diana Townsend finally had enough of her husband's philandering? Tommy said she hadn't been too broken up about his death, plus she'd planned the funeral so fast it made my head spin.

If someone had deliberately struck Everett Townsend, his death hadn't been accidental at all.

He'd been murdered.

# TEN

I woke up exhausted, just as I used to during those early weeks after Nick died when my dreams had been filled with Rated-X-for-Violence scenarios imagining what had happened to him, how he had died. No matter what I listened to on headphones before I went to sleep – a calm-you-down session from a meditation app I bought, the sound of a gurgling stream or chirping birds or peaceful night noises – the nightmares haunted me.

Last night, the movie reel changed, and instead of Nick, I dreamed of Everett Townsend and Javi Aguilera. Why I connected them, I have no idea.

If I ever decided to see a therapist for dream analysis, they'd have a field day with what was going on inside my head. *I* probably wouldn't want to know what they discerned about my mental state. Just how close I was to the edge that separated sanity from whatever was over the precipice.

Grace called when I was already on my second cup of coffee and she was on her way to work.

'Any news?'

'You know I would have called you.'

'I know, I know. Jesus, where *is* he? I hope he's OK.'

'Me, too. Finn didn't call, so that must mean he doesn't have any news, either,' I said.

'Are you going to call him to make sure?'

'Right after we hang up. What about MPD?'

'What about them?'

'What do you mean? You work at the *Trib*'s Metro desk. You work with the Metropolitan Police Department all the time. You must have a list a mile long of detectives and police officers and people on speed dial who can find out things if you ask them. Can't you call in a favor, see if Javi turned up on anybody's radar?'

'I could,' she said. 'But if someone broke into Javi's place and he's on the run – instead of calling the cops like a normal person would do – I'm not sure getting the police involved would be such a good idea. Looking at it from his perspective, that is.'

She had a point.

After we disconnected, I called Finn who was already in his office at Streetwise. He confirmed what I'd told Grace: he had nothing new to report.

'Sorry, no news. Nothing. Just . . . nothing,' he said. 'None of the vendors know where he is or have seen him around the past few days.'

'Do you think no one *really* knows anything – or that they're protecting him by keeping quiet?'

'Your guess is as good as mine.'

'What about Tessa Janko? Yesterday, we thought she had some idea of what happened to him. She said he was looking after his sick landlady. Who was also missing when I stopped by.'

'I'll talk to Tessa again,' he said. 'I'll see what I can do.'

'Let me know?'

'Of course,' he said.

So there we were. Nowhere. Nothing.

I stuck my breakfast dishes in the dishwasher and poured the last of the coffee in the pot into a to-go mug to bring over to the studio. I had finally begun putting up some of what I thought were the best photos from my series on homelessness in DC on one of the studio walls, trying to figure out an order or a thread running through everything that would turn the photographs into a story. Maybe something or some*body* in one or more of the pictures would jog my memory, offer some clue as to who might know something useful about Javi.

It was another gorgeous Indian summer morning with a soft breeze, cotton-ball clouds, brilliant blue sky, and the sun warm on my face. I unlocked the door to the little carriage house – which, increasingly since Nick's death, had become my refuge. A sanctuary.

Before I moved in, Max had rented it from our landlady, using it to store furniture that either needed a bit of repairing or sprucing up or that he didn't yet have room for in his Georgetown antique gallery. When he found a bigger space that could accommodate both the antique store and the to-be-repaired furniture, he left behind a few pieces he'd decided he couldn't sell because of dents, scars, or other imperfections and practically gave them to me at a fire-sale price. What I bought was an oval oak dining-room table with carved cabriole legs, four almost-matching dining chairs that looked like thrones, a dark-green velvet Chesterfield sofa, a club chair covered in rust, green, and cream striped fabric, and – best of all – an Amish Mission-style trestle table that I used as my desk. I also bought an antique Jenny Lind spindle double bed I found at an estate sale to put upstairs in a loft area that I turned into a bedroom. My final acquisition had been an ivory hand-knotted Persian rug with a geometric pattern for the main room downstairs. Since the carriage house also had a kitchenette and a small full bathroom, I had the perfect guest house for visitors.

The tenant before Max had painted three walls of the main room a deep Venetian red, which I immediately painted white, although it took three coats and a couple of cans of Kilz to cover the brownish-red. The fourth wall was the original exposed brick.

My homeless photos were on one of the white walls, where I'd been arranging and rearranging them as I added to the collection. Only a few were of women: most of those who lived on the street in DC were men. The city tried to get women, especially if they had children, into a shelter. And if they were families – mother, father, and kids – they most definitely tried to get them in a shelter so they weren't on the streets or, as often happened, living in their car.

The project began as a by-chance photo opportunity, but it had turned into something much bigger after I stopped on my way home from a photo shoot at the Kennedy Center one brutally cold December day, when I saw a young Black man shivering while begging near the yield sign where cars came off the Teddy Roosevelt Bridge at the entrance to Rock Creek Parkway. I pulled off under an overpass bridge, which was where he and a small community of homeless individuals were living. Their camp, not far from the banks of the Potomac River, was a stone's throw from the Lincoln Memorial. This wasn't the poor side of town. People zipped by on their way to offices on Capitol Hill every morning and drove to homes in upper Northwest or the Virginia suburbs every evening. *I* had driven by dozens of times and never stopped until now.

The young guy and I got talking, he let me take his photo,

and I gave him the loaded Starbucks cards I had just bought, intending to put them in Christmas cards for a few friends who simply *could not get through the day* without a caramel macchiato or a tall flat white or a pumpkin spiced latte.

I kept going back to the bridge, getting permission to take more pictures, bringing more Starbucks cards, which bought not only coffee but the time and dignity to stay inside – as a paying client – and get warm. I listened to stories that alternately made my skin crawl because they were so awful or else made me want to weep because they were so heartbreaking.

And then I went back to my studio and started studying the photos of two female photographers whose work I admired because they took such honest pictures of those who, like these homeless individuals, were marginalized by society: Diane Arbus and Vivian Maier. Arbus was best known for shining a spotlight on people who were considered freakish or odd: carnival performers, dwarfs, strippers, the elderly. As for Maier, no one had paid attention to her because of who she was: a nanny, a paid household servant, who managed to take more than 150,000 photos of street people mostly in New York and Chicago. Vivian Maier's story especially fascinated me because she was a complete unknown until after her death in 2009, when her work was posted on the Internet and went viral. Like Arbus, Maier's most compelling photos were those of marginalized or unnoticed individuals – street bums, Black maids, children, people who lived in the rough parts of town.

No one had seen my photos until about a week ago when I invited Max to the studio. Typically, he arrived with a bottle of champagne and two Waterford flutes.

'These,' he said after he'd studied the wall of pictures, 'are incredible. *Powerful.* I had no idea you were working on something like this.'

He opened the champagne and we sat side by side on the Chesterfield sofa where we could stare at the photos.

'What are you going to do with them?' he asked.

'I've been thinking about talking to an editor I know at *National Geographic*,' I said. 'He might be interested. Or possibly the *Times* or the *Post* or the *Tribune* – see if I could sell the series along with a story for their Sunday magazines.'

Max clicked his tongue against his teeth and shook his head. 'That's all well and good, but these need to be exhibited in a gallery. In Washington absolutely, but also in New York. I'm talking about galleries where you'd get great exposure, get your name out there – I have friends who can help.'

Of course he did.

'Let me make some calls,' he said.

I couldn't let him call in favors like that. *Huge* favors like that. 'Max, you can't.'

'Darling,' he said. 'I *can* and I *will.*'

By ten thirty, my eyes were crossing after editing the photos I took yesterday at the tent camp under the L Street bridge, plus finishing up the last batch of photos I'd taken on Monday when I was at Fernway. Talk about opposite subjects.

Maybe if I went back to some of the homeless camps and took my camera, I could ask around about Javi. But if the Streetwise vendors hadn't found out anything, why would someone talk to me? Besides, the camps – and there were a lot of them – were scattered throughout the city. It could take *days* to find someone who knew where Javi might be. Or had been. He could be moving around, especially if whoever came to his house was still hunting for him.

My mobile rang. The display read *Darius Zahiri.*

Director of the Dupont Underground. We hadn't spoken for a couple of weeks after Knox Porter called me from Connecticut to pitch the idea of me giving the talk my grandfather would have given at the opening of his photography exhibition in a few weeks. I am not great at public speaking – I'm better behind a camera than a microphone – but Knox had sold Darius on the idea as well. This was probably a final arm-twisting call because Darius needed a fish-or-cut-bait commitment. They wanted to print the exhibition programs.

Darius had the kind of devastating good looks that not only turned women's heads but kept them staring. He was of medium height, slender, and well built, with the noble bearing of a Persian prince. He had a thick mane of jet-black hair, piercing blue eyes, a hawk-like nose, and skin a bit darker than mine. But it was his voice that got your attention instantly. Deep and sensuous, it sounded like a sexy growl wrapped in a warm caress.

Although he was born in Iran, he grew up in London when his parents left after the ayatollahs came to power, so he'd also acquired a cut-glass British accent to go with that great voice. I was never sure how or where he'd made his fortune; he was vague about his wheeling and dealing. But he had also founded a publishing company specializing in gorgeous coffee-table art books that could be found in museum gift shops like the National Gallery, the Smithsonian, and the Library of Congress – as well as the Louvre, the British National Gallery, and the Prado. He was the editor as well as the publisher, which meant he knew a lot of up-and-coming artists around the country and throughout the world. It also meant he was the perfect person to be the director of the Dupont Underground, which he'd added to his already-full portfolio.

'Sophie,' he said when I answered the phone, 'how are you, my love? I'm calling to ask if you might be free for coffee today. Tatte Bakery and Café, as usual? I have something that belongs to you and I apologize for not getting it to you sooner. You must let me make it up to you. I'm buying. Two house lattes and your favorite pastries.'

I smiled. Darius *always* bought. We *always* shared pastries. His favorites were the decadent ones filled with cream or custard – *mille-feuille*, profiteroles, eclairs – so that's what we always had. I would have a sugar buzz for the rest of the day. The house lattes were made with honey halva and cardamom. The pastries were out of this world. The bakery was a ten-minute walk from my house and not far from the Dupont Underground and Darius's office in a beautiful Beaux Arts building on the corner of Massachusetts Avenue and Dupont Circle.

'I'm fine,' I said. 'And I'd love to see you. I just finished up some work, so I could meet you now if you like.'

'Excellent,' he said. 'I'll meet you at Tatte. Your latte and pastries will be waiting.'

He disconnected before I realized that I'd forgotten to ask him what he had that belonged to me.

The bright-red railings around the staircases at the two entrances to the Dupont Underground stood out from the otherwise gray

landscape of sidewalks and the pinwheel of streets that inter-
sected Dupont Circle. Originally DC's only underground trolley
station, it was a cavernous 75,000-square-foot space with a network
of tunnels that was gradually being transformed into one of the
city's most avant-garde art galleries. Abandoned for years when
buses and the Metro replaced the trolleys, it had been repurposed
twice: as a fallout shelter in case of a nuclear war with the Soviet
Union and later as an underground food hall that lasted mere
months because it was too dark, dank, and creepy. In 2016, devel-
opers got the idea to transform the nearly forgotten massive space
into an arts center – a quirky plan that quickly took off.

With so many miles of drab, dull concrete, its owners turned
to graffiti artists to help fill the space with elaborate paintings and
words or slogans – whatever they wanted to do. The brilliantly
colored walls that were the result – and there were still more
tunnels to paint – had become the Underground's most distinctive
feature. What made it truly unique was that when there was an
exhibition, the art was hung on those graffiti-filled walls rather
than expanses of pristine white.

My grandfather's exhibition was going to be a big draw for
the Underground, the first real event since the pandemic shutdown,
and I knew Darius was counting on folks packing the place. I
walked by one of the entrances on my way to Tatte Bakery and
Café. A chain-link fence had been placed over the opening
and tethered to the red railing, the only way to keep folks from
going down the stairs and sleeping there or shooting up or peeing.
A *Closed* sign with a warning about the dangers of walking or
lying on the barricade was attached to the fence with wire.

The bakery was a block further south of Dupont Circle. When
I walked into the light-filled, noisy restaurant a few minutes later,
Darius was already there. He waved at me from a corner table
surrounded by windows and stood as I walked over to him,
leaning in to kiss me on both cheeks. I kissed him back, breathing
in the faint scent of his musky, woodsy cologne and the Cuban
cigars he occasionally liked to smoke.

We sat and he pushed my latte over to me. As for the pastries:
an eclair, a *mille-feuille*, and a profiterole, as expected. Three of
the most sinfully rich confections in the pastry case.

'Shall we share?' he asked.

We always shared because I knew he wanted to sample everything.

'Of course.'

He cut the *mille-feuille* in half and set the pieces on our plates. I picked up my fork and took a bite. 'I'll take these as an apology any day – they're so good. And just what is it you need to apologize for? I forgot to ask.'

He stopped mid-bite and looked chagrined. 'A letter. Addressed to you, care of the Dupont Underground. I'm so sorry. I've had it for a week – maybe a bit longer. A woman gave it to one of the tour guides. She said she knew you'd be by because of your grandfather's exhibition. I took it back to my office, intending to call you and let you know, but I got distracted and forgot. No excuse. I hope it isn't something urgent or with a deadline.'

'A letter from a woman? Who was she?'

And why would she hand-deliver a letter meant for me to the Dupont Underground? I have a website. Anyone can contact me there. What was wrong with an email that would land directly in my inbox, rather than a letter left at a place this woman knew I'd come by but not *when*?

Darius licked custard off his finger. 'No idea who she was. The guide said she looked as if she were in her late seventies or maybe eighties, with a faint accent she couldn't quite place – she thought either Spanish or Italian. Utterly charming but very determined to leave the letter. Apparently, she wouldn't take no for an answer – and wouldn't leave her name, either.'

'It's probably someone who knew my grandfather.'

He attacked the eclair, slicing it in half. 'Damn. The halves are uneven. Take the big one.'

I switched the plates around. '*You* take the big one. Going out with you is bad for my waistline. I'm trying to watch my weight.'

He flashed a mock-leering suggestive grin at me. 'There's no need for that, darling. You look gorgeous as usual. Though a bit tired. Is everything all right?'

He slipped the letter out of the inside pocket of his navy blazer and set it down next to my plate. I glanced at it. No return address. As Darius said, just my name, care of the Dupont Underground. The handwriting – a flowery old-fashioned script – was a bit shaky.

'Not really. A friend of mine is missing. And I suppose you heard about Everett Townsend.'

His eyebrows went up when I mentioned Townsend. 'I'm sorry to hear about your friend. And even if you lived in a cave, you heard about Everett Townsend. His death, his potential successor, what it means for the future of the Supreme Court, which way it's going to tilt now. What impact it's going to have on the future of America, the planet, the entire solar system. It's getting to be a bit much. Why do you bring him up?'

'A friend of mine and I found him when we were out for a run on Capitol Hill the other night. I called nine-one-one and we stayed with him until the ambulance got there.'

In the clear bright light streaming through the windows, Darius's blue eyes turned icy. '*You* found him? Are you serious?'

'I am. I would say *deadly* serious, but that's not the best choice of words. I'm grateful our names were kept out of the news. So please don't mention this to anybody, OK?'

He made a zipping motion across his lips with a finger. 'What happened?'

I told him.

When I was done, he said, 'I knew him.'

'You did? How?'

He huffed out a breath as if the memories weren't exactly pleasant. 'We saw each other at parties and fundraisers on the DC social circuit. His wife is a big philanthropist.'

'I know. What did you think of them?'

'She's stunning – a knockout.'

'I know that, too. I *mean* as a person.'

'Diana's a real do-gooder. But she's also quite strong-willed and very well connected. I wouldn't exactly call her an operator, but she knows what buttons to push to get things done and the people to call to do them.'

'What about him?'

Darius's eyes flashed. 'I didn't like him.' He placed a hand over his heart and said, without an ounce of sincerity, 'God rest his soul.'

'Why not?'

'He was condescending and patronizing. He could be cruel and cutting to anyone he thought wasn't bright enough to engage in a conversation with him. I saw him put someone down more than once, humiliate them in front of others. He could be a mean-spirited bastard. Brilliant, though – I'll give you that. An absolutely brilliant mind.'

Jack had said the same thing, and for the dozenth time I couldn't figure out what Vicki Russell had seen in Townsend. He didn't seem like her type at all. *Her husband* seemed like her type. Funny. Charming. Compassionate. Intelligent. Kind.

'I've heard that assessment of Townsend before,' I said.

'Plus he was a hypocrite,' Darius said. 'He was Justice Law-and-Order, the by-the-book justice on the Court, but he ran with a fast, hard-partying crowd. Kept it under the radar, of course. Although with a lifetime appointment to the Supreme Court, what did he have to worry about? He didn't need to run for re-election or please a constituency.'

'Wow. That's harsh.'

'True, nonetheless. He developed a taste for the good life and got paid piles of money to give speeches for which he was always flown first-class and stayed in five-star hotels. The usual. He just landed a seven-figure book contract to explain that, in his opinion, the Court has *not* become politicized.' He stabbed what was left of his *mille-feuille* with his fork, shredding the flaky pastry into crumbs.

I watched him, trying to figure out what he *wasn't* saying. 'You're not . . . jealous of him, are you?'

Another huff of air, this time disdainful. 'God, no. I just hate to see someone exploiting a position of power and authority for personal gain. A judge – especially a Supreme Court justice – is someone you expect to be above the law, not to use that legal acumen to get away with actions or behavior that would have consequences for the rest of us.'

'What did he do, Darius?' Because even though Darius was talking in generalizations, reading between the lines, he was referring to something quite specific.

Darius set down his fork and looked me in the eye. 'His position on the Supreme Court made him a very rich man. A very *entitled* rich man. A sense of entitlement like that – you're on the *Supreme Court*, for God's sake, one of the nine and the ultimate arbiter of the law and the Constitution – can make you reckless. It can make you believe you can get away with something because of who you are.'

'Most of the country thinks that's what Washington's all about anyway,' I said. 'Greed. Money. Power. Everyone's on the take, thinking only about what's in it for them. Townsend isn't any different from everyone else according to the *vox populi*.'

Darius reached for the plate with the profiterole on it.

I held up my hand. 'It's all yours. I couldn't.'

'You must.'

I shook my head, but he had already cut the profiterole and set half on my plate anyway. 'Maybe so, but rumors were he had gotten careless. Thought he was above it all.'

'What do you mean?'

'Rhett Townsend was quite pally with a Russian oligarch named Alexey Ozupov. They went to private school together when they were both growing up in London. Ozupov's father was the Soviet ambassador to the Court of St James. Later, he was Soviet – then Russian – Foreign Minister. Now Ozupov Junior owns the biggest private bank in Russia. He still lives in London – or, at least, one of his homes is there. Knightsbridge. He owns a football team, too. Dover FC. Townsend was a huge fan. If you follow English Premier League football, every so often you see the owners in their boxes on television. With their trophy wives and best pals.'

'Ozupov's best pals included Everett Townsend?'

Darius nodded.

'What of it?'

'Ozupov is a huge philanthropist. He's also an astute businessman who knows how to capitalize on the economic misfortune of others. He was one of the oligarchs who snapped up Soviet-owned energy and mining companies in the 1990s, loaning millions to Boris Yeltsin who was desperate for funds for his nearly bankrupt new country. That's where Ozupov made his fortune – and then kept growing it. In the meantime, he began writing sizeable checks to major British, French, and American museums, universities, and cultural institutions. He's also one of the billionaire philanthropists who signed the Giving Pledge that Warren Buffett and Bill and Melinda Gates established, promising to give away half of his money to charity.'

'Are you serious?'

'I am indeed. The next conquest he's set his sights on after endearing himself as a generous donor to so many American charities and worthy causes is . . . guess what?'

'No idea.'

'Politics.'

I set my fork down and folded my hands. 'I suppose I shouldn't be surprised.'

'Well, it won't be as easy as it is in other countries because of our restrictions on campaigns taking foreign donations. Although you can get around them, as a few recent presidential candidates have proven. And look what happened to them.' Darius paused, waiting for my rhetorical answer.

'Nothing.'

'Exactly. Big shoulder shrug, we didn't do anything wrong, next subject, please. So who better to help Ozupov meet the people he needs to meet than his old school friend who is now a Supreme Court justice?'

'And no one's saying anything about it.'

'More like no one's *doing* anything about it. In return, Townsend was always welcome at any Dover game as a guest in the owner's box whenever he was in Britain. Plus, Ozupov owns a superyacht where he parties hard. Of course, he keeps the Love Boat in international waters so anything goes and nothing is against the law.'

'Townsend was welcome there, too?'

Darius nodded.

'Not to defend him,' I said, 'but he's not the only justice with a questionable past. And like you said, nothing happens. No one cares – or seems to.'

'I know. Which is why Townsend got away with it.' He raised an eyebrow. 'Until . . .'

'Until what?'

'There were rumors that he and Ozupov had a falling out recently.'

'Over what?'

'That I don't know.' He looked over at my plate. 'You didn't finish your profiterole.'

'You eat it while I look at this letter.' I pushed my plate over to him and he didn't object.

There was a single sheet of paper inside the envelope. I unfolded it and started reading.

> *Dear Sophie,*
>
> *You don't know me, and what I am about to tell you will probably be quite a surprise, but now that your grandfather is dead, I believe there is something you need to know about him – and me.*
>
> *Charles Lord and I were married many years ago when he was twenty and I was eighteen. We were young and foolish, and believed we were deeply in love. Unfortunately, because we were young and foolish, the marriage didn't last, and we separated after a few months.*
>
> *We never saw each other again.*
>
> *As these things happen, we also never bothered to get divorced. In other words, I am legally still Charles Lord's wife, now his widow.*
>
> *I would like to discuss this further with you, so I am inviting you to lunch at my home in Georgetown on Wednesday, October 12th. Please come at noon.*

There was an address, but no phone number. And the letter was signed 'Oriana Neri Lord.'

# ELEVEN

'Is everything OK?' Darius asked as he signaled for the check. 'Are *you* OK?'

'Yes. Fine. No.'

'Pick one.'

'The letter is from a woman who was a . . . friend . . . of my grandfather's. She invited me to lunch.' I glanced at my watch. 'In ninety minutes.'

'Damn,' he said as a young woman with a sexy cold-shoulder top that showed off an elaborate tattoo of intertwining roses laid down the bill and smiled at us. Darius set his credit card on top of the bill without looking at it and smiled his heart-melting smile right back at her.

'I won't be a moment,' she said, though she lingered to cast another look at him over her shoulder before she left.

'I'm so sorry, Sophie,' he said. 'I should have given you that letter when I got it. What are you going to do?'

'You mean, besides regret eating three pastries and now I'm not hungry for lunch?'

He grinned. 'You only ate half of each one. So it's one and a half, not three.'

'Still.'

'You're going to go.'

'I am,' I said. 'First, I'm going home to change.'

Our waitress returned, her eyes fixed on Darius. He signed the receipt and set a twenty on top of it for her tip.

'Thank you, my love,' he said, flashing another smile. Then he turned to me. 'We should go. You haven't got much time.'

When we were outside on Connecticut Avenue, I said, 'You broke that poor waitress's heart, you know. She's smitten.'

'I rather doubt that. I'm too old and grizzled for her.'

He slipped an arm around my waist and we started walking up Connecticut Avenue. 'I hope your luncheon goes well,' he said. 'And while we're generally on the topic of your grandfather,

I'm counting on you to give the talk at the opening of his exhibition.'

I stopped walking and turned to face him. 'Knox Porter should give it. He's setting up the Charles Lord Museum and the photography program at CIFA . . . he'd be the perfect person to give that talk.'

'You're Charles Lord's granddaughter. I want you.' His blue eyes burned into mine and for a moment I didn't know if he meant me speaking at Chappy's exhibition . . . or something else.

'Darius . . .'

'Come on, Sophie. You know I'm right.'

We started walking again.

'All right, I'll do it, even though I get incredibly nervous when I have to speak in public,' I said. 'And I have a condition.'

'Tranquilizers? I can arrange that.'

'Very funny.'

'Sorry. You'll be fine. You'll be brilliant.'

'We'll see about that. But here's my condition: I'm working with a group of people at Streetwise, the media company that puts out the homeless newspaper. They also sponsor a lot of workshops, including a photography workshop. I help out the Artist-in-Residence sometimes,' I said. 'I've seen some terrific photographs. I want you to come to one of the sessions and see them, too. You'd be amazed.'

'All right,' he said. 'Set it up and I'll be there.'

'There's something else.'

'What?'

'I want the Underground to sponsor an exhibition of their work. Not photographs *of* the homeless, photographs *by* the homeless.'

He gave me a long, assessing look. 'I'm interested, but let's discuss it.' He paused. 'Over dinner.'

We had reached the corner of Mass Avenue and the Beaux Arts building where his office was located.

'Dinner. You mean, like a business dinner?'

'No,' he said. 'I mean like a date. That is, unless you're involved with someone already. Then it would be a business dinner. Unfortunately.'

'No, no, no,' I said. 'I'm not. I just . . . haven't gone out on a date . . . with anyone . . . yet.' Outings with Jack and grocery shopping with Max didn't count. Even I knew that.

He leaned over and brushed my cheek with his lips. 'So it's about time, don't you think?' he said in that low, sexy voice that sent shivers down my spine. 'I'll call you.'

My phone dinged with a text as I unlocked my front door. I elbowed it open and checked the message: *I'll be in town Friday all day for meetings at the DC bureau. Leaving Saturday afternoon for London. Have dinner with me Fri nite? It's been so long that I've forgotten what you look like. P.*

I smiled and felt a tug of old memories.

Perry DiNardo, the bureau chief for IPS's London bureau and my former boss. Actually, the best boss anyone could ask for, someone who would do anything for his reporters and photographers. Back you to the hilt if the suits in New York squawked over something they didn't like. I adored him.

I texted back. *I would love to. Where and when? I'll wear a red rose so you'll recognize me. S.*

A moment later he replied. *Iron Gate on N Street 6 p.m. Don't forget the rose. P.*

I sent him a smiley face and went upstairs to my bedroom to change out of jeans and a short-sleeved top into a V-neck coral-and-white floral-print dress with a side slit. Three-inch black heels, bare legs, my hair pulled into a high ponytail, black eyeliner, mascara, a bit of blush, tinted lip balm, and the braided yellow-white- and rose-gold necklace Nick had given me for my birthday one year that I never took off.

I was ready to meet the first Mrs Lord.

I took an Uber to Georgetown. First, because it was Georgetown, where you were guaranteed to get a ticket if you parked in a residential zone without a proper sticker – presuming you even found a spot – and second, because riding a Vespa while wearing a dress and heels is never a good idea, especially if it's a bit windy. Oriana Neri lived on 29th Street between Q and R in a small brick row house painted a luscious pale butter-yellow with black shutters, a black front door, and white trim. I used the polished brass door knocker because I didn't see a doorbell.

The woman who opened the door was beautiful. Eyes the color
of pale jade, snow-white hair pulled into a chignon, blood-red
lipstick, perfect skin, slim and elegantly dressed in a smart-
looking Chanel pantsuit the same color as her lipstick. Diamond
tear-drop earrings and a large pale-green emerald-and-pearl ring
on her wedding-ring finger. 'Sophie,' she said, her eyes flitting
over me. 'Please come in.'

She fiddled with her ring, turning it around and around on her
finger as I walked inside. So I wasn't the only one who was
nervous about this meeting.

Her Italian accent was faint but distinctive. I wondered where
Chappy had met her and when. She had written that they were
eighteen and twenty when they got married. She must have been
a knockout. No wonder my grandfather fell for her.

We walked into her living room. Oil paintings and watercolors
hung on the walls; a built-in bookcase was filled with books that
looked as if they'd been read and weren't there for decoration.
Comfortable furniture, a few antique pieces. A Sarouk carpet that
I guessed might be more than a century old; although it was a
bit threadbare in a few spots, it was perfect for the cheerful,
sunny room. A cut-glass vase filled with pink hydrangeas on the
coffee table. Framed photographs on the grand piano: rosy-
cheeked children and good-looking adults in matching shirts
and chinos at a beach and gathered near a Christmas tree next
to a cozy winter fire. An oil painting of Oriana, much younger,
hanging over the fireplace when her hair was flaming red and
she was wearing a black velvet cocktail dress that showed off
white porcelain shoulders and an enticing amount of décolleté.

'Your home is lovely,' I said.

She smiled. 'Thank you. Come, we are having lunch on the
terrace because it is too nice to be inside.'

I could see the terrace through the French doors in her dining
room. Also perfect. High ivy-covered walls, a patch of bright-
green lawn, shade trees now in fall colors of red and gold on
either side to guarantee total privacy from the neighbors. A well-
cared-for garden in a serpentine bed that wound around her
backyard. A glass-topped wrought-iron table was set with china
and wine glasses. Two wrought-iron chairs with cushions were
pulled up on either side of the table. Lunch was hidden under a

fabric-covered dome on another small table, and a bottle of wine was chilling in a wine cooler. Behind the table, a fountain gurgled pleasantly, and on either side of it, two large urns were filled with pink pansies still rioting even though summer was long gone.

'It is peaceful here,' Oriana said. 'I spend a lot of time on this terrace with my morning coffee or a glass of wine in the evening or just reading. I and a pair of cardinals who believe it is *their* garden.'

I listened; sure enough, the familiar cheep-cheep song of a cardinal came from somewhere in the trees. A moment later his – or her – mate answered. Virginia's state bird. Cardinals were like that, very territorial. My arrival had not gone unnoticed.

'My mother and stepfather also have a Mr and Mrs Cardinal who believe our backyard belongs to them,' I said. 'It's nice yours keep such a close eye on you.'

'Yes. They do,' she said with a soft smile. She indicated one of the chairs. 'Please have a seat. Lunch is simple – a salad, pasta, and homemade gelato with fruit. I thought we might also have some prosecco.'

I sat. If I drank alcohol at lunch, it made me sleepy and I'd need a nap later. It was a good thing I'd taken an Uber. She reached for the bottle, which wasn't quite full. I wondered if she'd fortified herself with a glass before I arrived. She caught me noticing the bottle and her self-conscious smile said I'd guessed right.

'I didn't get your letter until this morning,' I said as she filled my glass. 'In fact, I got it about an hour and a half ago. There was no phone number to RSVP, no email address, no way to get in touch with you. If I hadn't gotten it when I did, I wouldn't be here because I wouldn't have known about your invitation.'

'I don't email. But you should have this.' She reached over and picked up a calling card that was sitting on the table next to the wine cooler. 'Now you will know how to get in touch with me in the future.'

I took the card. Embossed with her name, address, and a phone number. And no email address.

'This would have been useful if you'd put it in your letter. I could have called.'

'It wasn't necessary. Besides, I knew you'd come.'

'What made you so certain?'

'You would be too curious. I knew you weren't going to turn down an opportunity to meet me, to know more about me.' She picked up her glass. '*Cin-cin*.'

I raised mine, relieved she hadn't said something mawkish or awkward like 'to family' or 'to our first meeting.' Also annoyed at her flippant assessment of me. She had no idea who I was.

We drank and then she set her glass down so she could lift the fabric dome to reveal two small salads. She handed me a plate. I waited until she raised her fork and then took a bite of my salad. Baby greens, pomegranate arils, feta, and toasted pistachios with a citrusy dressing.

'It's delicious.'

'Thank you,' she said. 'My partner – Gianni – and I used to cook together. Now I rarely have anyone to cook for since the children live so far away – Italy and California – so I'm a bit rusty, I'm afraid.'

'Your "partner"?'

'Yes. We were together for more than fifty years. Fifty-six to be precise.'

She noticed my surprise and confusion because she added, 'It's complicated.'

Nothing about Oriana Neri – who had dropped into my life out of the blue less than two hours ago – seemed as if it wouldn't be complicated.

'Because you were . . . married . . . to my grandfather for a couple of months?' I asked. *Days? Weeks?*

Her eyes flashed. 'No, not at all. It was Gianni. He was married to a woman who had serious mental health problems. Unfortunately, it meant that she was unable to keep a job for very long, plus she suffered from severe, crippling depression. They separated, but Gianni wouldn't abandon her – divorce her – so she could continue to have coverage under his health insurance. I admired him for his devotion to her, but that meant it was out of the question that we would ever marry as long as she was alive. Happily, he had a son and daughter who I came to think of as my own children. They practically grew up in our home. And now I'm a grandmother as well.'

I thought of the photographs on the grand piano. 'How long ago did Gianni pass away?'

'Two years last June.'

'I lost my husband fifteen months ago. It's hard.'

'I know about your husband,' she said. 'Nicholas. I'm sorry for your loss as well.'

She pronounced his name the Italian way. *Nee-ko-las.*

'You seem to know quite a lot about me and my family.'

'I do,' she said in a matter-of-fact tone. 'You probably won't be surprised that I followed Charles's career over the years. So, of course, I learned he had remarried and that he and his wife had a daughter. When you became a photographer – Charles's granddaughter – I followed your career as one can these days thanks to the Internet.'

She didn't email but was savvy enough to find out about all of us by searching the Internet. And the word *remarried* stung.

'Oriana,' I said, 'my grandfather never – and I mean *never* – mentioned you. This meeting today – meeting you – has been a complete surprise.'

I didn't intend to deliberately hurt her – I'm not like that – but I caught the flash of pain in her eyes. Still, it was true. Chappy was dead. Why did she have to stir up ancient history *now*?

Her voice turned frosty. 'Of course he didn't. Why *would* he tell your grandmother he was still married to me?'

'I'm sorry,' I said, 'but I think I knew my grandfather better than you did. I also knew him *longer* than you did. I don't believe he would marry my grandmother and have a child – my mother – if he was still legally married to you. He just *wouldn't*. Chappy was a casual Catholic, but he believed in the sacraments, and he and my grandmother got married in the church. *She* was the devout one. But he still went to confession and communion. A priest friend of mine said his funeral Mass. You're talking about him committing *bigamy*.'

'I'm sorry you're so angry,' she said, 'but it wasn't like that.'

'Then please tell me what it *was* like.'

She reached for her prosecco and sat back in her chair. 'Different. Those were different times, the 1950s. The war had been over for more than a decade. Charles moved out to California. To LA. He was hoping to make it out there as a photographer, work for one of the big studios. I had just immi-grated to the US from Italy and thought I could become a successful actress in America – people told me I was talented. In the meantime, I had all the jobs starving actors get while waiting for the big break, which is how I met Charles. One evening, I was a server at a party in Beverly Hills where he was one of the photographers. He asked if I'd let him photograph me – you know, as a model. Of course I said yes because he was going to pay me.'

She helped herself to another glass of prosecco and tilted the bottle at me.

'No, thank you,' I said. 'Please go on.'

'I modeled for him a couple of times – he didn't have a studio, so it was just his apartment. His bedroom. One thing led to another . . . and we became quite friendly,' she said, with a just-between-us-girls look that said *friendly* meant 'friends with benefits' and they were having sex. 'One weekend, on a crazy impulse, we decided to go to Las Vegas. Neither of us had ever been.'

She drank more prosecco. I tried to keep my face as expres-sionless as possible, but you'd have to be clueless not to know what came next. A weekend in Sin City. Probably with fake IDs since they weren't even twenty-one yet.

'As you probably already guessed, we drank and gambled.' She had the guilty look of a teenager who had just crashed the family car and came home to confess what had happened to an irate parent. 'We drank quite a lot.'

'And you got married when you were drunk.'

'I found the license in my purse the next morning. We went to one of those twenty-four-hour marriage chapels. Charles bought the license with his gambling winnings.'

Too bad he hadn't lost. 'Then what happened?'

She shrugged. 'We went back to LA and I moved into his place. It wasn't long before we were arguing all the time. We knew the marriage had been a mistake.'

'Why not get a quickie divorce to go with the quickie marriage if you were that unhappy?'

'*Cara mia*,' she said, 'we were *Catholic*. It was the *1950s*. Do you have any idea what kind of stigma that would have been?

Besides, no one knew we were married except the two of us. Not even our families. It was our secret.'

'So what did you do?'

She gave a one-shoulder shrug. 'Charles started coming home later and later. I met a director not long after that who promised he'd make me a star. I moved in with him and then I heard Charles moved back East. To New York.'

'Did you ever get in touch with each other after that?'

'Never.'

'Did you tell Gianni you were married to my grandfather?'

'By then, so many years had passed, and the circumstances of Charles's and my wedding being what they were, I never brought it up.'

'But you are bringing it up *now*. With *me*.'

'Yes.'

'Why?'

'I saw the announcement about the exhibition he was going to have at the Dupont Underground,' she said. 'And that the photos are going to be never-before-seen pictures he's taken that are a bit . . . erotic.'

'The exhibition is still going to take place,' I said. 'It was already planned before he died.'

'I know that.' Oriana stood and gathered our salad plates. 'Give me a moment. There's something I want you to see.'

She returned holding a large envelope and set it down in front of me.

'Please. Have a look.'

I opened the flap and slid out the contents. She sat down and watched me. The marriage license was on top. I recognized Chappy's signature. It was genuine, all right.

The rest of the contents were photographs of Oriana. She was nude.

'Your grandfather took these,' she said. 'I think they belong in the exhibition.'

I studied the pictures. The photographs Chappy had chosen for the Dupont Underground were sensuous and erotic, but these seemed almost pornographic. Not his style at all.

'They don't look like his pictures,' I said. 'The lighting, the poses – it's not him. Erotic and explicit are two different things.'

Oriana stiffened. 'Of course he took them. What are you talking about? They're *Charles's* photos. Don't be absurd. Why would I show them to you if they weren't?'

'I don't know why but I disagree that they're his.'

'Wait here.'

I wasn't going anywhere. She left. It was my turn to reach for the prosecco bottle. When she came back, she was holding more photos. 'I wasn't going to show you these,' she said, clearly upset. 'They're very private and, shall we say, rather more explicit. But since you seem to need *proof* . . .'

They were in bed, facing the camera – or, rather, facing a mirror. He was reclining against the headboard, propped up by pillows cocooning her body into his. She leaned back, head resting against his chest, legs splayed open, a lazy, suggestive post-coital smile on her face. He held the camera over their heads, aiming it at the mirror as though he was hoisting a trophy. Both of them, of course, completely naked. She was smoking a cigarette, and a curl of smoke slightly obscured their faces.

Her flaming red hair, my grandfather, younger than I'd ever seen him, almost unrecognizable with dark, curly hair and a deep tan that made his skin almost as dark as mine. There were more pictures. Selfies in the days before anyone knew what that word meant.

'Please tell me you're not asking me to put these photos in the Dupont Underground exhibition,' I said. 'There's no way . . .'

'Of course not,' she said, sounding irritated. 'But the others that he took of me when I modeled for him – those I do want you to put in the exhibition.'

'Why?' I said.

She gave me a calculating look, and that's when I knew exactly why I was here today and what she wanted.

'You want to sell them, don't you?' I said. 'If they're in the Dupont Underground exhibition, they'll be much more valuable. They're originals. No negatives or copies, I'm sure. Plus, there's the cachet that they are photos of Charles Lord's previously unknown first wife taken years before he was famous. Collectors would pay a lot of money for photos like that.'

And having them in the exhibition would give her the imprimatur she needed.

'So do we have an agreement?' she asked.

'What belongs in the exhibition is not my decision. In fact, my grandfather chose what photographs the Underground could use shortly before he died. As for these – I doubt he'd be in favor of having them displayed with his other photos, don't you agree?'

She reddened. 'It doesn't matter what he would have wanted any more. You're Charles's granddaughter. Whatever *you* want to do will be acceptable to the organizers at the Dupont Underground.'

Bingo.

Get me on board and her photographs would be in Chappy's exhibition.

'Oriana,' I said, 'this . . . *situation* you've just presented to me is going to be complicated, too. My mother doesn't know you exist. I'm sure you can imagine what a shock and a surprise – an unhappy surprise – it's going to be when I tell her about you, never mind when – or if – I show her these photos. Second, my grandfather left his entire estate and photo collection to a small school in Connecticut near his former home. It was his intention that whatever they choose to sell of his collection would bring in the money to establish one of the top – if not *the* top – schools of photography and photojournalism in the country. That's his *legacy*, and those people need to be involved in this decision as well.'

She crossed one slim leg over the other. 'You're so much like Charles. The similarities are quite amazing.'

'I'll take that as a compliment.'

She still sounded irritated. 'Do what you have to do, but I rely on you to persuade your mother and these other people to put my photos in the Dupont Underground exhibition.'

'I don't guarantee anything.' *And I'm not in your corner, either.*

She gave me a sly look. 'Don't be foolish, Sophie. The photos of me will be a huge draw. Everyone is going to be curious about Charles Lord's secret life. And a wife no one knew he had. The pictures are . . . incredibly erotic.'

They were.

'You're talking about exploiting my grandfather's reputation. I can't imagine my mother will be happy about it, or in favor of it. No matter how much money your photos bring in.'

Oriana steepled her fingers. 'But the director of the Dupont Underground and the people at the Connecticut photography school would be delighted to include them. For *exactly* that reason. More money.'

I said, knowing she was going to turn me down, 'I'll need to take these photos with me. Everyone involved is going to want to see them.'

'Absolutely not. The photos stay with me. They're originals. But if you wish, you may photograph them. Use your camera phone. They will still be good-quality photos and that will be proof enough.'

'What if the answer is no? Because it probably will be.'

'I hope it is not.' Her voice hardened. 'Don't forget I am still legally Mrs Charles Lord. I could, if I chose, contest his will. As his wife who survived him.'

I felt the blood leave my face. Sam Constantine, our lawyer, had said that Chappy's will was legal, but just barely. Written on a piece of notebook paper and witnessed by a waiter and one of the managers in the restaurant where he wrote it. Oriana could tie my grandfather's estate in knots for months. Maybe even *years*.

'That's blackmail.'

She stood. 'It doesn't have to come to that. What I'm asking will benefit everyone. More money for the school and the Dupont Underground. Your mother wasn't exactly a saint when she married your father, was she? I'm talking about your *biological* father. And apples don't fall too far from the tree, as they always say. So let's not split hairs over matters of legitimacy. Of course learning about me will be a shock to Caroline, but I'm sure she'll come around once you talk to her.'

It felt as though Oriana had just slapped me hard across the face. The fact that she knew such intimate details about my mother, my birth – things *no one* knew – was voyeuristic, as if she'd been spying on us through some peephole we hadn't known existed.

'Don't talk about my mother and my father. Just *don't.*'

'I'm sorry you're upset,' she said in a mild, dismissive voice as though we had just argued over something trivial. 'Let me go see about lunch, and while I'm gone, you can take your photographs.

I'm also bringing another bottle of prosecco. I have a feeling we both could use another drink.'

By the time she returned carrying a tray with a steaming bowl of pasta and a bottle of prosecco, I had taken all the photos I needed.

When she set the tray down, she took one look at me and said, 'You're not staying for lunch.'

'No.'

'As you wish.'

'I can see myself out.'

'Very well.'

I gave her a long hard stare and said, 'If Gianni had divorced his wife or if she passed away and he asked you to marry him, you would have said yes in an instant. Wouldn't you?'

She answered right away. 'I don't know.'

Which meant she did.

'You do know,' I said. 'And if you had married him, we wouldn't be having this conversation. You would have torn up that marriage license and pretended it never existed.'

'I also think you should leave. The next time we have a conversation, I expect you'll tell me that my photos belong in Charles's exhibition.' She gave me a triumphant look. *'Out of the Public Eye: Exposing the Unknown Side of Charles Lord.* These photos would truly be exposing a side no one knew about him.'

'Don't get your hopes up. I don't guarantee anything.'

'You might want to think about that.'

I heard her voice, shouting after me as I walked through her beautiful living room.

'Don't do anything you'll regret, Sophie.'

I closed the front door behind me.

Too late for that.

I already had.

# TWELVE

My Uber – a red Honda Accord – arrived in front of Oriana's home three minutes after I sent a request. I climbed in and leaned my head back against the seat.

'Are you all right, miss?' the driver asked as we pulled away.

I looked up and our eyes met in the rearview mirror. He was older, maybe late fifties, kind face. I guessed by his accent that he came from one of the French-speaking African countries.

'Yes, thank you. I'm fine. Thank you for asking.'

Of course, the correct answer was that I *wasn't* fine after my meeting with Oriana had quickly deteriorated into a series of veiled threats about just how miserable she could make my family's life if I didn't do what she wanted me to do.

I also wished I hadn't drunk so much prosecco.

The Uber driver looked as if he didn't believe my response, either, but he nodded without saying anything. I closed my eyes and my phone rang. The old-fashioned bell – which I had apparently set on full volume – drowned out the classical music on the car radio.

'I'm sorry.' I sat up and pulled the phone out of my purse.

'It's OK,' he said. 'No worries.'

I was about to decline the call when I saw the name that flashed on the screen. *Quill Russell.* I touched the green button and said, 'Quill. How are you? *Where* are you?'

'Sophie. Good to hear you. I'm at the house in Georgetown,' he said. 'I cut the trip short by a day. I finished my meetings ahead of schedule, so I came home early.'

What a coincidence. Here I was in Georgetown as well. 'Is everything all right?'

'Yes, yes, fine. I was wondering if you might be free to have a drink tomorrow night. I saw the last photos you sent of the ginkgoes. They're gorgeous.'

The ginkgoes. It felt as if a millennium had passed since I'd been out to Fernway. Those pictures had been taken the day Vicki was making out in the pool with Everett Townsend. And now he was dead.

'Thank you.'

'So . . . are you free?'

'Oh, sorry. Yes, of course. Tomorrow night would be fine. What time and where?'

'How about the bar at the Jefferson Hotel at six? I have a meeting at the White House before that. It shouldn't take long.'

The Jefferson was just down the street from the White House. 'That would be great. I'll see you there at six tomorrow.'

'Good,' he said and disconnected.

The driver had to wake me when we pulled up in front of my townhouse on S Street. I gave him a generous tip and thanked him. He helped me out of the car – the prosecco had definitely gone to my head – and I walked, somewhat wobbly, up the steps to my front door. As soon as I got inside, I went straight to my bedroom, kicked off the heels, and threw myself face down on the bed.

I slept.

When I woke up, the light coming through my bedroom window was a pale silky gray. It was getting dark. It took a moment before my memory kicked in and I remembered Oriana's luncheon and the prosecco. I checked my watch. Six thirty. And I had a splitting headache.

I stripped off my dress and pulled on a pair of yoga pants and a sweatshirt I wore to work out in. In the bathroom, I got a couple of aspirin out of a bottle in the medicine cabinet, threw them down, and went downstairs because I was famished. My phone buzzed with a text as I was looking in the refrigerator.

The text was from a number I didn't recognize and it made no sense.

*James Buchanan wants to meet tonight at 8.30. Wear black.*

James Buchanan. Did I know him? And what was wearing black all about? He'd also neglected to say *where* he wanted to meet. I closed the refrigerator door and leaned against the kitchen counter, staring at the text. It was a 202 area code, the original code for Washington, DC, so it was local. I pondered that for a moment, and then it hit me.

The message wasn't *from* James Buchanan because the James Buchanan the text had been referring to *was* the former President of the United States. He had preceded Abraham Lincoln, serving just before the Civil War. And, quite obviously, he had been dead for more than a century.

There was a monument to Buchanan in Meridian Hill Park, one of DC's most beautiful but less well-known parks, unless you were a local – few tourists visited it. Besides the memorial to Buchanan, there were also monuments to Joan of Arc and Dante – though why the three of them were grouped together remained one of the city's great mysteries. The park was also the location of a drum circle that had been meeting every Sunday afternoon for years – actually, it had been going on for decades. People showed up with djembes, bongos, timbales, or anything that made noise. You could play, dance, or just listen.

Javi Aguilera was one of the regulars at the drum circle.

The text was from him.

Either he had borrowed someone else's phone, which was why I didn't recognize the number, or he was using a burner phone. And he wanted to meet me tonight in Meridian Hill Park. *Wear black* hadn't meant to come in a Little Black Dress. He wanted me to blend into the night.

I texted a one-word reply: *OK.*

Three little dots appeared on my screen. He was writing back. Then the dots disappeared and, though I waited, there were no more texts. I set my phone on the kitchen counter in case he changed his mind, but still nothing came.

Since breakfast this morning, all I'd eaten were three half pastries and a coffee with Darius and a small salad and too much prosecco with Oriana. I found the bowl with last night's leftover pasta from my dinner with Tommy, heated it up, and ate the whole thing.

Then I went upstairs to change into black jeans, a black turtleneck, and my black Chucks. In the front hall closet, I found a black knitted cap, which I pulled on, tucking my hair underneath, and a pair of black gloves.

I was ready for my meeting with Javi.

At least I hoped I was.

\*   \*   \*

Meridian Hill Park, which sprawled across twelve acres on the edge of Adams Morgan and Columbia Heights, was a brisk fifteen-minute walk from my house up 16th Street. If you didn't know better, when you entered through one of the wrought-iron gates, you might think you were on the grounds of a beautiful Italian villa that dated from the era of the Borgias. The park was divided into two sections: an upper park with a large mall that was surrounded by woods, and a lower park, which had a dramatic cascading waterfall of thirteen linked basins that were flanked by symmetric staircases. At the base of the waterfall, a reflecting pool sat in the middle of a plaza. The Buchanan memorial was tucked into a corner of the lower park and was partially obscured by a copse of trees.

Javi had chosen well. We would have plenty of privacy.

I had realized that walking up 16th Street by myself at that hour of the evening would not be my wisest decision, and the red-and-white Mini would stick out like a sore thumb. Same with my mint-green Vespa. I ordered another Uber and hoped the driver wouldn't comment on my all-black attire.

He didn't, but he did give me an odd look. And when he dropped me off at the entrance to the lower park a few minutes later, he said, 'Are you sure you're going to be all right on your own here?'

'Thank you, I am,' I said and held up my phone. 'I'm a photographer. I'm going to take some night shots of the park. I'll be fine.'

As lies go, it was the best I could come up with.

'OK,' he said, though he still looked puzzled. Perhaps because he might have been expecting me to show him a camera, rather than a phone. 'But be careful.'

It was exactly eight thirty when I walked through the gate across from the Buchanan memorial; the park closed at nine. Whatever Javi had to tell me obviously wasn't going to involve a long conversation. Other than a pair of dog walkers and a young couple engaged in an intense discussion as they sat on the stone ledge surrounding the reflecting pool, the place was dark and quiet.

The bronze statue of James Buchanan, who was seated on a chair and dressed in what looked like flowing judge's robes, was flanked by two long, low granite benches. Two statues representing law and diplomacy bookended the benches.

Javi stepped out from the shadows next to Buchanan as I started to walk across the plaza. He, too, wore black. And to my relief, he didn't show any sign of having been wounded recently.

I gave him a quick hug and said, 'Are you OK? I went by your apartment and found blood. What happened? What's going on?'

He said, astonished, 'Why did you do that?'

'Because you didn't show up for work and no one knew where you were. Except maybe Tessa Janko, and she wasn't talking. What happened?'

'Jesus, Sophie. I wish you hadn't done that. I hope now he's not looking for you as well and maybe thinks you're involved.' He sounded panicked.

'*Who* is looking for me? Involved in *what*?'

He led me over to the bench next to one of the statues, so we were completely in the shadows.

'I'll tell you,' he said. 'Except I'm still trying to figure out what's going on myself.'

'OK,' I said, flicking a glance at my watch. Eight thirty-eight. We had twenty-two minutes. I needed to quit asking questions and let him talk.

'The other night, my landlady seemed like she wasn't doing too well, so I took her to the hospital,' he said. 'She wouldn't let me call nine-one-one.'

'Tessa told me you were taking care of her,' I said.

'I didn't know she talked to you.' He didn't sound happy about it.

'Finn and I practically dragged the information out of her because you didn't show up for work, didn't call in sick, and weren't answering your phone.'

'Oh,' he said. 'OK.'

'Go on,' I said. Eight forty-one.

'I took her to the Emergency Room at GW Hospital,' he said.

'When was that?' I asked, but I was starting to get an idea when it might have been.

'Monday,' he said. 'Monday evening around six thirty.'

About the time the ambulance carrying Everett Townsend would have arrived.

'OK,' I said, and now the hairs on the back of my neck were standing up.

'The doctors decided to keep her overnight, so I drove her car back home,' he said. 'A car followed me. I made a few detours just to make sure I wasn't imagining it. He hung back, but he was definitely on my tail. So I parked in the alley behind the house and managed to get inside before he came through the back gate. He must have cut his lights because I thought I'd lost him. Sophie, he had a *gun*. He picked the lock to the back door and came inside.'

'My God, Javi—'

He looked distraught. 'I had grabbed a butcher knife that was next to the stove just in case. Then I waited in the hall where he couldn't see me. When he walked through the doorway, I stabbed him. I got lucky. It was the arm that was holding the gun. The blood you found in the kitchen was his. Not mine.'

I was both relieved and appalled. 'You stabbed the guy?'

He nodded. 'I got his shoulder pretty bad and his arm. It all happened so fast.'

'OK. Go on.' Javi would have aced the hostile environment training course.

'I still had my landlady's car keys in my pocket. It's one of those cars you can start remotely with the key fob, so I did. The guy who came after me was older, overweight, and not fast on his feet. I took off before he could do anything else. I also got this off him.' He lifted his shirt and I saw the revolver tucked into the waistband of his trousers.

I said in a faint voice, 'Wow. OK. How did you manage that?'

'One of my foster families sent me to a martial arts academy, which they figured was better than street fighting. The guy who attacked me was counting on his gun, nothing else.'

'The kitchen was a mess with all that blood. I was afraid it was you.'

'Not this time.'

'What do you mean?'

'They'll try again,' he said in a cool, matter-of-fact voice that gave me chills.

'Who's "they"?'

'I don't know for sure.'

'But you have an idea. Look, the park is going to close in . . .' I checked my watch again. 'Fourteen minutes. Start at the beginning and tell me what you do know.'

'What I *do* know is that I was in the GW Hospital Emergency Room with my landlady the night the ambulance arrived with the Supreme Court justice who just died. Everett Townsend.'

A vein started throbbing in my temple. 'Go on.'

'I had to give the docs information about Maryann – my landlady – because there wasn't time to call one of her kids. I saw the stretcher with Townsend lying on it when they brought him in. He was in bad shape. Except it wasn't Townsend.'

'What do you mean it wasn't Townsend?'

'Just what I said. I don't know the guy's name, but everyone calls him "the Professor" because he's always dressed in a suit and he looks like a professor and talks like one, too. He's really smart, except . . .' He twirled a finger next to his temple. 'A little crazy. I don't know what's wrong with him – maybe Alzheimer's or dementia – but he's definitely got something wrong with his mind. It was him.'

'Are you sure?'

'*Of course* I'm sure. I've seen him in the camps. Talked to him.'

'This Professor is homeless?'

'Well . . . he was. Now he's dead. I also overheard one of the guys who brought him in mention your name. You and someone else. Jack Somebody. He said you two found him in an alley on Capitol Hill.'

'That's why you texted me?'

'Yeah. Because you saw him, too, right? You were with him for a while; you really got a good look at him.'

'We did. But Jack – my friend – *knows* Townsend and said it was him. Townsend's wife identified him, too. Javi, he had Townsend's ID on him. He was wearing an expensive suit, expensive shoes. He had his wedding ring, his watch, his wallet and his briefcase.'

The briefcase I'd seen at Vicki and Quill Russell's house.

Javi folded his arms across his chest and gave me a stubborn look that said he wasn't buying my version of the story any more than I was buying his. 'I'm telling you, Sophie. It wasn't

Townsend. I also heard from Tessa Janko that the Professor is missing.'

He had to be wrong. *Had to be.* 'Diana Townsend identified her husband's body. His funeral is Friday. She's already planned it. He's going to be cremated – if he hasn't been already. I just don't think—'

He snorted. 'Cremated. Of course. Then there's nothing left to identify him.'

'Javi—'

'Look.' He sounded exasperated. 'I told a couple of people at the hospital that they were wrong and that the guy wasn't Townsend. He just happens to look *exactly* like Townsend. I was pretty insistent, maybe a little loud. I also said that even though I didn't know his real name, everybody called him the Professor and he was homeless. Then, right after all that, someone follows me home from the hospital and tries to kill me. You think that's a coincidence? I don't.'

'You're saying someone wanted to shut you up?'

'You got any other ideas?'

'No . . . but this sounds – I don't know – just . . . crazy.'

'I know. But I'm right.'

'OK, say you are. Where's the real Townsend?'

'Beats the hell out of me.'

Me, too. If Javi was right, he was talking about an elaborate conspiracy to kidnap a homeless man who was a double for an Associate Justice of the Supreme Court, switch clothes, give him Townsend's wedding ring, watch – everything – and leave him behind his home on the Hill where he was supposed to die of an accidental insulin overdose. Except Jack and I came along and called nine-one-one. The EMTs who treated him discovered the head injury after they gave him two doses of D50 to counter his dangerously low blood-sugar level – which was what ultimately killed him. Then, boom, Diana Townsend gets his body released after it was determined there was no need for an autopsy. Next thing you know, she announces her husband is going to be cremated as he would have wished.

Jack identified the man we found as Everett Townsend and told the EMTs that's who he was. Plus, his wallet and briefcase had documents that confirmed it. But more to the point, Diana

Townsend, whom Jack described as a living saint because of all her charitable work, identified the man as her husband. Why would she lie?

'Was Diana Townsend in the ER when you said it wasn't her husband?' I asked.

He nodded. 'She showed up pretty fast.'

'Did she hear you?'

'I don't know. Maybe.'

'So who could have followed you home? Was anyone else there with her?'

'Some guy showed up about fifteen minutes after she got there. I don't know who he was, but I had a feeling he wasn't a family member just by the way he acted when he saw her.'

'The park is closing, folks. You need to make your way to one of the exits.'

A young guy with a German Shepherd on a leash shone a flashlight at our feet.

'We're leaving,' I said to him. 'Thanks.' To Javi, I said, 'Which way did you come?'

'I came in through a gate in the upper park,' he said. 'We can't leave together. How'd you get here?'

'Uber.'

'Call one now.'

I got out my phone and tapped in a request. A moment later, I said, 'A black Camry with DC plates will be here in three minutes.'

'Good,' he said. 'I'll wait to make sure you're OK, then I gotta take off.'

'I think we should talk again. Let me see what I can find out about what you just told me and then I'll be in touch.'

'Nope. Too dangerous.'

'Javi, we *have* to meet – at least one more time. You can't be on the run forever. Finn is worried about you, and Grace is worried sick. Where are you staying?'

He avoided my eyes. 'Here and there. It's better if you don't know. And I'm sorry everyone's worried.'

The flashlight beam swung around on us again. 'Folks?'

'We're leaving,' I said. 'Right now.'

I tugged the sleeve of Javi's black sweatshirt before he could take off. 'Meet me here in two days. Same time, same place.'

He nodded. 'OK, but look, be careful. Your Uber should be pulling up right about now.'

'It is. And don't worry, I'll be careful. Same goes for you.'

'I've lived on the streets long enough, I'll be OK. But watch it if you start asking questions and nosing around about Townsend. I don't want you to get hurt.'

He slipped away and disappeared into the shadows.

He was right. If he had accidentally stumbled on a conspiracy to fake the death of Justice Everett Townsend by substituting someone who looked just like him in his place, there had to be a few people who would go to any lengths to keep that secret.

Starting with Everett Townsend, who must have orchestrated the whole thing. And maybe got his wife to go along with the scam as well – though that didn't fit with her profile as St Diana, which is what Jack called her.

I sprinted across the plaza to the gate where a black Camry with DC plates was waiting.

On the short drive back to S Street, I kept my eye on the rearview mirror. No one followed us.

But Javi was right: if whoever was after him found out that I knew about Townsend's supposedly faked death, sooner or later I'd be in their crosshairs as well.

Someone had tried to kill Javi.

They wouldn't hesitate to kill me, as well.

There couldn't be any loose ends.

Javi.

And now me.

# THIRTEEN

I heard every car that drove down S Street for the rest of the night, bolting upright in bed and listening to make sure the driver wasn't slowing down in front of my house. After the sound of the engine receded – which it always did – I would resume breathing and try to talk myself into going back to sleep. Nobody had followed me to or from Meridian Hill Park.

No one was stalking me. I was making myself crazy for no good reason.

At five, I finally gave up and went downstairs to make a pot of coffee. I took a notebook and pen from a desk in a living-room alcove that I'd turned into a small office, got a mug of coffee, and threw myself into an oversized armchair in front of a bay window that had a perfect view of the street below.

In the middle of the first page of the notebook, I wrote Everett Townsend's name and drew a circle around it. Then I started adding the names of everyone who had been involved with Townsend the day he died, putting them in random places on the page and drawing circles around their names as well until it looked as if I'd drawn a page of thought bubbles. Jack. Me. Diana Townsend. The guy who showed up at the hospital. The EMTs. Javi. The Professor. I chewed the tip of my pen for a moment and added Vicki Russell and my brother Tommy. Then I drew lines connecting each person to everyone they knew until what I had – which was a mind map – resembled a spider web. I stared at it, looking for connections I hadn't yet considered as well as who might have more information about the identity of the man who had died in the Emergency Room at George Washington University Hospital three days ago.

The first and easiest person to reach out to was Tommy. He could find out who else had been in the ER that night and when Townsend's body left the morgue for the funeral home – and which funeral home it was. Someone or more than one person took care of Townsend, or the Professor, before he was cremated.

I added 'funeral home' to my spider web and connected it to Tommy, Diana, Townsend, and the Professor.

Then there was Vicki.

She didn't know I'd seen her and Townsend together the morning he disappeared. If I confronted her and started asking questions, a lot of things would unravel. The least of it was that I'd blow the surprise Quill and I had been keeping for more than a year, and everything would go downhill from there. Far more important was that I'd be the one who outed her affair with Townsend. It would destroy Quill and I couldn't do that. But I did wonder whether Vicki had known what Townsend had intended to do.

Next was Diana Townsend. Her husband couldn't have pulled off his disappearing act by himself. He had to have help. Otherwise, how could he have known there was a homeless man who looked like his identical twin? What were the odds?

I nearly spit out a mouthful of coffee when I figured it out.

*Jack* had explained it to me. My God, *he* knew. He'd told me as we walked back to Gloria House. after the ambulance left to take 'Townsend' to GW, that Diana did a lot of charity work with the homeless and what an angel she was.

Jesus. Diana Townsend knew the Professor from her work in the homeless community. And either she had told her husband about the uncanny resemblance between the two of them or maybe Everett Townsend had met the Professor himself.

That had to be the connection.

I drew a line connecting Diana with the Professor and another connecting Townsend and the Professor. I stared at my web, which had suddenly grown more intricate and complex.

Was *Diana* the link between the Professor going missing and whoever dressed him in Everett Townsend's clothes and gave him Townsend's wallet, watch, briefcase, and phone – and then gave him an overdose of insulin? Somehow I couldn't imagine Diana Townsend actually committing murder. But she *must* have played a role. Like insisting there be no autopsy and that her husband's body be immediately released to the funeral home before anybody changed their mind and decided his death should be investigated. Maybe she and her husband were working together on his scheme.

I turned another page and wrote Everett Townsend's name again, drawing another circle around it. This time I wanted to figure out what he could have possibly done, or been involved in, that made vanishing *forever* – a respected, erudite judge with a lifetime position as one of the nine justices on the Supreme Court – a better alternative than staying to tough out whatever or whoever was after him. And killing his lookalike as part of the getaway plan. I began writing down anything I'd learned about him recently. He was a womanizer, according to multiple sources, including a former law clerk who worked with Grace's husband, Ben. He was having an affair with Vicki Russell – that *I* could corroborate first-hand. He didn't seem to have a particularly close or even happy marriage. See womanizing above. That was the personal stuff.

Professionally, he'd been raked over the coals during his Supreme Court confirmation hearing for giving a mere rap on the knuckles while he was a DC District judge to a real estate businessman who'd been accused of laundering money. He'd dismissed that by claiming the prosecution hadn't made a good case and he was a by-the-books judge. Finally, Darius Zahiri said Townsend was 'pally' with a Russian oligarch named Alexey Ozupov, partying with him on his superyacht and as a frequent guest in the owner's box at Dover football matches. In return, Darius said Ozupov was counting on Townsend to be his entrée to the Washington political scene after establishing himself as a generous philanthropist to American charities and committing to the Giving Pledge. Then unexpectedly Ozupov and Townsend had a recent falling out. Over what, Darius didn't know.

I tapped the eraser end of my pencil on the notebook and looked at what I'd written. What was I missing? None of this looked like dire enough circumstances for Townsend to fake his death and disappear. Why couldn't he have just toughed it out and waited until the dust settled – whatever 'it' was? People in Washington had short memories that lasted a couple of news cycles, if that. Anyone, however heinous the deed they'd done, could be rehabilitated in this town. Forgive and forget. The guilty person left behind the detritus of whatever scandal or illegal or nefarious activity they'd been accused of and went on with life as usual. That is, after going on whichever cable news channels leaned their way politically, telling their sob story, eliciting sympathy by claiming it wasn't true, moaning about unfairly being maligned, and insisting the 'other side' was out to get them. Then, after waiting an acceptable amount of time so as to seem properly rehabilitated, re-emerging into the public eye, bright-eyed and bushy-tailed, ready to start again with a clean slate. Yadda, yadda, frickin' yadda.

Why not go that route?

Maybe because of all the people Townsend could have had a falling out with, getting on the wrong side of a Russian oligarch – even an old friend like Alexey Ozupov – could have serious repercussions. If Ozupov had dirt on Supreme Court Justice Everett Townsend – say, something that happened on his super-yacht that Townsend might not want to come to light – Ozupov could have him over a barrel.

I knew that only too well.

My husband had gotten on the wrong side of the Russians by trying to find out something they didn't want him to know, and he paid for it with his life.

The Russians played for keeps.

Napoleon Duval must have been reading my mind – I'd often wondered if that was one of the superhuman skills he possessed as such a high-ranking spook – when I stepped out of the shower a few hours later and my phone rang. I'd been in full free-association mode, my thoughts swirling around, pinging from Townsend to the Russians to Nick and how little I knew about what had happened to him in Vienna. The display said *Private Caller.* Somehow I didn't think it was Lexie, so I took a guess Duval was finally getting back to me after the message I left the other day.

I picked up the phone, still dripping wet, and said, 'Hello?'

And waited. I was right.

'I just got back in town,' he said. With Duval, that could have meant he'd been in Detroit or Djibouti. 'Have you ever seen the Blue Rooster?'

'Do you mean the one that sits on top of the East Wing of the National Gallery?' I wiped water off the screen with my bath towel, careful not to accidentally disconnect the call.

The fourteen-foot-high rooster, known as Hahn/Cock and painted a brilliant shade of ultramarine blue, had originally been commissioned to sit on one of the plinths in Trafalgar Square during an exhibition of contemporary art. I'd seen it when I lived in London. A few years ago, it had been loaned to the National Gallery of Art – the one in Washington. During Covid, the museum in Potomac, Maryland that had acquired it decided to make it a permanent donation to the NGA in recognition of the resilience of the American people during the pandemic.

'That's the one,' he said.

'I've seen it.'

'Nice view of the city from that rooftop.'

'Yes, it is.'

'I could meet you there at eleven,' he said.

'I'll be there.'

'Good,' he said and disconnected.

My heart did a few flip-flops. Duval wouldn't meet me for no reason. With any luck, he had information about Nick that he was willing to share, so maybe I'd finally get answers to my many questions.

Or at least some of them.

Duval was already there when I opened the door and walked outside to blindingly bright sunlight glinting off the white marble of the Rooftop Terrace of the East Wing of the National Gallery of Art shortly before eleven o'clock. He was staring at the Capitol, with his back to both me and the enormous bright-blue rooster. The Capitol, also, dazzled in the brilliance of the almost-midday sunshine.

He turned around as I approached him and I saw my reflection in his mirrored aviator sunglasses. Typical Duval. It was easier to hide emotions – if he had any – behind those opaque shades, and make it harder for me to try to suss out what he was really saying. Or thinking.

He had changed since the last time I saw him when Nick had gone missing in Russia three years ago. His hair was grayer, buzzed military-short, and he had put on a few pounds, though he carried it well with the ramrod-straight posture and commanding physical presence of someone who'd served in the Marines.

Nicely dressed in a navy blazer, sharply pressed chinos, and white dress shirt, no tie. He folded his hands together and looked me over. Missing nothing.

I had lost weight on the 'grief diet' as I'd called it – eating by myself – so I was thin. And now I was a widow.

'Ms Medina . . . Sophie.'

'I prefer Sophie, Mr Duval.'

'Call me Leo, Sophie.'

'Leo,' I said. 'All right.'

Somewhere a huge chunk of the polar ice cap had just melted. Napoleon Duval had never been anything but extremely formal with me, even a bit chilly. *Call me Leo* was a rare sign that he might actually be human.

I walked over and stood next to him. We both stared at the Capitol.

'Thank you for meeting me,' I said.

'You're welcome. And just why is it we're meeting?' he asked as if he didn't know.

I turned so I faced him, and the pent-up anger I'd felt about being stonewalled by the CIA spilled out. 'I want to know what happened to my husband. And please don't give me any BS about him being hit by a car in Vienna. I already know more than that. He was supposed to meet someone who never showed up. A Russian. He walked into a trap.'

Those sunglasses did an outstanding job of hiding any reaction in his eyes to what I'd just said. He also had perfected his poker face as every spy learned practically on day one, so I couldn't tell whether he was surprised or not by how much I knew.

'OK,' he said.

'OK, I'm right, or just "OK"?'

'OK, you're right.'

Yeah, well I knew that already. 'Did his trip have anything to do with the Russians trying to hack into OPEC's computers?'

That *did* get a reaction. 'Can I ask where you got that information?'

'You can. The newspaper. Specifically, *The Washington Tribune*. I put two and two together and it added up. The timeline fitted with Nick's last-minute trip to Vienna. Crowne Energy, his former employer, was based in Russia searching for oil – which, as you know only too well, they found – so Nick knew all the players. Plus, he had a lot of connections in OPEC, especially once he started working for Quill Russell.' I folded my arms across my chest. 'How am I doing so far?'

'You're doing fine.'

'Good. Please feel free to chime in if you've got something to add.'

That got me a ghost of a smile. 'I can't say much more except to confirm everything you just said.'

I gritted my teeth and said, 'Leo, please. There's no one else I can ask. You're my last hope. I'm not asking you to compromise anyone else in the field, but if your' – I glanced at his left hand; still no wedding band – 'if someone in your family came to someone like you, wouldn't you want that person to help your parent, your sibling, your . . . whoever . . . find closure over their loss so they could finally be at peace?'

'It's not that simple.'

As if I hadn't expected *that* answer. 'It never is. What was he doing there? *Really* doing there?'

Duval stared over my head at the giant rooster as if Hahn/ Cock, who was looking benevolently down on the traffic along Pennsylvania Avenue, might turn toward him and impart a few words of wisdom. Tell her or don't tell her?

Duval let out a long breath. I held mine.

'OK,' he said, 'OK. He was supposed to be meeting an asset. You know that already. It was someone he'd turned, someone he worked with extensively while he was in Abadistan – and Moscow – during the days when he was with Crowne Energy. One of our people learned that she wanted to talk and that she had information about the hackers. Except the only person she would talk to was Nick.'

'*She?* This asset was a woman?'

'That's right,' he said. 'I thought you knew.'

'I didn't.'

He seemed to consider that for a moment. Then he said, 'Nick was OK with that when he found out, so he said he'd do the meet-up. There was some concern that the Russians were starting to suspect her of spying for us, and he wanted to persuade her that it was time to let us extract her.'

'I was told she never showed up.'

'That's right.'

'Where is she now?' I wanted to know and didn't.

This time, I could feel the heat of his stare through the glasses. 'Either in the bowels of some prison after having been mercilessly tortured or they're done with her and she's been executed. My guess? She's dead.'

I closed my eyes. 'If Nick were alive and he knew what you just told me, he'd blame himself. *Forever.* He would never, ever be able to let it go.'

'Sophie,' he said, 'they knew to come after Nick. There's only one person who could have given them that information. The time and place of their meeting.'

'She . . . betrayed him.'

'More than likely, the torture broke her. I'm sure she held out as long as she possibly could.'

My God. 'Can you at least tell me her first name?'

He shook his head. 'Sorry. No can do. It wouldn't be her real name anyway. Any more than the name she knew Nick by was his.'

'You said they were close.'

He gave me a wary look, but he nodded.

'How close?'

'Sophie . . .'

'Close, as in she and Nick were romantically involved?' My voice shook, but I couldn't help it. I had to know. Because Duval did. Probably more than a few people in the Agency knew as well. Everyone except the wife. 'You people know everything, even the most intimate private details. Nothing is a secret. So I know you know the answer.'

'Are you asking me if he was in love with her or are you asking me if they had sex? Because they're two different things.'

'Both,' I said, lifting my chin and giving him a defiant look as Jack's voice from the other night rang in my head. *What if you find out something you wish you didn't know? Haven't you been through enough?*

Duval echoed Jack's words. 'What difference does it make . . . now?'

*It makes all the difference in the world.* 'I want to know.'

'It won't change anything.'

'Not for Nick,' I said. 'But it will for me.'

He held out both hands, palms up, like a reluctant witness who had been told to explain something he didn't want to explain. 'Unless you've been there, you can't imagine what it's like when you're in the field on your own with no safety net. Pretending to be someone else, some made-up fake identity. You do what you have to do, not necessarily what you want to do. And you try not to let it mess with your head. Because the bottom line is that it's all about the mission. It's all about doing your *job*.'

He was equivocating, stalling. He hadn't answered the question, but then again he had.

'They had sex,' I said in a hard, flat voice. 'They were lovers.'

'Yes.' After a moment, he added, 'I'm sorry.'

It felt like the worst kind of gut punch, but I managed to say, 'Don't be. I suppose I'd be incredibly naive not to be surprised.'

'For what it's worth,' he said, 'she was married, too.'

I nodded because the lump in my throat had become so big I didn't think I could speak anymore. Finally, I said, 'And then she betrayed him.'

'It would seem so.' He laid a hand on my shoulder. His touch was surprisingly gentle. 'The Agency is really rough on marriages, Sophie. The pressure, especially when you're in the field, living under a false identity, is unimaginable. Relentless. Ruthless. You can never slip, never make a mistake, because it could cost a life. Maybe yours, maybe someone else's. It can be brutal.'

'Is that why you're not married, Leo? Because you've seen what the life can do to someone you love, how it can warp a relationship and destroy a marriage?'

He seemed taken aback, but he said, 'Yes.'

I chewed on a fingernail and willed myself not to cry.

'Are you going to be all right?' he asked.

I nodded. Eventually, I would be. But not right now, not this instant. Not today. A Russian woman, whose name I would never know, had been my husband's lover and then betrayed him. And he had betrayed me. It hurt. I'd never had a clue.

What other lies had he told me?

Duval took off his sunglasses and looked me straight in the eye for the first time. I had forgotten what a deep, intense blue his eyes were, especially against his warm mahogany skin. 'I could have lied,' he said. 'I could have told you they weren't intimate, that their relationship was strictly business. But I thought you deserved the truth if you were gutsy enough to ask for it.'

'Thank you.'

'You're tough, Sophie. You *will* get through this.'

'Thank you for that, too.'

'You've got my number,' he said. 'Don't lose it.'

'I won't.'

'Good.' He put the shades on again. 'I might stick around and enjoy the view for a while.'

He wanted me to leave first. 'Before I go,' I said, 'I want to ask you something else. It's not about Nick.'

He cocked his head, a curious look on his face. 'OK. You know there are no guarantees I can answer you, though. Depending on what it is.'

Jack kept secrets because he had taken a sacred vow to do so. Duval kept secrets, too, but for a very different reason.

'It has to do with Everett Townsend.'

He gave me a sharp look. 'What about him?'

'I heard that he was good friends with a Russian oligarch named Alexey Ozupov, but that they recently had a falling out. I was wondering if you knew anything about it – whether it was a big deal or not?'

You would have thought I'd just told him Townsend had been whisked onto an alien spaceship and was on his way to a distant planet. Duval looked stunned.

'Even if I did know, I couldn't tell you. What makes you ask something like that? *Now?* Townsend's dead. And where did you get that information?'

It sounded as if we had reverted to Agent Duval and Ms Medina.

'A friend of mine and I found him unconscious in that alley on Capitol Hill. I called nine-one-one and we stayed with him until the ambulance got there.'

That clearly was news to him. 'Go on.'

'Someone who saw him in the ER at GW Hospital said the man who was there wasn't Townsend. It was another person who looked just like him – a doppelganger. Practically an identical twin, except they're not related. The other man was a homeless man.'

'A homeless man? Are you *serious*?' He gave me such a ferocious look that I nearly took a step backward.

'I am.'

'You're suggesting that an Associate Justice of the United States Supreme Court faked his death? That he committed pseudocide?'

'Pseudocide?'

'Yeah. That's the fancy term for it. Usually, men do it; more often than not, an insurance policy payout and some big debts are involved. Or if a woman does it, she's trying to get away from an abusive relationship. Justices of the Supreme Court generally do *not* do it.'

'I see. Well, strictly speaking, I'm not suggesting it. I'm *telling* you that's what happened. Everett Townsend committed pseudocide. He was an exception to your rule.'

Duval shook his head, still incredulous. 'Do you have any idea how hard it is to pull off something like that – especially someone as well known and recognizable as Everett Townsend?'

'I can't imagine it would be easy. But it wouldn't be impossible, would it? His body is being cremated, or maybe it already has been. There'll be nothing left to identify.'

'Sure, but the real Townsend – if you're right – will still be alive and well. Somewhere. Except he'll be in hiding – and that's what doesn't sound logical or plausible to me. Where's he gonna go? How long can he stay off the grid? And for God's sake, *why*?'

'I don't know. At least I don't know for sure.'

'You said you saw him. Stayed with him until the ambulance got there. You tell me if it was Townsend or not.'

'He had Townsend's ID, his wallet, his wedding ring, his phone, and his briefcase,' I said. 'I didn't recognize him, but my friend did. He's the one who ID'd him as Townsend. And he's a Catholic priest.'

'Who is this person who says it's *not* Townsend?'

'Someone who used to be homeless – which is how he recognized the guy in the hospital.'

I could almost hear the gears whirring inside Duval's head.

The validation of a priest who said it was Townsend versus a homeless man who said it was not. I could tell he was coming down on Jack's side – which, to be fair, was probably the logical conclusion to reach.

'Ozupov writes big checks to a number of charities in the US. He also serves on boards of cultural organizations and makes donations to universities and museums. He's got a lot of friends, a lot of influential contacts in this country. He's no angel – he acquired his billions during the Yeltsin years when everyone was making a grab to privatize the former Soviet energy companies. He's ruthless just like all those oligarchs are, but somehow he's managed to thread the needle and not end up on anyone's bad side. The Americans because he gives so much money and he's well liked, or the Russians because he still supports their corrupt government. I don't get where you're going with this.'

'I'm just trying to figure out why someone like Everett Townsend would fake his death. I'm looking for a reason.'

He kept shaking his head. 'There is no reason because he probably didn't fake anything. Townsend's dead. And trying to link your theory based on something a homeless guy told you to someone like Alexey Ozupov is really far-fetched, you know?'

I did know. Still, I believed Javi. 'You are going to look into it anyway, aren't you?' I asked.

He gave me the dumb-question look, and that's when I knew he'd whip out his phone before I made it halfway across the terrace and said goodbye to Hahn/Cock. And start asking questions.

'You know what I think?' he said. 'I think you're trying to tie this – in some kind of convoluted way – to what happened to Nick, his involvement with the Russians. And they're not related, Sophie. They're not.'

'I know they're not.' He was right. I was probably grasping at straws. 'For what it's worth, though, I believe my homeless friend.'

'Because?'

'Because someone who had a gun broke into his apartment after he got back from the hospital. My friend got away but thinks whoever it was wanted to shut him up, probably because he was overheard saying the guy in the hospital wasn't Townsend.'

That got his attention. 'Where is your friend now?'

'I don't know. Somewhere in the homeless camps.'

'Has he told anyone about this besides you?'

'No. And you're the only person I've told.'

'Keep it that way,' he said. 'Look, you brought this to me, so let me handle it from here on out, OK?'

'I will,' I said. 'But you have to tell me what's going on. My friend can't keep running. Please help me out here.'

He looked up toward the sky, probably eyes closed behind the mirrored aviators, probably deciding what his reply would be. Follow the rule book or, because I told him something he hadn't known, keep me informed so I had something to give Javi. The slippery slope. I didn't know which way he would go.

Finally, he said, 'I'll do what I can.'

'OK,' I said.

I hoped it would be enough.

Because Javi was running for his life.

# FOURTEEN

After I left Leo Duval on the terrace of the East Wing of the National Gallery of Art, I wasn't sure what I was going to do or where I was going to go, so I just started walking. And tried to make sense of what Duval had just told me about Nick during that conversation and how my life – which I had so carefully put back together after he died – was once again splintering into a million tiny shards.

Maybe I should have listened to Jack. Maybe it would have been better not to know about Nick's secret life, about the other woman he loved who ended up betraying him – which was why he had been executed – because she herself had been tortured so brutally. Why couldn't I have just left it at what Quill said to me: your husband made the ultimate sacrifice for his country and died a hero?

Quill. Damn. We were supposed to meet in the bar of the Jefferson Hotel after his meeting at the White House this evening. He wanted to talk about the Fernway book. My photos. Wrap up our year-long project. Tonight, though, I couldn't face him. Not with what I'd just learned about my husband. Not with what I knew about his wife. And then there was this: was Quill among the inner circle who knew that Nick and his Russian asset had been lovers? I'd thought that sort of thing was forbidden if the Agency found out. You couldn't be objective anymore if there was a personal relationship between the two of you, so you were reassigned.

My aimless walk had taken me down the Mall in the direction of the Lincoln Memorial. When I looked up, the Smithsonian Castle was across the way and I was standing next to a bench under one of the large old American elms that lined the walkway. I sat down and pulled out my phone to call Quill and beg off for tonight. I had turned on *Do Not Disturb* during my talk with Leo to avoid the increasing number of scam calls from sharp-voiced IRS agents who were turning me over to a collection agency for non-payment of taxes, or a friendly guy with an easygoing manner informing me of the horrors that would befall me because my car warranty was about to expire. I turned off *Do Not Disturb* and saw four missed calls from someone at *The Washington Tribune* that wasn't Grace. Her calls would have gone through. There were voicemails with three of the calls, increasingly agitated – and they *were* from Grace who obviously was not in her office.

*Call me ASAP.*

She picked up right away. No greeting. 'Where have you been?'

'I'll tell you another time,' I said. 'It had to do with Nick. Why?'

'Oh.' She sounded chastened. 'I'm sorry. It's just that I have been trying to reach you for the last hour.'

'I could tell by the number of missed calls and voicemails. I had *Do Not Disturb* turned on. You're not at your desk or your calls would have gone through. What's going on?'

Her voice went ragged. 'I needed to go someplace where no one would see me lose it. I'm in one of the conference rooms. Soph, it's Javi. A friend in MPD told me that his body was found this morning in an alley behind Lanier Place in Adams Morgan. A gunshot wound to the head. He probably – mercifully – died instantly. Oh, my God . . . *why?*'

She sounded so bereft and anguished. I closed my eyes and saw Javi dressed completely in black last night, telling me to take care. To be careful. More concerned about me than himself. Then disappearing into the shadows as the night swallowed him up. Now he was dead. Had someone seen him – or maybe seen the two of us – in Meridian Hill Park and then followed him? Was that where whoever was hunting him had picked up his trail?

Leo had just told me to keep what I knew between the two of us. To tell Grace anything would only put her in danger as well. So I lied and said, my own voice unsteady and filled with sorrow, 'I don't know.'

But I did.


After I hung up the phone with Grace, I walked across the Mall to the Smithsonian Metro station near the Castle. A couple of stops later, I was at Metro Center, from where I walked over to the Church of the Epiphany and the entrance to Streetwise. This time, I didn't text Finn to let him know I was coming because I was hoping to see Tessa Janko alone. And I didn't want Finn to know what I wanted – needed – to ask Tessa about Javi. Fortunately, the woman at the entrance had been there the other day and knew me well enough from helping out at workshops that she badged me through the door in the lobby leading to the offices upstairs.

'I'll only be a minute,' I told her. 'I just need a quick word with someone.'

She clearly didn't know about Javi. But it wouldn't be long before word would get around the homeless community and everyone would know.

I took the stairs to the second floor. Tessa was at the App Desk by herself, head bent down, long dark hair swinging forward so it obscured her face. When she looked up, her big dark eyes were red-rimmed. She already knew.

No need for pretense or conning each other. I walked in and said, 'How did you find out?'

'From a friend who works at MPD.'

'I'm so sorry,' I said. 'Did you get a chance to talk to him before . . .?'

She cut me off. Curt. Angry. 'No. But you did.'

I had just lied to Grace, but I couldn't face down Tessa's uncompromising stare and her righteous anger. 'Yes. How did you figure that out? Who told you?'

'I just *knew*. The way you blasted in here.'

'I saw him last night.'

'How was he?'

'Scared. Someone with a gun broke into his apartment after he got home from taking his landlady to the ER. He saw the guy coming and caught him off guard. He had enough time to grab a carving knife and at least slow down whoever it was. He also got the gun.'

Which he hadn't been able to use in time to stop someone in that alley in Adams Morgan.

'Good for him.' She smiled briefly, but then her face closed down and she gave me an unflinching stare. 'Do you know why?'

I did. I couldn't tell her any more than I could tell Grace.

'He didn't know.'

She said in a hard, flat voice, 'He knew and you know, too. You're lying, Sophie. Don't mess with me. I mean it.'

'All right,' I said. 'I am lying. But I'm *not* going to tell you because you'll end up like Javi if I do. So tell me what you know because I have a friend who can look into this and find out who killed Javi.'

She folded her arms across her thin chest. 'All I know is that whatever happened has to do with the Professor.'

So she *did* know something. 'OK. Do you happen to know the Professor's real name?'

'He used to be a vendor, so it's in the computer. It's Paul Smith.'

'Do you know anything else about him?'

'Only that he disappeared a few nights ago. No one knows where he went or what happened to him. I've been worried because he has . . .' She twirled her finger next to her temple. 'He forgets things. The name of someone he knows. A place he's been. Sometimes he just seems . . . lost.'

'Alzheimer's.'

She shrugged. 'Well, it's not like he's been to a doctor to diagnose it, but my nana had Alzheimer's, and he reminds me of her. Eventually, she didn't remember anything or anyone. She didn't even know my mom, her own daughter. I'm worried that's what's going to happen to him.'

'Alzheimer's is cruel.'

Chappy had started to have memory issues before he died. Alzheimer's was soul-destroying for anyone who had to watch someone they loved literally lose their mind.

'It's horrible,' she said. 'I'm trying to get the word out to anyone who comes in here that he's missing. He could get into trouble without meaning to. He could get hurt. He could end up like Javi.'

If Javi was right, no one would ever find the Professor. He was already dead and that's why Javi had been killed.

I nodded and thought about the life Nick must have led when he knew something but couldn't talk about it or say anything to help. Did he feel as utterly, utterly miserable as I did right now?

Did he ever stop feeling guilty about lying and just do what he had to do?

'You've taken a lot of photos of people at the camps, Sophie,' Tessa was saying. 'If you had one of Paul, we could make copies and pass them out – the vendors would help – and folks could start looking for him.'

I had taken thousands of photos over the past year. Some were crowd photos where I hadn't identified each individual. But if I had taken a photo of a particular person, I had asked permission and gotten a name. I didn't remember 'the Professor' or 'Paul Smith.'

'I'll check,' I said. 'And if I do, I'll make enough copies for you to give out.'

Which obviously would be pointless if he was dead.

'Thanks.' She flashed a quick, grateful smile.

'I'll be in touch,' I said and left.

Yet one more lie I had told today. One more person I had deliberately deceived.

I'd make a lousy spook because the guilt was eating at me already. How Nick had managed to live a double life, a life of deception, for so many years – even for the noblest of reasons – was something I would never really understand.


I had been inside the Church of the Epiphany a number of times over the last eighteen months. After I left Streetwise, I let myself in through one of the arched red doors and sat by myself in a pew in this peaceful holy place, where I hoped the cacophony of voices that had taken up residence in my head would quiet down so I could think through everything that had happened ever since Jack and I had found Everett Townsend, aka Paul Smith, three days ago.

Whoever killed Javi – or ordered his death – had wanted to make sure no one could cast any doubt that the man who had been brought to the ER on Monday night was Associate Supreme Court Justice Everett Townsend and that he had died of complications related to diabetes. And although I didn't want to think about it, a niggling worry that I *had* been seen with Javi last night had started to haunt me. Silencing him had been priority number one. So now that Javi was dead, had I bumped to the head of the line?

Would someone be coming for me next? And if so, who was it?

Who, besides Townsend himself, had a vested interest in silencing Javi? I'd been over this before. And the first name that came to mind – again – was Diana Townsend. Saint Diana, according to Jack. Except that it was impossible for her not to realize – *to know for a fact* – that the man she saw in the ER that night wasn't her husband. And because of her charity work with the homeless, she knew *exactly* who he was.

She had to be in on this, too.

If anyone would know about Diana's involvement, Jack would. Since I moved home from England, I had watched his reputation blossom as a respected public speaker and author on issues involving ethics and morality. *How to Live Morally in an Amoral World. The Importance of Integrity in Leadership. Listening to – and Heeding – Our Better Angels*. His phone had begun lighting up as more and more people – particularly high-ranking politicians and government officials – called on him to discuss the moral and ethical challenges they faced in the often murky and sometimes distasteful world of Washington politics. Lexie had once let it slip that she'd seen Jack's name in the White House Visitor's Log, though she never revealed who he'd come to see. The Vice-President was Catholic, but so were a number of senior West Wing advisors. And being Catholic wasn't a prerequisite for asking for Jack's counsel.

After what I learned the other night, I had no doubt Diana Townsend was one of the people who sought Jack's guidance and spiritual advice. I also didn't doubt that he probably heard her confession from time to time and knew intimate things about her that he would take to his grave. He might even know why she lied about the man in the ER at GW Hospital being her husband. And yet he couldn't say a word about it.

But I knew Jack better than Diana did. If I told him there were already two deaths because of Everett Townsend's deception, he would surely want to do the right thing. He could talk to Diana without betraying the sanctity of the confessional. He could persuade *her* to do the right thing.

Although what, exactly, *was* the right thing if you had just lied to cover up your husband's elaborate hoax to fake his death?

Flip on him suddenly and turn him in after a crisis of conscience? Then what came next?

If you were Diana, nothing good.

Everett Townsend might have managed to go to ground, but once word was out that he was really alive and well, there'd be no corner on earth remote enough and no hole deep enough where he could hide. Diana would get dragged through the mud of whatever he was involved in – which almost certainly involved a murder charge. Possibly two. Would capricious, mercurial Washington forget something like *that*? The answer was probably no. Not murder. And if Diana had lied to cover up for her husband, that made her an accessory to murder or maybe an accessory after that fact. I wasn't exactly fluent on such matters, but I did know this: she was in a lot of trouble now, too.

I got up from the pew, genuflected, and made the sign of the cross – old habits – and left. When I got outside, I did two things. First, I checked the *Tribune* website and, sure enough, there was already a story about Javi's murder last night in Adams Morgan. I clipped it and forwarded it in a text to Leo. No explanation needed. He'd know why I'd sent it.

Then I called Jack.

He answered on the second ring. 'Hey, what's up? I've been thinking about you. Hoping you're OK after what happened the other day. I know it was pretty traumatic.'

'I've been thinking about you, too. And I was wondering if you might have some time to see me today?'

'Sure. Everything OK?'

'I need to talk.'

If he was surprised by my request, he didn't let on. 'I'm done teaching for the day and my office hours end in thirty minutes. I could meet you somewhere.'

The law school wasn't far from Gloria House, but I didn't want to meet in his office.

'How about back at the house?' I said.

'Sure,' he said again. 'Give me an hour.'

'I'll see you then.'

My stomach rumbled as I disconnected. It was going on two o'clock and I'd missed lunch. I found a little deli-cum-grab-and-go near Metro Center and got an iced green tea and a pre-packaged tuna salad sandwich, which I ate perched on a high stool at a long, narrow counter that looked out on G Street. When I was done, I walked to the Metro station and took the Red Line four stops to Union Station. Gloria House was about a ten-minute walk. There was no sign of the homeless camp that had been cleared out of Columbus Circle in front of the train station a few weeks ago – the plaza was swept clean. But it didn't mean those people were gone – that they had vanished.

They had just migrated somewhere else.

Jack answered the door when I rang the bell, still wearing his blacks after a day of teaching but with the dog collar off and his shirt collar open. He gave me a one-armed hug and bussed my cheek. I hugged and kissed him back.

'Come on in,' he said. 'I need to get out of these clothes. Can you give me a minute to change?'

'Of course.'

We went upstairs to his suite and he disappeared into the bedroom. I opened the door to his terrace and stepped outside. The air still smelled sweet and warm, but Indian summer was waning and the weather forecast already predicted cooler air moving in as soon as tomorrow. No more bare arms and legs and sandals. Fall would be here in full force and then a gallop to the holidays and the cold weather season.

Jack joined me a moment later dressed in jeans and a polo shirt with the Jesuit logo embroidered where a pocket would have been. 'You want something to drink? I can make coffee. And I've got sparkling water or orange juice. I'm afraid that's it. Unless you want booze.'

With what I had to ask him alcohol was tempting. 'Sparkling water would be great.'

'Stay here. I'll be right back.'

I was leaning on the parapet overlooking Stanton Park when he plunked down a glass of sparkling water next to me.

'You want to talk?'

'Yes.'

He gestured to the pair of comfortable lounge chairs and ottomans with their ticking stripe cushions where we always sat. 'Shall we?'

We sat and he said, 'OK, spill it.'

'I don't really know how to say this, so I'm just going to tell you straight out,' I said.

He tugged on a lock of his wavy brown hair, which he often did when he was thinking, and gave me a bland look. 'OK. That's probably the best way.'

He was really good at this. I'd bet money people told him way more than they ever intended to say because of his friendly let-me-help-you demeanor as he listened, absorbing everything with calm, non-judgmental equanimity.

'Someone I know was at GW the night the ambulance brought Everett Townsend into the ER,' I said. 'This person happened to see him as his stretcher was wheeled in and recognized him. But not as Townsend. As a homeless man everyone calls "the Professor," who happens to look exactly like Townsend. They could practically be identical twins. I think the word for it is doppelganger. Someone who looks just like you but isn't related.'

Jack was nodding as I talked, but I thought I saw him grow a bit tense The tension vanished and he said, in a matter-of-fact tone, 'Diana Townsend identified her husband's body.'

'I know that. But my friend – Javi Aguilera – who also used to be homeless and still has lots of friends in that community, told a few people in the ER that it was the Professor,' I said. 'Not Everett Townsend.'

He shook his head and said more firmly, 'I'm sorry, Soph. Your friend – Javi – was mistaken.'

'Then why did someone follow him home from the hospital and break into his apartment?' I said. 'With a gun.'

'What?'

'You heard me.'

'How do you know this?'

'I met Javi last night in Meridian Hill Park and he told me. He was terrified. He overheard one of the EMTs mention our names to someone in the hospital as the people who had found Townsend – or Paul Smith, which is the Professor's real name – so he wanted me to know.'

'Where is he now?'

'Grace called me a few hours ago. He was found dead with

a gunshot wound to his head in an alley in Adams Morgan this morning.'

Jack sucked in a quick, harsh breath and made the sign of the cross.

I waited a beat and said, '*Javi wasn't mistaken.*'

'Diana is planning her husband's funeral. How could *she* be mistaken?'

'Why are you defending her?' My voice rose. 'Come *on*, Jack.'

'There's *nothing* to defend,' he said, his voice a bit sharp. 'Your friend is wrong. I'll remember him in my intentions at Mass. My condolences, Soph. I gather you were close. But I've known Diana Townsend for years. She is a *good* person. Decent, kind, compassionate, caring. And she's mourning the death of her husband, whose funeral is going to be this Friday.'

'It's a memorial, *not* a funeral, because she's having his body cremated.'

'What of it?'

'Don't you think it's odd how quickly this is happening? That there's going to be no body at the Mass?'

'What I think is that Diana is honoring her husband's wishes.' He wasn't budging an inch.

I tried again because this conversation was going nowhere. 'Look, you told me yourself that Diana does charity work in the homeless community. Don't you think it's possible she already knew Paul Smith?'

'Maybe. Maybe not. The homeless community in DC is, unfortunately, very large, with numbers in the thousands. I seriously doubt Diana knows everyone.' He shook his head again; I could tell his patience was wearing thin. 'And I don't understand why you think she would lie about something like this. You're talking about taking the word of a homeless man over a wife's in identifying the body of her husband. Sorry. Not buying it.'

'Ask. Her.'

'Why? Why should I upset her? Come on, Sophie. You of all people asking me to do something like this? You know what she's going through. I'm not going to ask a woman who just lost her husband if she lied about it.'

'It's called pseudocide,' I said. 'It's when—'

He cut me off. 'I know perfectly well what pseudocide is.'

'You've known me longer than you've known Diana,' I said. 'Do you really think I would come to you with a half-baked theory – *especially* something like this?'

Jack stood up and folded his arms across his chest. 'I've seen Diana's grief. It's real. And what reason would Rhett Townsend have for faking his death anyway? It doesn't make sense.'

'I'm not sure. It might have something to do with a falling out he had with a man named Alexey Ozupov.'

'Soph,' he said, 'you're talking nonsense.'

'All right, I don't know why he did it, but now Javi's dead, too. Please talk to her, Jack. Do the right thing.'

'I am doing the right thing. Drop this, Sophie. Don't pursue it. Don't push it.'

'Don't tell me what to do.'

'If you don't tell me what to do, either.'

I set my empty glass down on a side table between our chairs and got up. 'I need to go. Thanks for the water. Be seeing you, Jack.'

He didn't reply. I looked back as I let myself into his apartment and saw him leaning over the parapet, shoulders slumped, head down.

He might not believe me now, but I had gotten under his skin. I knew Jack. He might not ask Diana Townsend outright if she lied about identifying her husband's body, but he was going to look into what I'd just told him.

At least I hoped he would.

# FIFTEEN

I took an Uber back to S Street. It was faster than the Metro and all I wanted to do after that disturbing argument with Jack – if that's what we'd just had – was get home.

Besides, I had forgotten to call Quill and cancel this evening's drink date in the bar at the Jefferson Hotel, and now it was too late to back out. He was at his meeting at the White House. I'd have to go through with it, except I was underdressed for the Jefferson, one of Washington's beautiful, posh Grand Dame hotels.

I put on the sleeveless black V-neck sheath I always wore when I needed something dressy without going overboard, my favorite black heels again, ran a brush through my hair, added a slash of bright-red lipstick, and spritzed on some perfume. When I pulled up in front of the century-old Beaux Arts building on 16th Street half an hour later, a valet took the keys to the Mini and a doorman held the front door for me. The hotel lobby was surprisingly quiet, and my heels made an echoing staccato noise on the highly polished black-and-white harlequin tile floor.

The bar, which I'd forgotten was appropriately called the *Quill* Bar, was sumptuous and cozy. Dark wood paneling, Oriental carpets, paintings of Thomas Jefferson – the hotel's namesake – a collection of old maps on the walls, comfortable leather chairs you could sink into, and subtle lighting. I felt as if I were back in London.

A middle-aged man with heavy horn-rimmed glasses and a well-lined Mediterranean-complexioned face looked up from polishing a glass at the bar and smiled. 'Can I get something for you, miss?'

'No, thank you. I'm waiting for Quillen Russell, though obviously he's not here yet.'

No one was here, but it was still early, especially in Washington where there had always been a perverse prestige in being the last to leave the office in the evening. Especially if you worked on

Capitol Hill or down the street at the White House or next door at the EEOB – the Eisenhower Executive Office Building – where no one wanted to be the *first* to say goodnight. A little games-manship in the power-play pecking order of whose work was more important, who was closer to the boss. Lexie talked about it all the time. It drove her nuts, but she played the game, too.

The bartender's dark eyes lit up when I mentioned Quill. He smiled, showing two gold teeth. 'Mr Russell always takes the table in the corner over there.' He pointed to the table he meant. 'If you would like to have a seat, I can bring you a cocktail while you are waiting.'

'Thank you. I think I'll hold off until he arrives.'

He nodded. 'Of course. As you wish.'

But a moment later, he showed up with a bowl of mixed nuts and pretzels and a glass of sparkling water with a lime twist. 'A little something to tide you over so you don't perish from hunger or thirst while you wait.'

I laughed and said, 'Thank you. I definitely won't perish.'

I resisted the urge to pull out my phone and uselessly scroll until Quill got there – I could feel brain cells dying every time I did that – and instead leaned back into my chair and thought about my conversation with Jack. Maybe Diana hadn't told him anything and he truly had no reason whatsoever to doubt the man we found in the alley *was* Everett Townsend. Lying in front of Townsend's pied-à-terre, next to Townsend's car, wearing Townsend's clothes, his watch, carrying Townsend's wallet, phone, ID, and briefcase with his insulin medication inside. Jack hadn't sounded as if he was trying to cover up something or put anything over on me.

So could Javi have been *wrong*?

If he was, then who had broken into his apartment on Monday evening with a gun and then shot him last night in that alley in Adams Morgan? He had been running for his life – *that* was real. Was he mixed up in something else I didn't know about?

And what about the Professor? Where was *he*? If the real Paul Smith turned up somewhere, then Javi had pulled me into an elaborate game of cat and mouse that had nothing whatsoever to do with Everett Townsend. Plus, now I'd gotten Leo Duval involved. And Jack.

With accusations and theories about a Supreme Court justice that might be nothing more than a case of mistaken identity gone very, very wrong.

Jesus. What a mess.

'Manny, good to see you.' I heard Quill's pleasant baritone before I saw him.

'You, too, Mr Russell. Your guest is waiting at your table. Can I bring you your usual?'

'That would be great. And we'll have two menus when you get a chance. Does Ms Medina have a drink?'

'No, sir. Ms Medina was waiting for you.'

Quill's face lit up when he caught sight of me. 'Sophie. My dear, you look gorgeous.'

He flung his briefcase down on an empty chair and we exchanged hugs and kisses. He was dressed in a three-piece bespoke navy pin-striped suit that exuded power and confidence, probably from a London tailor by the looks of it, pale-blue dress shirt, a burgundy-and-blue paisley tie, sharply creased pale-blue pocket square, and expensive, highly polished black brogues.

'And look at you,' I said. 'Don't you look handsome?' He grinned an aw-shucks grin and I added, 'No, I mean it. You look terrific.'

He took the seat across from me and reached out, squeezing my hand. 'It's good to see you. It's been too long. We need to catch up.'

'It's good to see you, too. How was your meeting at the White House?'

'Good, good. The President and I have a sort of regular get-together every couple of months, so it was one of those. We sat in the Rose Garden and discussed what in the world is going on in the world. Solved all the problems.' He rolled his eyes skyward and gave me an ironic *as if* smile.

'The President? Wow, you didn't say who your meeting was with. It must have been a fascinating conversation. I wish I could have been a fly on . . . a rose.'

He grinned again and shook his head. 'It's an impossible job, being President of the United States. *In*humanly *im*possible. So much to grasp, understand, analyze, parse, decide. It comes at you at the speed of light. And it ages the hell out of everyone who takes on the job, the weight of so much responsibility.'

He had been staring, unfocused, over my shoulder as he spoke, and I could tell his mind had wandered back to the Rose Garden. What he and the President had discussed: impossible problems, incalculable variables, uncertain outcomes in a world where nothing was a zero-sum game anymore. And, of course, how could they not take into account how it would play out in the media? The must-feed-the-beast, unrelenting, quixotic mixed bag of self-appointed social media pundits and the actual, genuine accredited press.

Especially with the midterm elections coming up.

'You must have carried your fair share of weight as Secretary of State,' I said.

His eyes shifted to mine. 'You're right. I did. The United States is a big player on the world stage. The biggest. You've got to do your damnedest to get it right one hundred and ten percent of the time. Or else. And believe me, there were more than a few "or elses" on my watch. Every one of them weighed heavily on my soul, kept me up at night.'

It was a raw, candid admission from Quill. It must have been a hell of a session in the Rose Garden.

'All of which makes you the perfect person to be a foil and a counselor to the President,' I said. 'I know you well enough to be sure you gave him your straight, unvarnished opinion. You don't sugarcoat anything.'

He cut me a look as if he wondered whether there might be a double meaning in what I'd just said, but before he could ask, Manny showed up with a drinks menu for me and two dinner menus. Both had the bar's logo on them – an old-fashioned quill pen. He set down a martini glass in front of Quill.

'They've got a great menu of seasonal cocktails, Sophie,' Quill said and, thankfully, we were back on neutral territory. 'Really inventive and unusual. Manny makes the best cocktails in DC.'

I smiled at Manny. 'I'm sure he does, but I drove here. I think I'd better stick to a glass of Pinot Grigio. And, Quill, please don't wait for me to start drinking that martini. You look like you're ready to dive in.'

He raised his glass. 'Don't mind if I do. You'll have something to eat, won't you? I'm starved as well as parched. Vicki's out in Middleburg at Fernway, so this is dinner. Although I'm sure we could get a table in the restaurant, the Greenhouse, once we finish our drinks. The food's great here, but the menu there is more substantial fare. I want to feed you properly.'

'No, this is perfectly fine. And the menu here looks great.'

'You sure?'

'Absolutely.'

We ordered sirloin burgers with fries, both medium rare, and Manny left to get my wine and give our order to the kitchen.

After Manny brought my Pinot, Quill raised his glass and said, 'A toast to the Fernway project. You did a terrific job, Sophie. I can't tell you how pleased I am with the way it turned out.'

'Thank you. I really enjoyed it.' We clinked glasses and I thought, *Well, most of it.*

He reached into his inside jacket pocket and pulled out a folded check. 'Here you go. Final payment. And thank you.'

I didn't look at the check, but I knew he almost certainly added to the amount we'd agreed on. I slipped it into the small black Chanel bag I'd found at a consignment store and took out his housekey with the jeweled Hamsa key chain.

'And I'm returning this.' I held it out and he took it. 'So now we're officially finished.'

'I'd still like you to look at the book layout before it goes to the printer.'

I wasn't sure I could go back to Fernway after that last visit. It would feel too weird.

'Why don't I drop by your office since we don't need to sneak around Fernway any more?'

'Sure, fine,' he said. 'Probably in a few weeks, maybe before Thanksgiving.'

Our burgers – with tomato confit and caramelized onions – and fries arrived, and for a few moments we were busy eating.

'This is delicious,' I said.

'The food here is always good.'

'Tell me about your overseas trip.'

'This one was a little more hectic than usual. I'm glad to be home. I'm beat.'

I waited while we both took bites of our burgers and then said, 'I was wondering whether you learned anything new about Nick while you were there?'

He set his burger on his plate and folded his hands together. 'I'm afraid not. It's kind of a closed case now, Sophie. I'm sorry.'

Like I said, he didn't sugarcoat anything.

A closed case. The end. Finished.

*We've moved on.*

There was no point beating around the bush with him anymore. 'You knew Nick was having an affair with the woman he went to meet in Vienna.' A statement. But I still added, 'Didn't you?'

He didn't even blink. 'How did you find out?'

'A good journalist never burns a source. Just like a good spy.'

He gave me an unflinching look. 'Yes. I knew.'

'And you didn't tell me.'

'No.'

'Why not?'

'I'm sure you can guess why not. What would be the point . . . now? I didn't think you needed to suffer any more unnecessary pain and grief than you already had to bear,' he said. 'As it is, you haven't even been able to tell your family or your closest friends what happened to Nick. Why put more on your shoulders?'

I slumped in my chair, uncomfortably aware of how close I was to tears. 'Did you know how long it had been going on?'

'No. To be honest, they managed to keep it a secret until the end, which is no small feat in the spy business. I didn't find out until that last assignment when he agreed to go to Vienna out of the blue. It didn't take a genius to figure out the reason the only person she would talk to was Nick. That there was something going on between them,' he said. 'By then, Langley wanted the intel she had, and if that was the only way to get it, they OKed it.'

'Did Nick ever say anything to you about her? Hint at anything?'

He shook his head. 'No. No, no, no. He loved you, Sophie. He was crazy about you. He never said anything about . . . anyone . . . else to me. *Ever.*'

'I see.'

He drained his martini and signaled for another. 'There is one thing.'

My heart skipped two beats. 'What is that?'

'The last trip. Before he left, he asked me to look after you while he was gone. I said I would, of course, but I thought it was odd because you're one of the most resilient and strong women I know, and you can take care of yourself perfectly well without help from me.' His smile was rueful. 'It never occurred to me that he was talking about longer than two weeks.'

My breath gave a little hitch. 'Do you think he knew what might happen?'

Manny set down the fresh martini and removed Quill's empty glass. To me, he said, 'Can I get you another glass of Pinot, Ms Medina?'

I covered the rim of my wine glass with my hand. 'No, thank you. I'm fine.'

After Manny left, Quill said, 'I've gone over and over it, but yes, I think Nick might have had a premonition about this trip, maybe realized he needed to be extra careful. That incredible intuitive sixth sense he had. Although I don't for a moment believe he thought he was walking into a trap. He would have pulled out if he did.' He took a long drink of his martini. 'What about you? What do you think?'

I shrugged one shoulder. 'I thought it was odd the way the trip came up so suddenly. And, of course, I thought it was QUORA business – that he was working for you – and nothing more. But Vienna . . . city of spies? I did wonder.' My turn to drink some wine. 'I wished I'd asked more questions, though you know as well as I do that he wouldn't have told me anything.'

'He wouldn't and he couldn't.' He picked up his burger and said in a gentle voice, 'Your dinner is getting cold.'

I gave him a wan smile and stabbed a few French fries with my fork. My phone vibrated in my purse. I had set it on *Do Not Disturb* again. My list of downtime contacts consisted of my family, Grace, Jack, Max, and, for old times' sake, Perry when he had been my boss in London.

Quill heard the buzzing sound as well.

'I'm so sorry,' I said. 'Do you mind if I check . . .?'

'Go right ahead.'

I took a quick look at the display and shut it off. 'It's Harry. I'll call him later.'

'Everything OK at home?'

'Fine. Isabella Filippova, the woman who has been sorting through my grandfather's photos and personal effects, told me she'd be finishing up any day. I need to collect the photographs Chappy chose for what's now his retrospective at the Dupont Underground. Harry probably wants to tell me I can drive out there and get them,' I said as a little stab of guilt went through me and I thought about Oriana Neri for the first time in twenty-four hours.

I still had to face Mom and Harry and tell them about her – and her ultimatum. Show them the photos she demanded be part of my grandfather's exhibition. Show them the Las Vegas marriage license that Oriana said was still legal. My mother would totally, totally unravel.

'I'm really looking forward to seeing that exhibition.' Quill sounded enthusiastic. 'I've already booked tickets for Vicki and me for the opening.'

'You have?'

'Of course. Why?'

'You get to hear me. The director of the Dupont Underground and the head of the school in Connecticut twisted my arm to give the talk Chappy would have given that evening.'

Quill's eyes lit up and he said, 'That's terrific. What an accolade, Sophie. You'll be brilliant. Wait until I tell Vicki.'

'I'm a terrible public speaker. I'm always a bundle of nerves.'

'I doubt that. Have a glass of wine before you go on stage to take the edge off. Everyone's going to love you. You've got nothing to worry about.'

Manny came to take away our empty plates and said to me, 'What can I bring you for dessert, Ms Medina? Mr Russell, here, knows what we have by heart. But I can also bring a menu if you would like to study it. Or Mr Russell can just recite it for you,' he said, and Quill grinned.

I laid a hand over my stomach. 'I couldn't possibly. Dinner was wonderful, but I'm completely, totally full.'

'They make their own ice cream,' Quill said, giving me an evil look. 'And their own sorbet. You have no idea.'

I glared at him.

He got the ice cream: a scoop each of bourbon and cocoa nib.

I had scoops of chocolate and raspberry sorbet. Two espressos afterwards.

The sorbet was, as promised, out of this world. So was the homemade ice cream. We traded bites from each other's dishes.

After Manny brought our coffee, I said to Quill, 'What's next for you? Any more trips?'

'Maybe one more to Asia before Thanksgiving. I'm also taking Vicki to Germany in early December so we can visit the Christmas markets. You know how she adores Christmas.'

'How lovely,' I said. 'Those markets are wonderful. No one does Christmas like the Germans. Or the Austrians. It's magical. Nick and I went as often as we could when we lived in Europe.'

'We're looking forward to it,' he said, smiling.

'What are you doing for your twenty-fifth – besides giving Vicki the book?'

'Celebrating at home with the kids – we're always home for Christmas and New Year, as you know. But in January I'm taking her to Anguilla. I've rented a villa for us on a private beach with a chef and household staff. Total luxury.' He put a finger to his lips. 'It's also a surprise. She knows we're going to the Caribbean, but she doesn't know where or any of the details.'

'My lips are sealed. Quill, you are such a romantic. You two will have the perfect second honeymoon.'

He smiled, but his eyes seemed to darken briefly as if a shadow crossed them, and I wondered if he knew, or maybe sensed, that his wife had been intimate with another man while he was away.

As if he read my mind, he said, 'Vicki's coming into town tomorrow since we're going to Rhett Townsend's funeral.'

Thank God I'd worked on that poker face. Because what was I going to say: I didn't know *both* of you knew him?

'Lexie said the President and the First Lady are going, too. She wrote his press statement when the news broke that Justice Townsend had passed away. She told me he ordered the flags flown at half mast, but that Townsend wouldn't lie in state in the Capitol because he was cremated.' I was babbling, but I didn't know what else to say that didn't involve possible self-incrimination.

Quill beamed like an indulgent parent. 'Lexie, that sweet girl. Next time I'm in the West Wing, I need to make a point to drop by her office and say hi, see how she's doing. I can't believe she's working at the White House. I still think of her as the scrappy little kid who took a tumble off her horse when he didn't clear a fence at the Upperville Horse and Colt Show, then got up, and took the jump again.'

'She broke her arm that day. She still has a nasty scar. And she's still scrappy, except she's not a kid anymore.'

Quill's smile was rueful as he signaled for the check. 'I know she's not. But in the blink of an eye, you've all grown up. Our kids. You, Tommy, Lexie. It goes too fast. I have moments now when I wonder if I wasn't gone too much, missed too many ballet recitals, soccer games, the school play, an awards ceremony. Vicki, too; her job was just as demanding. Still is. Plus, we've always had such an active social life because of our careers. Washington's known for that.'

He'd given me an opening. 'I remember you showing up at lots of school events, Quill. Both you and Vicki. I don't think you have anything to reproach yourself for. So is that how you and Vicki know Everett Townsend? The usual Washington social circles?'

He nodded, pulling his wallet out of his pocket. 'That and Rhett has – *had* – a case coming up before the Court later this session on soft money and campaign financing. Vicki knows that stuff inside out – as you probably know if you've seen her on television or read her pieces – so a few months ago, Rhett asked her to meet him and then picked her brain. She has some very definite opinions on some of the Court's most recent rulings that she says are going to make it easier for dark money to make its way into political campaigns. Apparently, the two of them are . . . *were* . . . having some mano a mano conversations on this particular case.'

'I had no idea.' Mano a mano. Yup, they were physical, all right.

'Well, you wouldn't,' he said. 'No one did. Rhett's brilliant – he had an incredible, erudite mind – but he could be a real prick when he thought he was smarter than you were, which was most of the time. And Vicki, who is as stubborn as the proverbial mule when she wants to be, was determined not to back down or be cowed by him.' He shrugged. 'Of course, now it doesn't matter anymore, does it? The President is going to nominate a successor and, as is well known, he and Rhett didn't see eye to eye politically, to put it mildly. So the new nominee – if the Senate confirms him or her – is likely going to cast votes that would be very different from Justice Townsend's. I'm sure you read in the press that someone leaked a draft of the opinion statement on the soft money case showing the vote was going to come down five-four against making the rules more lenient. And that Rhett was one of the five.'

I had read about the leaked document – who hadn't? It had been splashed all over the front page of all the major papers and covered ad nauseam by the cable channels and other media outlets. First *Roe v. Wade*. Now this case on campaign financing. The Supreme Court was leaking like the proverbial sieve.

'You'd have to be living on another planet not to have heard about it,' I said. 'That story has been everywhere. And it's the second time there's been a leak about a major Court decision in almost as many months.'

Quill frowned as if I'd said something amiss, so I said, 'What?'

Manny had arrived with the bill, setting down a leather folder on the table next to Quill. No rush,' he murmured. Quill pulled a bright-blue credit card out of his wallet and slid it into the leather folder.

After Manny said thank you and departed, Quill said, 'The draft statement may have been leaked, but Vicki had a strong feeling Rhett was going to change his vote and go the other way. So it would be five-four *in favor* of soft money.'

'Wait. Are you saying he was going to switch his vote because of the leak?'

'No, no, not for that reason. To be honest, Vic didn't understand the about-face at all, but she was almost one hundred percent certain that he was going to flip his vote. Which why there was a major shitstorm raining down from Townsend's office when he found out the press had gotten hold of that draft statement. Because now he was going to have to dig his way out of a massive sinkhole for supposedly' – Quill made air quotes – '"changing his mind".'

'I read about his temper tantrum, but I thought it had to do with the leak.'

Manny came back with the folder. Quill opened it and signed the bill after doing some mental math for the tip.

'Thank you again for dinner, Quill,' I said. 'And for the check.'

The two of us stood up and he reached for his briefcase. 'You're more than welcome. Just because this project is done doesn't mean we shouldn't continue to get together every now and again, you know?'

'I'd like that, but you don't need to feel as if you've got to be my guardian angel forever. You've done more than enough keeping an eye on me these last eighteen months.'

He laid a hand on my shoulder. 'Vicki and I think of you as another daughter, Sophie. You're very dear to both of us.'

'Thank you,' I said. 'I mean it.'

'The valet parked your car?' Quill asked as we walked out to the lobby. I nodded.

'Where's your ticket?' He held out his hand and I passed it to him.

He reminded me so much of Harry, the quietly commanding way they both took care of little things like that, because that's the way they'd been brought up, as old-school Southern gentlemen.

Quill gave the doorman my ticket, along with his own. Then he pulled out his wallet, taking out two bills which he folded to slip into the hands of whoever showed up with our cars. His black Lexus arrived first; the Mini was right behind it.

We exchanged hugs again and he said, 'I meant to tell you. Those photos of the ginkgoes – the ones that line the driveway – were gorgeous, Sophie, more beautiful than I ever remember them. I'm sorry I wasn't home to see them this year. When were you out at the house? When did you take those pictures?'

'Um . . . the beginning of the week. Monday, I think it was. Yes, Monday,' I said and hoped we could leave it at that.

'The light was stunning.'

'Thank you. I drove out early so I could be there as the sun came up. You know, the golden hour.'

'I wish I could have been there with you,' he said as the valet held the car door for him.

*No, you don't.* For a horrified moment, I thought I'd said it out loud. In reality, I just stood there with a smile pasted on my face and said nothing. As he pulled out of the driveway, he powered down his window. In the soft eerie glow of the dashboard display, his strong profile was in silhouette. He turned his face to me, and there was no mistaking the sadness in his eyes.

Which is when I thought, *He knows something happened at the house that day.*

*And he knows I know what it is, too.*

# SIXTEEN

I didn't listen to Harry's message until I was home and had changed out of my dress and heels into the tee-shirt and sweatpants I wore as pajamas. He'd called, as I'd told Quill, to let me know that Isabella had finished sorting through Chappy's photo collection and belongings, so I could come and pick up the photos Chap had chosen for the exhibition at the Dupont Underground whenever I wanted. I found an open bottle of a French Sauvignon Blend from Slater Run Vineyards, a family-run vineyard up the road from Mayfield, in my refrigerator, so I poured a glass and settled into my favorite armchair in the living room, feet tucked under me. The light from the streetlamps on S Street poured in through the bay window, bathing the alcove in soft, diffused light. It was unexpectedly quiet and peaceful – no wailing sirens, no distant bustle of traffic from Connecticut Avenue – except for the metronome ticking of the grandfather clock behind me.

I sipped my wine and leaned back in the chair, closing my eyes.

Twenty-four hours ago, I'd been at Meridian Hill Park with Javi. In spite of what Jack said about not looking further into whether the man who'd been brought into the ER the other night was Everett Townsend or an elaborate charade to deceive everyone that a homeless man named Paul Smith had taken his place, I intended to do exactly that and find out for sure who he was. Tomorrow, as I promised Tessa, I'd start going through my photos to see if I could find a photo of Paul Smith.

In the meantime, I needed to call Harry and tell him about Oriana Neri so he could prepare Mom before I drove out to Mayfield to pick up Chappy's photos. If anybody could calm my mother down after hearing news that would absolutely devastate her, Harry could, though I knew it would be a shock to him, too.

He answered on the second ring. 'Hi, sweetheart,' he said. 'You got my message.'

'I did. Are you and Mom having your after-dinner drinks in the library?' I asked. 'And before you answer, I need to talk to you when she isn't around. It's important. So maybe you could call me back when you're by yourself?'

I'd guessed right. Mom was in the room with him. Harry didn't miss a beat. 'Good,' he said, 'glad to hear that. Thanks for returning the call. We'll talk soon. Love you.'

He called back half an hour later. By then, I'd poured another glass of Sauvignon Blanc.

'OK,' he said, 'your mother went upstairs to do her nighttime beauty routine. I told her I'd be along shortly. I'm outside on the back porch with a cigar and a whiskey. What's going on?'

I told him about Oriana's letter, how I hadn't gotten it until literally just before her luncheon, and the news she had for me about still being married to Chappy.

There was a long pause before he said, 'Do you *believe* this woman? I mean, could she be a gold digger who maybe knew Chap a hundred years ago and is hoping she can stake a claim to part of his estate with some document no one can substantiate?'

'Well, there's more.'

'Lord, of course there's more. Go on. I can't wait to hear it.'

I told him about the pictures and he groaned. 'How bad are they?'

'I'm going to text them to you. Along with a photo of the marriage license. Then you tell me.' A moment later, I said, 'I just sent them.'

Another pause. I could hear the ice cubes tinkling in his glass as he waited. I didn't think much could shock Harry who was pretty worldly-wise. I heard his sharp intake of breath and a muttered swear word. 'These are . . . pretty explicit, Sophie. They don't look like Chap's photos at all. He wasn't into pornography.'

'I know. That's what I told her.'

'What'd she say?'

'Harry, she has more photos. The second set is . . . really explicit. Photos of both of them. She brought them out when I told her I didn't believe Chap took those nudes. They're her proof that the other photos are legit.'

'Damn. Send them.'

'All right,' I said. 'These are sort of blackmail, I guess you'd say, for ensuring the other photos end up in the Dupont Underground exhibition.'

I hit send and waited.

He let out a long, explosive breath and said, 'Sweet Christ Almighty. When your mother sees these . . .'

'I know, I know. That's why I wanted to talk to you first and tell you. Maybe you could prepare her before I come out there? I was thinking of driving out tomorrow.' *And getting this over with.*

'There's no good way on earth to prepare your mother for *these.*'

'I know that, too,' I said. 'Oriana's waiting for an answer. What do you want to do?'

'First thing tomorrow, I'm calling Sam,' he said. 'I'm gonna send him this whole sordid package you just sent me, along with that marriage license. It could be bogus, you know. People fake documents all the time. A marriage license would be dead easy.'

'The signature looks genuine enough.'

'A good forger could easily fake that, too. As famous as your grandfather was, enough people will have seen his signature to be able to copy it.'

He was right. But after meeting Oriana, I don't know why, but I doubted she'd faked the marriage license. My question was the photos. Had Chappy really taken them? The marriage license might be legit and she was using it as leverage to get the photos in the exhibition so she could cash in as Charles Lord's previously unknown first wife. I could see that scenario a lot more easily. Plus, she had to know there'd be plenty of juicy tabloid interest in *that* story, maybe even a book deal. She could riff off the title of the Dupont Underground exhibition: *Really* Out of the Public Eye: Exposing the Unknown Side of Charles Lord Nobody Knew . . . *Except Me.*

'What about Mom?' I asked Harry.

I heard him exhale and could almost smell the pungent scent of his Montecristo No. 2 cigar. He would have his feet up on the coffee table since Mom wasn't there to tell him not to, one booted leg crossed over the other, stretched out long and lean, phone clamped between his shoulder and his ear, whiskey and cigar in one hand, stroking Ella's sweet head with the other.

'Let me see what Sam says before I say anything to your mother.'

'OK, but we can't keep this from her too long, Harry. She'll be furious at both of us for going behind her back to Sam.'

'I know,' he said. 'I'll handle that; don't worry. You drew the short straw. You're the one who has to tell her about Oriana . . . and show her the photos. I'm sorry, Sophie, but I think the news has to come from you.'

'I know it does. You can't tell her. I have to do it.'

'Are you going to be OK?'

'Do I have a choice?'

'I wish you did. And now' – I could hear the creaking of the wicker chair as he stirred – 'I'd better get upstairs before your mother starts wondering what I've gotten up to. Let me talk to Sam and then I'll call you tomorrow to let you know when you can come out to pick up the photos for the exhibition . . . and tell Caroline about this awful woman.'

'I'll wait to hear from you.'

'Get some sleep, honey.'

'I will, Harry. You, too.'

He disconnected. I knew for sure that I wouldn't get much sleep. And what sleep I did get would be roiled with dreams.

I suspected Harry's would be as well.

I tossed and turned for an hour before I finally got my laptop and brought it into bed. Tonight, Quill had told me about Vicki's relationship – her professional relationship – with Everett Townsend and how she thought Townsend was going to flip his vote on a case before the Supreme Court, making it easier for political campaigns to accept soft money. Wouldn't that benefit someone like Alexey Ozupov, who wanted an entrée into American politics? I started searching for Ozupov and found plenty about his philanthropic donations in the US and abroad. He'd even donated paintings to the Louvre. Jeez. The guy was full of surprises.

An article about superyachts showed up, so I clicked on that. Sure enough, there was a photo of Ozupov's latest toy, a long, sleek yacht known as a 'white boat.' Other names were superyacht and megayacht. Also, gigayacht, which applied to anything over two hundred and ninety-five feet long. Ozupov's boat, which had been designed in Monaco and built in Italy, was a gigayacht. A fifth of all gigayachts were supposedly owned by oligarchs because of something of crucial importance in that testosterone-fueled world known as LOA. Length over all. The bigger and longer the better, especially for the Russians, who wanted to outdo each other in excess and crass opulence. If you could dream it, they wanted it. The boats might have been designed to ensure maximum privacy, but they were built to show off the incredible wealth and flamboyant lifestyle of their owners. There was also a list of some of the most over-the-top features found on Ozupov's yacht: his personal submarine, a Van Gogh in the master bedroom, a spa, an IMAX theatre, a small hospital clinic (apparently, Ozupov was a hypochondriac), a helicopter hangar, and a swimming pool set on a gyroscope so the water wouldn't slosh out of the pool in heavy seas.

Townsend had partied with this guy.

I turned off my computer. I'd seen enough for one night.

Indian summer vanished in the blink of an eye, ushered out unceremoniously by autumn, which decided to make its presence known by staging a cold, sharp entrance. My bedroom felt like the inside of a freezer when I woke up. I found my bathrobe on a hook in the closet and pulled it on. Then I shut the windows and went downstairs to turn on the heat for the first time in over a month.

After breakfast and a shower, I put on jeans, a long-sleeved shirt, and a jacket and took a mug of coffee over to the studio – which was also freezing. It didn't take long to warm up the little cottage; I turned on the space heater next to my desk, which made the room pleasantly toasty in no time. Although Harry and I both had Oriana's pictures and her marriage license on our phones, my mother was analog all the way. I printed out copies of the black-and-white pictures – *all* of them – plus the marriage license and put them in a large envelope.

Then I started going through the photos I'd taken at homeless camps and on the street over the last few years, looking for a photo of Paul Smith, known to his friends as 'the Professor.' A search of all the pictures I'd taken of individuals turned up nothing, which was what I'd expected. I would have remembered someone as distinguished-looking and well dressed as he was: not too many members of the homeless community wore business suits. And the name, as I'd told Tessa yesterday, didn't ring a bell. So now I had to start going through group photos one by one, checking to see if I had captured a picture of him without realizing it.

In the middle of my search, my phone dinged with a text message. I opened my phone and smiled. A red rose emoji and *See you tonight at 6* from Perry. Dinner at Iron Gate. I sent back a heart and a rose.

Harry called just before ten.

'I heard from Sam a moment ago.' He sounded grim, so this was going to be bad news.

'He did some research, called in a favor, and found the record for the marriage license. Las Vegas, Nevada, May third, 1958. It's legit.'

I groaned. 'I'm sorry, but I'm not surprised. I don't suppose he found a divorce decree?'

'Nope. Nothing. Nada.' Harry exhaled a long, frustrated breath. 'He also looked up Oriana Neri. Nothing to find there, not so much as a parking ticket. She's squeaky clean. He did come across a "Gianni Paolini" at the same address. Deceased about eighteen months ago.'

'Her partner of many years. She mentioned him, but not his last name. They never married.'

'Because?'

'He wouldn't divorce his wife who was mentally unstable and wouldn't have been able to get medical insurance on her own. So although he lived with Oriana, he continued to care for his wife.'

'Sounds like a good man.' I could hear the grudging admiration in Harry's voice. It would be easier to dislike them both if Gianni had been a cad and Oriana was a gold digger.

'Oriana said the same thing about him, though I gather she was disappointed he never made an honest woman of her, so to speak – she's that generation. Of course, if they *had* married, I doubt we would have heard from her because she'd have to admit that she, too, had committed bigamy,' I said.

'Bigamy,' Harry said. 'I still can't believe this.'

'Me, neither. By the way, I just finished making prints of Oriana's photos. And the marriage license. I know how Mom hates staring at little phone screens. She claims it ruins her eyes.'

That made him chuckle. 'Are you ready to drive out here and face the music?'

'No, but I will.'

'I'll tell Caroline you're coming out to pick up Chap's photos,' he said. 'And staying for lunch.'

'What about Oriana?'

'I tried to broach the subject so she'd have an idea you had something you wanted to discuss with her. In the end, there was no good way to do it without making her suspicious, and then she'd be primed for who knows what. So I figured it was better if you just show up and lay it all out. We'll take it from there,' he said.

'Right.' He didn't have a plan for how we should bring this up with Mom. Neither did I. What we *did* have was a prescription for disaster: wing it and hope for the best.

'See you in about an hour?' he said.

'Yes,' I said. 'But I'm not looking forward to it.'

I arrived at Mayfield just before noon, taking care of Ella's requisite head-scratching when she met me at the front door before calling out that I was home.

I heard Harry holler, 'We're in the sunroom. Come on back.'

I set my purse on the antique Windsor bench in the front hall and pulled out the envelope with Oriana's photographs. Then I took a deep breath and hollered back.

'I'll be right there.'

My mother had recently redecorated the sunroom – Mom was never happier than when she was picking out paint and fabric or choosing new furniture, and Harry, who was a total pushover for anything Mom wanted, unfailingly indulged her. Now the room looked like a lush English country garden. She had one of the walls painted a soft mossy green and hung on it a series of prints by Margareta Haverman and Rachel Ruysch, two eighteenth-century female Dutch artists known for their beautiful paintings of flowers. Two other walls were mostly windows with south- and east-facing views, which were ideal for the large plants – a money tree, a ficus, a dracaena, a fiddle leaf fig, and a bamboo plant, along with numerous smaller plants – that sat in colorful pots and on plant stands, all clearly thriving. The sofa, where Harry sat reading his newspapers – the *Post*, the *Times*, the *Trib*, the *Journal* – as he did every morning, was upholstered in a nubby cream fabric. All the other furniture was covered in a pleasing combination of botanical fabrics, white or cream backgrounds with ferns and plants in every shade of green. A large, low vase of pink roses sat in the middle of the bamboo-and-glass coffee table, a perfect contrast to all the green and white. The room was lovely.

Harry looked up, instantly alert, when I walked in. His eyes lasered in on the envelope I held by my side. My mother, who was seated on a chaise longue with a quilt my grandmother had made over her lap as she worked on a floral needlepoint canvas, looked up as well.

'Mom,' I said, 'that needlepoint is going to be beautiful.'

She smiled. 'Thank you, sweetie. It's eventually going in here if I ever get it finished.'

'You will.'

'We'll see. Harry said you'd be out here today to pick up Chap's photographs for the exhibition. Isabella left everything labeled on the kitchen table in the cottage. Of course, she wants you to sign some paperwork confirming that you're in possession of the photos.'

'Don't worry, I'll sign everything.'

'You'll also stay for lunch.' Not a question but a command.

'Yes. Thanks.'

She set her needlework on her lap and gave me a quizzical look. 'What's up?'

'Pardon?'

'I'm your mother. You've been restless and distracted since you walked through the door,' she said, her eyes straying to the envelope. 'What is it?'

I moved an ottoman covered in a twining vine fabric that was in front of a matching wing chair so it was next to her chaise. I sat down facing her and said, 'All right, there is something. I don't know an easy way to tell you about it, either.'

She cut a look at Harry and said with acute perception, 'You know what this is about, don't you, my love?'

He nodded. 'I do.'

She folded her arms across her chest, not happy. 'Well, maybe you two want to clue me in, then? Since I'm the last to know whatever it is?'

'OK,' I said and told her.

You can read my mother like a book. At first, she was horrified. Then she grew angry.

'It's impossible,' she said in a hard, flat voice when I was done. 'Your grandfather never – and I mean *never* – would have done something like that. He would not have married my mother when he was legally married to another woman. This Oriana Neri woman has got to be making this story up.'

'I'm afraid she's not, Caroline,' Harry said. 'I called Sam first thing this morning. He did some checking. The marriage license is legal. And Sam couldn't find any record of a divorce.'

My mother turned pale and her hand went to her throat as if she couldn't breathe. I had put the marriage license on top of all the photos and I took it out of the envelope and set it in front of her. Harry got up and left the room, returning with a shot glass filled with a golden-brown liquid.

He handed it to my mother. 'You might need this, sweetheart. It's brandy.'

She took the glass but didn't drink. Still, her hand shook. 'I need to talk to her. This woman.'

'Mom. There's more.'

'Drink the brandy, Caroline,' Harry said, and this time she did.

I pulled out the photographs – just the nudes of Oriana – and explained what she wanted. My mother held out her empty glass; Harry took it, leaving the room and returning with the bottle of brandy and the glass, which he refilled.

'We couldn't possibly agree to this blackmail,' my mother said.

Harry and I exchanged anguished looks. I handed my mother the envelope so she could look at the rest of the photographs for herself.

In the silence that followed as she flipped through the most explicit photos one by one, I knew her heart was breaking because of the secrets my grandfather had kept and what this meant to her and my grandmother. He had lied. He had another wife. He had deceived them. He had committed bigamy and never said a word.

After he died, she discovered he had bequeathed his estate to a small arts school whose benefactor had known Chappy's plans all along while she'd been completely in the dark.

Now this. I knew something of her heartache after what I'd learned about Nick. The hurt runs deep.

Chappy and Nick were gone. Neither Mom nor I were ever going to be able to ask *Why?* or *How could you?* We would never have a knock-down, drag-out cathartic fight where we got everything out of our systems and then tried to fix what they'd broken: our trust. And that, to use the technical term for it, just sucked.

'What do you want to do, Mom?' I asked.

She was still holding on to the photos and her hands shook. 'I need some time.'

Harry extracted the photos from her hands and put them back in the envelope, which he set on the coffee table. 'Of course you do, sweetheart.'

'What was she like?' my mother asked me. 'Tell me.'

She already knew from the photographs that Oriana was a stunner, a beauty, someone who absolutely would have captivated her father's attention. But as for what the woman herself was like? I'd spent an hour with her. I didn't really know.

'We didn't part on the best of terms,' I said, evading her question. 'But she clearly wants to be recognized as Chappy's first wife. Even if they got married on a drunken whim in Las Vegas and regretted it almost immediately afterwards.'

'That woman's photographs are *never* going to be in my father's exhibition. I promise you, it's never going to happen,' she said. 'Harry, Sam must be able to do *something* about this.'

'We'll talk to him,' Harry told her. 'We'll see what our options are.'

'Tell her,' my mother said to me, her voice quaking with rage, 'that there is no way in hell she's going to get her way. Tell her that from me.'

I took a deep breath and said, 'OK. I'll tell her.'

But I also knew that this would be the beginning of an all-out war between Oriana Neri and my mother. And it wasn't going to end well.

Mom went up to her bedroom to lie down after that bombshell news. Harry gave her a sedative and came downstairs when she started to drift off to sleep. The two of us had a quiet lunch in the kitchen – spinach quiche, a tossed green salad, and a bowl of fresh cut-up fruit with mint and clotted cream.

'She'll be OK, sweetheart,' he said. 'Once she gets over the shock of learning about Oriana and seeing those photos. Your mom is pretty tough.'

'I hope so. She's ready to do battle with Oriana, though.'

Harry said in a soothing voice, 'Let's see what Sam has to say. Oriana could screw up the whole ball of wax if she decides to get legal – but if she does, Knox and CIFA will get involved as well. It could end up being a big friggin' mess where the only winners would be the lawyers. Sam will know what to do to keep this as civil as possible.'

'I wish the will weren't handwritten on a piece of notebook paper and witnessed by a waiter and a manager in a diner. Thank God Sam said holographic wills are legal in Virginia,' I said. 'But I could very easily imagine Oriana challenging its validity.'

Harry nodded. 'I know.'

I got up and began clearing our lunch dishes.

'Leave those,' he said. 'The housekeeper will be in shortly. It all goes in the dishwasher, anyway. You need to go by the guest cottage and get Chap's photos. I'm going to go down to the stables. One of the horses has an injured foot – Maestro. I want to check on him. We had the vet in this morning.'

'Is he going to be OK?'

'I think so. It's a sprain, but not a bad one, fortunately. Say, how are you going to fit all those photos in that little toy car of yours?'

I grinned. 'Oh, I thought I'd stick them on the roof.' His eyes widened. 'I'm joking. Max loaned me his Range Rover this morning.'

'Range Rover, huh? Nice car.'

'It is. A bit of a step up from the Mini. Oh, and I need the key to the guest house, please.'

He got it for me and we walked outside to where the khaki-colored Range Rover was parked behind Harry's Jeep. Ella trotted along behind us, sure of a ride to the stables.

'You know, it's not entirely Mom's call about whether those photos belong in the exhibition,' I said. 'Chap left his collection to CIFA. Knox is going to have something to say about this – when he finds out,' I said. 'Plus, I think Darius Zahiri needs to be clued in. He can't be blindsided, either.'

'I've been thinking about that,' Harry said. 'I didn't want to upset your mother even more than she already is.'

'Are you going to talk to her about it?'

'I think Sam and I need to do that together. I also think Oriana needs to deal with Sam from here on out. Not Caroline or you.'

'That's going to escalate everything as far as Oriana is concerned if we lawyer up, Harry.'

'I doubt she'd be surprised. Sam told me the other day he rarely handles an estate settlement where some contentious issue doesn't rear its ugly head among the heirs before the money is doled out. Squabbling over who gets a favorite antique rocking chair or the pie server Mom used every Thanksgiving – little stuff that ends up in a legal battle with siblings no longer on speaking terms over some perceived transgression or inequity. Money makes people do crazy things, honey.'

'I know,' I said. Nick's estate had been simple: he left everything to me. His older sister, who lived in San Francisco and worked for a tech firm in Silicon Valley, had begrudged me nothing. She had flown to Washington as soon as I told her the news, accompanying me to the funeral home, by my side for all the plans and preparations. Then she had insisted on writing the check to pay for everything. We were still in touch, still close, and I was grateful.

Harry opened the door to the Range Rover for me and I got in. 'I'll be by to drop off the key once I'm finished,' I said. 'This shouldn't take long.'

'Do you need any help getting those photos to the car? They're good-sized.'

I wanted – *needed* – to do this by myself. It would be the first time I'd been in the cottage since Isabella had finished going through Chappy's possessions, putting into neat, tidy order what had been the pleasantly messy, slightly chaotic space where he did his best creative work. I wasn't sure what emotions would bubble up inside me. I wanted to be alone.

'No, thanks. I'm fine. You go see Maestro. He needs you.'

'OK, but we'll talk,' he said. 'I'll let you know what Sam says and when we're going to call Knox and tell him about this as well. He may want to talk to you since you're the only one who actually met Oriana.'

'Sure. No problem.'

I followed the Jeep out of the circular driveway; at a split in the road, he went left toward the stables, and I went right to the guest cottage.

I wasn't sure what to expect when I opened the front door, whether I would sense Chappy's presence – what Nick said the Russians called his *dusha*, his soul – or whether, after all those weeks of someone cleaning, tidying, and organizing his possessions, there would be no trace of my grandfather in these rooms anymore. The cottage smelled vaguely of something pleasant and floral, a scent I didn't recognize, until it occurred to me that it was probably Isabella's perfume that still lingered. As for Chappy's *dusha*, it had departed.

Isabella had been considerate enough to put all the photographs he'd chosen for his exhibition on the kitchen table, as my mother had said, as well as to put protective paper between each one. Nothing was framed yet – which wouldn't have been the case if Chappy had still been alive – but Knox and Darius had worked something out, and CIFA would pay for framing everything if Darius would take care of having it done. After the exhibition, the photos would then be shipped to Connecticut for a reprise of the Dupont Underground exhibition on the campus of CIFA.

Once I put everything in the trunk of the Range Rover, I went back inside to sign Isabella's paperwork. The keyring Harry had given me had both the key to the guest cottage and the key to the barn. Most of Chappy's photo collection and all of his papers were in the barn. I drove over and let myself in. Isabella had been as thorough and meticulous here as she had been in the cottage. Chap had already labeled the archival boxes that held his actual photos, which had made things easy. Same for the zippered binders that held the negative strips and the cases with his slides. The digital photos were backed up on several hard drives – those were in the cottage.

His papers and documents were another matter; they were nowhere near as organized as his photos. Isabella had put everything in boxes on which she'd written a date range and *Miscellaneous Papers and Diaries*. The photos were more important to CIFA; I knew they'd go through the papers later, once everything was shipped to Connecticut. I found a box labeled *1957–1960* and pulled it off the shelf. Isabella probably hadn't given what was inside more than a cursory glance – plus, she wouldn't have known about Chap's marriage to Oriana.

Maybe she'd overlooked something.

Like divorce papers.

I was only going to borrow the box for a few days and look through the contents. It would be right back here before Isabella realized it was missing. And it wasn't as though I was stealing it. I carried it out to the car and set it on the back seat. No point telling Harry or Mom I'd taken it, either.

At least not right now.


The Jeep was back at the house when I drove up to drop off the key. Either Harry had been really quick at the stables or I'd taken longer than I expected with the side visit to the barn and my errand there.

Ella barked happily when I opened the front door, and my mother called, 'Sophie? Is that you?'

'I'm just returning the key to the guest cottage, Mom.'

'We're in the library,' Harry said. 'You want to come say goodbye to your mother?'

Which meant *Come say goodbye to your mother.*

'Sure.'

She looked a lot better than she had earlier, this time propped up on the sofa holding a mug of green tea. A plate of English shortbread cookies was on the coffee table. Harry sat at the other end of the sofa, with Mom's feet draped across his knees. The television was on and a choir was singing 'Ave Maria' as a camera pulled back to take in a crowd of worshipers inside the ornate Italian Renaissance Cathedral of St Matthew the Apostle in Washington, DC.

'That's . . .' I began as the camera suddenly zoomed in on the profile of Diana Townsend, looking remote and exotic, as if she'd stepped out of the 1940s in a black pillbox hat with a black netted veil that billowed around her face. She looked even more beautiful than I remembered . . . beautiful and tragic.

'It's Everett Townsend's funeral,' Harry said. 'The Cardinal is saying the Mass. It's almost over.'

'Lexie told me about it. The President and First Lady are there. I think everybody in official Washington is there.'

The focus shifted from Diana to some of the other famous guests in the crowd, as if to validate what I'd just said. The President and First Lady. The Chief Justice. Members of the Supreme Court. The Senate Majority Leader. The Speaker of the House.

The Cardinal, resplendent in dark-purple vestments, sat behind the altar, his head bowed as the choir continued singing the beautiful hymn, a final meditation after communion.

> *Ora, ora pro nobis peccatoribus*
> *Nunc et in hora mortis*
> *Et in hora mortis nostrae.*

Pray, pray for us sinners, now and at the hour of our death . . . the hour of our death.

'Jack's there,' my mother said. 'I was surprised to see him. He's one of the concelebrants with the Cardinal. And the Papal Nuncio – he's on the altar, too. That's quite an honor.'

I stiffened, but I said, 'Jack is good friends with Diana Townsend, Mom. I think that's probably why he's on the altar.'

The hymn was over, and after a poignant moment of silence, the Cardinal got to his feet.

'Let us pray.'

This time, the camera panned the altar and, sure enough, there was Jack, head respectfully bent, hands clasped, eyes closed. Diana would have seen to it that he was one of the concelebrants of her husband's memorial Mass. She had arranged it.

I stared at Jack and wondered if he'd asked Diana to tell him the truth, offered her the sanctity of the confessional: was the man in the ER the other day her husband, the man he and everyone else had come to mourn today? Or was it someone else?

Once the Mass was over, the case would be closed.

Looking at him now, I doubted he had asked her anything. He wouldn't rock the boat, do anything to upset her.

Which made me even more determined to find out the truth. Because I thought Diana Townsend had lied.

And she was about to get away with it. With the blessing of the Cardinal and everyone else who had come to pay their final respects to a man who probably wasn't dead.

# SEVENTEEN

B y the time I got back to Washington, it was four o'clock, two hours before I was supposed to meet Perry for dinner at the Iron Gate. I decided to put Chappy's exhibition photos in the guest room rather than leaving them in the studio. The studio was safe enough, but both Max and I had decided to have alarm systems installed in our duplexes a year ago just because it was DC and violent crime had gone up at a crazy rate since the pandemic. It had everybody on edge from the mayor down – with more and more people becoming desperate as they lost their homes, their jobs, their health, and saw their lives changing at the speed of light with no idea what was coming next. Dupont Circle and our neighborhood was still relatively safe, but that could turn on a dime, and Chappy's photos were irreplaceable.

I also brought the box of memorabilia upstairs and put it in the dining room so I could lay out everything on the big table and survey it all at once. I meant to start doing that in the morning, but I couldn't resist lifting the lid – and promptly sneezed until my eyes watered after inhaling the dust and moldiness of papers and documents that were nearly seventy years old. The box was filled to the top as I'd guessed it might be because it had been so heavy and because my grandfather, a notorious pack rat, never threw out anything. I removed yellowed letters, bank statements, receipts from the camera shop where Chap bought his film and darkroom supplies, notebooks filled with lists of photos he'd taken, and – about a third of the way down this archeological dig – a stuffed-thick page-a-day calendar with a cracked fake-leather cover and *1958* embossed on it. Probably stamped in gold when Chappy bought it; now the numbers were a faint impression. I set the calendar on the table and turned the fragile pages until I got to May 3rd.

There were notes about an airline flight from LA to Vegas, a hotel reservation, and a rental car. Nothing about a wedding, not even the next day. After that, there were references on various days to 'O,' which, presumably, was Oriana. Chappy had combined their calendars during the brief time they were living together after their marriage. Studio auditions, her work schedule, and a doctor's appointment at the end of May with a big red circle around it and two exclamation marks. My mind immediately went where it shouldn't: an ob-gyn? Was Oriana pregnant? Was *that* why they got married in Vegas?

Then what happened? A miscarriage? An abortion? Two Catholic kids in the 1950s. An abortion would have been out of the question – even in Hollywood – especially if they'd gotten married so the baby wouldn't be an illegitimate love child. In the 1950s that would have been a huge scandal.

Today? Pfft. Nothing. Plenty of people had kids and then got married. Or didn't. No big deal.

Oriana hadn't said anything about a pregnancy, so maybe I was completely off-base about my theory. And by the end of June, the references to 'O' had stopped altogether. She'd moved out and they'd gone their separate ways.

The box was still two-thirds full, but it was time to get dressed and ready to meet Perry at the restaurant. I put the lid back on, left the documents I'd already removed on the dining-room table, and went upstairs to my bedroom.

It was about twenty degrees cooler than last night when I'd met Quill at the Jefferson Hotel. I looked through the warmer clothes in my closet and chose a silky-knit long-sleeved khaki wrap dress that tied in a self-knot at my waist. Nude heels. A belted black leather jacket and a favorite khaki, cream, and chocolate-brown animal-print shawl picked up at an outdoor market in Botswana that I wound around my neck. I wore my hair up, fixed in place with two art deco tortoiseshell combs, a find in a shop that sold vintage clothing and jewelry on the King's Road in London.

I walked to the restaurant. Perry was seated at the bar when I arrived precisely at six. It had been a while since I'd been here, but I loved the Iron Gate – or the Iron Gate *Inn* as a lot of folks still referred to it – because of its history, romance, and the stories of ghosts that haunted it. Also because it possessed the graceful patina of age and distinction as Washington's oldest restaurant until it had closed for the first time in eighty-seven years in 2010. The bar – an old cobblestone carriageway – led to a courtyard garden tucked away like the best surprise. The restaurant itself was a former carriage house that had been converted to stables by an army general who bought the house that went with it from a navy admiral at the end of the nineteenth century. If you requested it, you could eat in one of the old horse stalls.

A row of candlelit carriage lanterns hanging along a wall of the long narrow bar cast a golden light that made soft shadows and gave the room the gauzy, time-softened feel of a less complicated era when all life's problems could be solved by a good cocktail and the conversation of friends. Most of the bar stools were occupied by the well-dressed brainy crowd of diplomats, lobbyists, journalists, and think-tank wonks who worked nearby around Dupont Circle or Mass Ave. There was a pleasant buzz of conversation, laughter, and the soft tinkle of china and glassware.

Perry got up and came over to me, pulling me to him in a fierce hug. 'You look *sensational*,' he whispered in my ear. 'God, Medina, I have missed you.'

I hugged him back. We hadn't seen each other since he flew to Washington for Nick's funeral. My voice caught and I said, 'I have missed you, too.'

He stepped back and looked me over. 'How are you?'

'Fine. I'm fine.' I never could con Perry.

'Yeah, and I'm the King of England,' he said. 'Come on. Our table's waiting. We're sitting inside by the fireplace. I thought it was a little too chilly for the garden, as beautiful as it is with the fairy lights winding through the canopy of wisteria and grapevines. You can tell me everything over dinner.'

He slid an arm around my waist and walked me to the wrought-iron gates at the entrance to the restaurant. Our table was next to the fireplace as promised and Perry insisted I take the seat closest to the fire.

Our waiter showed up almost immediately with menus and the wine list. 'Can I get you folks a cocktail?'

'Just a glass of wine with dinner for me, please,' I said.

Perry gave me a meaningful look and said to the waiter, 'Actually, we'll have a bottle. Can you give us a minute and then maybe make some suggestions?'

After he left, Perry said, 'Greek or Italian?'

'Greek.'

'White or red?'

'What are you having?'

He looked at the menu. 'For the main course, Cornish hen. What about you?'

'The swordfish looks terrific. So how about white?'

The waiter astutely sent the sommelier to discuss the wine menu with Perry, which, to me, sounded as if the two of them were negotiating geographical boundaries for a complicated treaty. *What about Northern Greece? Perhaps the Peloponnese? How about the Islands? Something from Central Greece? Organic, yes or no? Sweet or dry? Skin contact or not? A bit of minerality?*

And most importantly, *Would you care to try a sample?*

In the end, we did sample the wine – a minerally white from Santorini that was delicious.

The waiter took our orders and returned with a bottle of sparkling water, a dish of olives marinated in garlic and herbs, a warm loaf of crusty bread, and a dipping bowl of flavored olive oil.

Perry tore the bread into chunks and pushed the breadboard toward me. 'Here you go. Eat up. You've lost a lot of weight since the last time I saw you, Medina. So tell me. What's going on?'

I wanted to ask whether he wanted it in chronological or alphabetical order. Nick. Oriana. Javi. Everett Townsend. Leo Duval. Jack.

Even though Perry had been my boss, he'd been someone I could confide in – we'd go for a pint at one of the pubs near the bureau after work and talk and talk. His advice and wisdom had never steered me wrong. He was older than I was by fifteen years, married and divorced three times, with a flock of girlfriends in between. His nickname at the bureau, behind his back, was 'The Chick Magnet,' and I wondered if he knew about it – though we were talking about Perry who had eyes in the back of his head, so of course he did. Probably enjoyed it, too. The London bureau of International Press Service was his to run as bureau chief until he didn't want it anymore because he was so damn good at it, and that would probably be when he retired – *if* he ever retired. Besides the three wives, Perry was married to his job, which came first – and also explained the divorces.

One thing I never wanted to do was whine or moan or cry in my beer over some little matter that was hardly worth bringing up when Perry and I had our heart-to-hearts in the pub. I wanted him to know – *needed* him to know so he would keep sending me out on the tough, gritty assignments – that I was strong and resilient. That I could handle whatever he threw at me. So I discounted just about everything that had happened in the last few days except one: had Everett Townsend faked his death and, if so, why? Leo Duval had instructed me to tell no one about Townsend possibly committing pseudocide while he looked into it. Jack just plain didn't believe me and wasn't going to say anything to anyone – especially Diana.

I needed to talk to *someone*, and Perry had good instincts and a good analytical mind – in fact, the best. He was also a shrewd judge of character, whose assessment of someone was rarely wrong. There was also this: telling him about Townsend wasn't going to put him in danger because in less than twenty-four hours he would be on a plane for London. The restaurant had a good crowd on a Friday evening, but as with every eating establishment in town, it hadn't returned to pre-pandemic numbers. There was no one sitting close by, so we had privacy.

The waiter brought our wine and opened the bottle, pouring a small amount for Perry to taste. He nodded and the waiter filled my glass and Perry's. After he left, I told him about Everett Townsend. All of it, beginning with Jack and me finding him outside his pied-à-terre on Capitol Hill to Javi's conversation in Meridian Hill Park and subsequent death, to Townsend's funeral yesterday. I broke off when the waiter brought our first courses – warm Medjool dates with blue cheese and pistachios for me, hand-pulled burrata with fennel, olive oil, and crostini for Perry.

He didn't interrupt or ask a single question while I talked, but his eyes grew darker and more intense as I went on. Once or twice, he glanced around the room as if making sure no one seemed to have tuned in to our conversation. When I was done, he set down his knife and fork.

'That,' he said, 'is a hell of a story and a hell of an accusation.

How sure are you that you're right? One hundred percent? Fifty percent? Twenty percent?'

'I don't know.'

'Why do you want to take the word of a formerly homeless kid who shows up in the ER, probably panicked because he's bringing in someone who is also in distress, over the wife of a Supreme Court justice?'

I gave him an unhappy look. 'You don't believe me, either.'

'I didn't say that. I'm just asking questions to which you don't seem to have answers that will back up your premise that Townsend is alive and well somewhere and is responsible for the death of someone who looked just like him. Or his wife is.' He ate a piece of burrata and then waved his fork at me, stabbing the air. 'Plus, you didn't answer the question. Why do you believe Javi over Diana Townsend?'

'Because someone went after Javi – he was pretty sure it was because someone heard him say that the guy in the ER wasn't Townsend – and now he's dead. And because the Professor is missing,' I said.

Perry looked shocked when I told him of Javi's death, but he said, 'Still circumstantial, but OK, let's say you're right. It would take a hell of a reason for a guy like Townsend – who has every-thing going for him, you have to admit – to decide that faking his death and being on the run for the rest of his life is preferable to what would happen if he stuck around.'

'I *know*. I *agree*. That's why I thought you could help me figure out a plausible reason why he might have actually done it.'

Perry reached for the wine bottle, which the waiter had put in a silver wine cooler next to our table, and refilled our glasses. The wine was making me a little woozy, but it went down easily and I knew Perry meant us to finish the bottle tonight. He'd insist on after-dinner drinks, too.

We clinked glasses and he said, 'What have you got as a possible motivation for Townsend to concoct this kind of crazy plot? Do you know how hard it is to disappear? I mean, *really* disappear? For the rest of your life. You have to become a totally different person, give up everything you care about – family, friends, your home, your possessions, and, often hardest of all, your hobbies or avocation.'

'Why are your hobbies hardest of all to give up?'

'Because that's how you get caught. You collect stamps or you're a fountain pen aficionado? Sooner or later, you'll buy something from a dealer or attend a show and it will fit your profile. Bingo. They've got you. You like NASCAR? They'll be looking for you at every race in the country. Your pursuers can be wrong a hundred times and you'll get away. But slip up once and *bam*. It's damn hard to stop being true to who you are, especially the things you're passionate about.'

'You're beginning to make me think that maybe I'm a little crazy. I know that's what Jack thinks.'

'I don't think you're crazy at all. I just think you need to be on more solid ground if you're going to throw mud at a now-dead-and-buried Supreme Court justice and claim he's alive and well and living . . . somewhere.'

'He wasn't buried. He was cremated. There's nothing left of whoever he was but ashes.'

'Sorry. Semantics. So, what motivation would he have for this whole charade?'

'OK, for starters, it's common knowledge that he's a woman-izer, that he cheated on Diana over the years.'

He shrugged. 'Big deal. A lot of men cheat on their wives, but they don't run off and disappear into the ether. Same with women who cheat on their husbands. Besides, can you actually back up that accusation?'

Here it was. 'Yes. First-hand.'

'Oh, yeah? Tell me.'

I did.

I also told him that no one knew I'd seen Townsend and Vicki Russell together in the Russells' swimming pool, although I couldn't say for sure about Quill, who possibly suspected some-thing was going on with his wife and that I might know what it was.

'Jesus, Medina. Did you take any photos?'

'God, Perry, how much of a no-scruples voyeur do you think I am? Of course not. I'm a photojournalist, not the paparazzi. There is a difference.' I banged my wine glass on the table, sloshing wine on the white linen tablecloth. 'Damn.'

'Sorry. Professional reflex.'

'Well, just forget it, will you?' I blotted the tablecloth with my napkin. 'I'm aggressive and I get the photos I need for the story – you know that – but I don't exploit someone in their own home who believes – rightly – that they enjoy total privacy to do whatever they want. I also didn't take any photos of Townsend or whoever he was when Jack and I found him unconscious and lying on the ground. Even after Jack told me who he was. *I'm not that person.*'

'OK, OK. I apologize,' he said. 'If you'll calm down, you were starting to go through reasons Townsend might have faked his death. Sex is always a good motivator – the best – but an affair with Quill Russell's wife seems pretty banal.'

Now my eyebrows went up, but he was probably right. It only mattered more to me because I loved Quill and Vicki so much – and I knew how much Quill loved his wife. But an affair like that making the rounds of Washington gossip circles . . . meh, so what? It was sad and a bit scandalous, but that sort of thing happened all the time, as Perry said. A few people got hurt. Life went on. Next subject, please.

'There's more,' I said. 'One of Everett Townsend's good buddies is a Russian oligarch.'

Perry shrugged one shoulder. 'And?'

'His name is Alexey Ozupov. They're old friends who go back to private school days in England. Now Ozupov owns the biggest private bank in Russia. He also owns Dover FC and a yacht that's bigger than the entire city of Baltimore where he throws a lot of parties. Out in international waters, where anything goes.'

'And Townsend is a guest on the yacht and at Dover football games?'

I nodded, but I could tell he still wasn't persuaded.

'Other than the optics not looking great, so what?' he asked. 'When did you become such a cynic?'

'I like to think I'm a realist. There might be smoke in what you're telling me, but I can't smell a fire anywhere.'

'OK, Ozupov is also quite the philanthropist. He's given a lot of money to American charities and cultural institutions, and ingratiated himself just about everywhere. Now he's got his sights set on becoming a player in US politics. And who better to help him meet the right people than his old school buddy who is now a Supreme Court judge? Ozupov's father was . . .'

'Georgi Ozupov. I know who he was.'

Perry had probably *interviewed* Georgi Ozupov. I'd been in middle school when he was already covering stories as a foreign correspondent.

'Sorry. Of course you know who he is.'

'It's OK. I know I look like I just got my J-school degree ten minutes ago, but I'm a bit older than that. And Ozupov wouldn't be the first Russian, or even the first oligarch, to show an interest in our politics. It's been going on for a while.'

Our dinners came and we stopped talking while the waiter served us, refilled our wine glasses, and wished us *bon appétit*.

'How's your swordfish?' Perry asked.

'Delicious. How about your Cornish hen?'

'Outstanding. So where were we?'

'Other than you bashing everything I just said?'

'Yes, but it was done with love. What have you *not* told me – yet?'

'Townsend and Ozupov apparently had a falling out recently.'

'Over what?'

'I don't know.'

'But you have an idea,' he said. 'Which brings us to why you think Townsend might have bolted.'

'Ta-da.'

I told him about the leaked opinion in the campaign money Supreme Court case, and Quill telling me that Vicki had said Townsend was livid because he planned to switch his vote, changing the outcome of the case in favor of allowing soft contributions to be made. Leaving Townsend with a whole heap of explaining to do in the court of public opinion.

That *finally* got Perry's interest. 'You think Ozupov might have been the one to put pressure on Townsend to switch his vote on that soft money case? And that's why he disappeared?'

'I don't know. It's all I've got.'

'If Ozupov all of a sudden put the squeeze on his old friend to change his vote – and I'm saying *if*,' he said, 'there has to be a reason he has the leverage to do it. More than football tickets and boat parties.'

'OK,' I said. 'That's something.'

'My first guess would be that whatever it is has to do with a woman. Sex and money are the two oldest motivators in the book.'

'Maybe Townsend needed to pay off someone and he went to Ozupov for the money.'

'So the woman's paid off and now Ozupov wants a favor. I repeat: why would Townsend take off?'

We were really reaching the outer limits of speculation about what Townsend – and Ozupov – might or might not have done.

'I don't know. But what if someone was blackmailing him because of what he did? *Not* the woman. Someone else.'

He shrugged. 'Maybe. Could be.'

'Although if it's something like that, you'd think Townsend could survive it – as you've been saying, it's Washington. Look at the Trump Administration and all the women who've tried to sue Donald Trump. He got away with everything,' I said. 'Townsend would come off like a choirboy, comparatively speaking, though his marriage would probably be a train wreck afterwards. Whatever happened, it's got to be something really bad.'

'Define *really bad*.'

There weren't too many options.

'Well,' I said, 'there is murder.'

Perry looked startled and then he nodded. 'OK, murder would definitely qualify. But seriously? Townsend *killed* someone? Who and how?'

'I don't know. Maybe something happened a long time ago when he and Ozupov knew each other in school. There's no statute of limitations on murder, you know.'

'OK, say you're right. Let's go back and talk about this Professor. Are you implying Townsend is responsible for *his* death as well? Staged it to look like his own? *Two* murders?'

'It sounds . . . awful, I know,' I said. 'But there's this: the Professor most likely had Alzheimer's. And he was homeless.'

'Which would justify killing him? Jesus, Medina.'

I set my fork down and felt as if I was going to be sick. 'No, of course it wouldn't. I'm just trying to think how Townsend might see it. If the Professor – Paul Smith – had Alzheimer's and was living on the street, he probably wouldn't survive for very long under those circumstances. He couldn't defend himself, wouldn't be able to take care of himself. He'd be terribly vulnerable and easy to prey on. But, my God, of course it wouldn't be right – a mercy killing, if that's how Townsend saw it. Doing what he did so Paul Smith wouldn't suffer unduly.'

Perry reached over and covered one of my hands with his. 'Sophie,' he said, 'you've been around, sweetheart. You know as well as I do that there are people in this world who believe that whatever they do – however wrong or cruel or corrupt – is justified because of who they are. That we're *not* all created equal, and there are people who are expendable if they're in your way. Because it's about the greater good – or *their* greater good as they see and define it.'

'Townsend is a *judge*. A man of the law. He sits on the highest court in the United States.'

'And all that notwithstanding, he's human. He's capable of being venal, selfish . . . corrupt. Believing he's *above* the law because of who he is. He wouldn't be the first person in Washington to have that thought. Or act on it.'

Our waiter came for our plates. 'Was everything satisfactory?'

I said, 'Delicious,' as Perry said, 'Wonderful.'

'I'll be right back with your desserts. Would you care for coffee or tea?'

Perry eyed me and I nodded. 'Two espressos,' he said. 'After dessert.'

The waiter left. Perry's hand still covered mine and he had begun absently stroking it with his thumb. I thought about extricating my hand, but I didn't.

'What are you going to do with this?' he asked.

'I don't know,' I said. 'We just concocted an incredibly unlikely scenario as to why a Supreme Court judge might fake his own death by substituting a homeless man in his place and then flee. A theory we can't substantiate because everything we know is hearsay or rumor.'

'All true.'

'So what if rather than trying to dig into Everett Townsend's past, we focus instead on the Professor? Find out what happened to him and see where that leads?'

'It would be a whole lot easier,' Perry said as the waiter arrived with our ice cream – espresso ice cream with chocolate espresso and marsala gelée for him and gianduja ice cream with hazelnut and bittersweet chocolate for me.

We traded tastes of each other's desserts, and when our coffees came, we changed the subject. Instead, we talked about London, what was going on in the bureau, and the latest IPS gossip about who'd been promoted, got fired, had an affair, got married, divorced, or had a baby.

'Have you given any thought to coming back to London?' Perry asked after a few moments when neither of us had spoken. 'You can have your old job back whenever you want it. Just say the word. New York is in favor of it; I just spoke to them yesterday. I'm *definitely* in favor of it. I miss you. I need you.'

I said, flustered, 'You brought up me returning to London to take my old job when you were in New York just now?'

He nodded, his dark eyes boring holes into mine.

'Perry . . .'

'What?'

He knew what. He'd already made it clear that he was interested in me – just before I left London when he thought Nick had been killed by kidnappers who abducted him from our home. But as my boss, we couldn't be involved romantically or someone would get sacked. Most likely him.

'I don't know,' I said as a stray thought of Darius Zahiri inviting me on a dinner date floated through my mind. 'I'm flattered, but right now I just don't know what I want. I'm still . . . dealing with a lot of things.'

'Will you at least consider it?'

'I will. And thank you.'

'Good.' He pushed his cup and saucer to the side. 'How about an after-dinner drink?'

'I couldn't. Besides, the wine has already made me a bit tipsy.'

'Did you drive here?'

'No, it's not far. I walked.'

'You're not walking home by yourself now that it's dark. It's DC, not London. I'm coming with you.'

'Where are you staying?'

'Across the street. At the Tabard Inn.'

Another Washington institution. Just as the Iron Gate had been DC's oldest restaurant, the Tabard Inn, a beautiful old building possessing the charm and atmosphere of an English manor house, was the city's oldest hotel.

'I can take an Uber. You don't need to walk me back.'

'Are you blowing me off?'

'Of course not.'

'Good,' he said. 'Then let's walk.'

Most of the old houses on N Street were now owned by businesses and were no longer residences, so except for the lights that shone from the windows of the Tabard Inn and the carriage lights at the entryway to Iron Gate, the car-lined street was mostly dark and quiet.

Perry draped his arm around my shoulder once again as we walked toward 18th Street.

'What time's your flight tomorrow?' I asked.

'It's—' He broke off as a car coming down the street suddenly cut its headlights.

It drew up alongside us and the passenger window powered down. Perry's arm became a vise around my shoulder, and I could feel my instincts from the hostile environment training course kick in.

I don't know which of us shouted *Gun!* first, but Perry yanked me down behind a parked car. We fell together and hit the sidewalk hard. He moved on top of me, shielding me from what was coming next as a spray of bullets rained over our heads, followed by the sound of shattering glass.

'Stay down.' Perry's voice was harsh in my ear. 'Don't move.'

'I won't. I can't.'

Which is when I knew that whoever had gone after Javi somehow found out there was one more loose end, someone else who knew that Everett Townsend might not be dead, after all.

Me.

# EIGHTEEN

A nother car drove down N Street and stopped.
'Don't move.' Perry's mouth was next to my ear, barely a whisper.

An accomplice? Were there *two* of them? Or maybe another car driving down the street, in the wrong place at the wrong time? An engine revved and took off with a screech of tires.

A moment later, someone slammed a car door and a male voice yelled, 'Hey! Are y'all OK? Is everybody OK? I heard gunshots. Anybody hurt?'

Perry had pushed my head down with such force that I felt as if I was suffocating. I tried to squirm out from under his grip, but it was like trying to defy gravity. 'The car with the shooter is gone,' I said, gasping. 'Let go. Let me up. I'm OK.'

He released me and I sat up. I hurt like hell, but at least I was alive. Perry had dragged us both down so we hit the ground pretty hard, but he had also saved my life.

'Thank you for what you did,' I said. 'I owe you.'

He gave me an unmistakable look and said, 'I'll collect.'

I could feel the heat flush my face. He meant it, too.

'Are you OK?' I asked him. I looked closer and said, 'You're bleeding. There's blood on your face.'

'I hit some gravel when we went down. I'll be OK. What about you?'

'I need to check.' My ribs hurt and my right leg felt like it was on fire.

'You folks OK?'

A kid who looked as if he couldn't be more than sixteen wearing dreadlocks and a black nylon tracksuit reached his hand out to me and helped me up. He'd been the one who called out, asking if we were all right. Probably – mercifully – scaring off the car with the shooter.

I wanted to kiss his hand, kiss *him*.

'Lady,' he said, 'y'all are bleeding. Your leg.'

I looked down. My right leg was covered in blood and stung like hell. My right shoe was gone, probably somewhere on the ground or under a car. 'I think it's road rash, or whatever you call it, from where I hit the sidewalk. It's just a bad scrape, but that's why it's bleeding so much. I'm OK. Thanks. And thank you for stopping. The other car left because you showed up.'

Perry got up, too. 'Did you get the plate number?' he asked the kid.

'Nah, when he cut his lights, I wasn't thinking about paying attention to the plate. But it was a black Subaru,' he said, adding, 'Outback. I'm pretty sure the plates were DC. Man, whoever it was shot up the Jeep right here pretty bad. Blew out the driver and backseat windows. You're lucky those bullets missed you.'

People had begun emptying out of the restaurant and the hotel on to the sidewalk and the street once they realized whatever had happened was over. I heard snatches of conversations. Angry. Scared. Irate.

*When is it going to stop . . . just having dinner for God's sake . . . too many weapons . . . we'll be the murder capital of the US again . . . the mayor needs to do* something . . .

Someone had called nine-one-one, because an MPD cruiser with full lights and sirens careened down N Street, turning from 17th and stopping in front of where we were standing. Another cruiser and an EMS van arrived from the other direction. A pair of EMTs took care of our cuts and scrapes, which turned out not to be as bad as they looked – although the antiseptic spray one of them used on my leg made it sting like crazy. Neither of them was happy when Perry and I declined their offer of a ride to the nearest ER to check us both out more thoroughly, even after they tried to sweet-talk us by throwing around phrases like 'possible concussion,' 'internal bleeding,' and – with a significant glance at me – 'broken or cracked ribs.'

When they found out we meant it – no hospital, no thank you – they left us to the questions of one of the officers who had also located my shoe. But as with the EMTs, there was nothing to say.

No, we didn't get a look at the shooter.

No, he or she didn't say anything to us before firing those shots.

And no, *absolutely not* – I nudged Perry hard, making sure the officer didn't see me – we didn't have a single clue why someone would drive down this quiet street and randomly start shooting at the two of us.

When the officer was done asking questions and the crowd had started to thin out – except for the distraught couple who owned the Jeep that had been shot up – Perry clamped his arm around my waist again and said, 'Let's go.'

'Where?'

'My hotel room. It's just across the street.'

'I, uh, probably should be getting home.'

'After what just happened? And that lie you told that nice police officer? Not a chance, sweetheart. You're staying with me tonight so I can keep an eye on you.'

He had a point. If that shooting wasn't random, then I'd been the target. And if the shooter knew how to find me tonight at a restaurant with Perry, then whoever it was absolutely knew where I lived. And possibly was now waiting on my street in that big black Subaru, biding his or her time until I came home.

Max had gone to New York for the weekend, thank God. I'd already put Perry in danger.

A shiver went down my spine. I'd never forgive myself if something happened to either of them on account of me.

'What?' Perry asked.

'Nothing.' Then, echoing him, I said, 'Let's go.'

The Tabard Inn, which consisted of three connected nineteenth-century townhouses, didn't have an elevator, so Perry helped me climb the stairs to the second floor since my leg still hurt and my ribs ached. His antique-filled bedroom, which was painted the color of sunshine, had a fireplace, a brocade-covered settee, a small writing desk and chair, a double bed with a brass head-board and footboard, and oil paintings of a ship at sea over the bed and a bucolic country landscape above the fireplace. There were also two large windows with views of the rooftops of the N Street townhouses and, silhouetted against the night sky, the lighted dome of St Matthew's a block away.

'There's a tub in the bathroom, one of those old-fashioned

claw-foot tubs,' Perry said. 'You might want to take a bath and soak that leg. I'll be back in a few minutes.'

'Where are you going?'

'To see if I can get a couple of brandies for us in the bar. I don't know about you, but getting shot at always makes me think about drinking. I also need to let them know at the front desk that I've got a roommate tonight.'

I filled the tub after he left, stripped off my clothes, and climbed in. My dress, which was blood-stained and abraded where I'd hit the pavement, was probably beyond saving, even by a good dry cleaner. Same with my leather jacket, which had a nasty tear in the right sleeve. Perry came back while I was still luxuriating in the tub. He knocked on the bathroom door and said he had our brandies, plus the staff was sending up a plate of cheese and crackers. And extra towels.

By the time I joined him, bundled up in the thick white terry-cloth bathrobe I'd found hanging on the bathroom door, he'd changed into a pair of jeans and a soft, gray tee-shirt that showed off the hard contours of his muscles. He still worked out when he was back in London and he looked good. He insisted I take the settee and put my legs up, so I did. Then he dragged over the chair from the writing desk so he was sitting across from me. His laptop was open on the bed; he'd been doing some work.

He handed me a brandy. Indicating the laptop, I said, 'Anything going on?'

'Nope, other than the usual stuff. I was just looking up Alexey Ozupov.'

'I did that, too. Find anything interesting?'

'Yeah. His boat – his latest one. Or, should I say, his ocean liner? Boys with toys. The Russian oligarchs do love their floating palaces. Of course, when they're out in the open waters, it makes life so much easier if you've got your own landing strip for planes, a heliport, and even a tower from where you can fire anti-aircraft missiles if you're being attacked. Oh, yeah, and a submarine. Total James Bond stuff. You can get away with murder and no one's going to stop you. Or find out.'

He showed me the picture he'd found. Different from the one on the website I'd found last night. 'I know. It's crazy. And that boat – *ship* – *is* bigger than the city of Baltimore.'

'Putin's superyacht is even bigger.' Perry closed his laptop.

'Putin probably has one that totally blocks the sky when it pulls into a harbor somewhere and makes you think an eclipse is happening.'

He grinned and clinked his brandy glass against mine. 'To being alive.'

We drank and he got the cheese-and-cracker plate from the desk, along with two small plates, and set them on a bench in front of the settee. He cut a piece of chevre from a small wheel and spread it on a sesame seed cracker.

'Here,' he said. 'Eat this.'

I hadn't expected to be hungry after our dinner at the Iron Gate, but I was. 'Thanks. This is great.'

'Good.' He leaned forward, forearms resting on his knees, giving me one of his intense, penetrating looks. 'Now, tell me how someone – with a gun – knew where you were tonight? How did they know where to find you? Because that shooter, as we both know, wasn't just some random guy looking for someone to pop.'

I set my brandy down on a small table next to a Tiffany lamp. It was as if he'd read my mind.

'I've been wondering that myself.' And I hadn't liked a single one of the answers that came to mind.

'Who did you tell about Townsend possibly faking his death? *Everyone*, Medina. Everyone.'

'It's a short list.'

'Good. That makes things easier.'

'Nobody on it would have a reason to want to take a shot at me – or *want* someone to take a shot at me.' That was a hill I was willing to die on.

No one.

'That can't be true.' He was insistent and I shivered. 'Someone killed Javi. And they *could* have killed you tonight, but they didn't. So it's possible they just wanted to scare you. Warn you off.'

OK, maybe. Someone I knew and trusted must have let something slip.

Unknowingly. I couldn't – wouldn't – believe it was deliberate.

'First of all, I'm pretty sure no one saw Javi and me in Meridian Hill Park the other night.'

'But not one hundred percent sure.'

Perry and his absolutes. 'OK, not one hundred percent sure.'

'Who else?'

I ticked them off on my fingers. 'Leo Duval. He knows everything. Jack, who, as I said, doesn't believe me. And Tessa Janko, who works at Streetwise. She knows that Javi's death has something to do with the Professor's disappearance, but she doesn't know it's also connected to Everett Townsend.'

Perry reached for his brandy. 'Any one of those people could have inadvertently mentioned you to someone who *was* interested in knowing you'd managed to make a connection between the Professor and Townsend. Even Tessa. Just connecting you to Javi and the Professor would be enough. And whoever they spoke to needed to do something to silence you.'

I closed my eyes and massaged my forehead. When I opened them, Perry was standing up and holding out his hand.

'Come on,' he said, his voice gentle, 'you should get some sleep. We're not going to solve this tonight.'

He pulled me up and went over and turned down the bed. I lay down on one side and he went around to the other. He stripped off his shirt and jeans until he was just wearing his briefs and I could see that he was aroused. He got in bed, lying next to me.

I pulled the belt of my robe until it untied. The robe fell open so he could see that I was naked.

'If you want to collect for saving my life tonight,' I said, 'this would probably be a good time.'

He smiled and rolled over, slipping off my robe and his briefs, and moving on top of me. I reached up and turned out the light. We had forgotten to close the curtains, so we could still see each other in the wash of pale-blue light, two ghostly figures who knew each other so well in every way but one. Until tonight.

He took my face in his hands and murmured, 'You're so beautiful. You know I've wanted to do this for a long time, Sophie. And you have been worth waiting for.'

Then he kissed me, tasting of brandy, and I was lost. I had been faithful to Nick for our entire marriage. There had been no one else, not ever. And there hadn't been anyone at all for the past year and a half since Nick died.

Perry was like finding an oasis after being in a desert for so long that I hadn't known how parched I was, how badly I needed him. We were quiet, speaking in whispers, as we explored each other, devoured each other, tasted each other, because we didn't know how thick the walls were in this old building. Our love-making went on for hours. He was careful of my bruised leg and gentle each time he entered me, considerate of my sore ribs. All I knew was that I didn't want him to stop.

When I finally fell asleep wrapped in Perry's arms, my dreams weren't of faceless men with guns or Javi lying in a pool of blood in an alley. Or even of Nick making love to some anonymous woman whom I could only conjure in my head.

I dreamed of Perry, his kisses, his touch, the words he'd whispered to me in the dark, his strong arms around me keeping me safe.

And I slept deeply and well.

Perry was already awake when I opened my eyes the next morning. It was barely light out, the sky still colorless since it was too early for the sun to be up.

He brushed a strand of hair off my face and said, 'Morning, beautiful. How'd you sleep?'

I kissed him on the lips and said, 'Really, really well. How about you?'

'I slept well, too.' He ran a finger from my neck between my breasts and down to my belly. I shivered.

'Come here,' I said and pulled him on top of me. 'I want you again.'

'I want you again, too,' he said, and for the next hour we made quiet, unhurried love as the room slowly filled with golden sunlight.

When my brain was finally functioning, I said to him, 'You never told me last night what time your flight is today. How much more time do we have together?'

He rolled over and looked at the clock on his bedside table. 'Less than I wish we did. It's just after eight o'clock. What if we take a shower and have breakfast in the restaurant downstairs? Then I'm afraid I need to pack, check out, and get a cab for the airport. First, though, we're going to your place so I can make sure you're going to be all right.'

'I'll be fine. You don't need to do that. You don't need to worry about me. I can take care of myself.'

'Oh, yeah? What's your plan? Wear a bulletproof vest any time you go out from now on?'

I smiled. 'It wouldn't be the first time.'

He wasn't smiling. 'You were in a war zone, not walking around goddamn downtown DC.'

'Max and I both had alarms installed in our places. If anyone tries to break in, I'll know. Plus . . . I have a gun.'

'Jesus. You have a gun?'

'A revolver. Harry gave it to me. He's been taking me for target practice fairly regularly when I'm out in Middleburg. He thought I ought to know how to shoot. I'm pretty good, in case you're wondering. Besides, I think you were right when you said last night that if that shooter wanted to kill me, he wouldn't have missed. Someone just wanted to scare me.'

'Which hopefully is what he did and why you're going to drop this and let Leo Duval handle everything from now on, OK?' he said. 'And you need to tell him about that shooter.'

I sat up on my haunches, hands on my hips, and stared at him. 'This from my ex-boss who used to quote the legendary Robert Capra, one of the original Magnum photographers? "If your pictures aren't good enough, you're not close enough to the story." You're telling me to *walk away*? Seriously, Perry?'

'I don't want anything to happen to you.'

I got out of bed and tried not to wince. I didn't want him to know my ribs still hurt.

'Look,' I said, picking up the bathrobe where it had fallen on the floor and pulling it on, 'if we hadn't slept together last night and you were still my boss, you absolutely would not be telling me to walk away from a story. "Be careful. Don't take chances." That's what you'd say. But *not* "Let someone else handle it." You'd *never* say that.'

'Sophie—'

'Perry.'

He threw up his hands. 'I need to pack. Why don't you take a shower first?'

'Fine.' I went into the bathroom and closed the door, probably harder than I needed to.

The sex had been great – actually, it had been amazing – but it had most definitely changed our relationship. I wasn't sure I liked the direction it was heading. Because if he was going to worry about me like a concerned parent from now on, there was no way I could go back to London and slip into my old job. He couldn't be my boss anymore.

I wondered if he realized that, too.

We were excessively polite with each other over breakfast and I hated it. Afterwards, I waited in the lobby while he ran up to the room and got his carry-on bag and the messenger bag he used for his laptop. The cab was waiting when we stepped outside.

'Dulles Airport,' Perry told the driver, 'but first we're making a stop at . . .'

'1821 S Street,' I said. 'Just around the corner.'

'OK, folks,' the driver said.

I'd caught him noticing my torn and blood-stained dress and my leg. He also saw me wince as I got into the cab. Our eyes met in the rearview mirror. His were concerned, and I could just imagine the thought bubble above his head, except there wasn't anything I could say that would sound like a logical explanation for why I looked the way I did at nine thirty in the morning. Not to mention the cuts on Perry's face.

The cab pulled up in front of my house less than five minutes later. I knew Perry had scanned the parked cars on the street as anxiously as I had. As expected, there was no black Subaru parked or idling nearby.

'Give me a bit of time to help my, uh, friend into the house and make sure she's all right,' Perry said to the driver. 'I'll be right back.'

We walked up the stairs to the front door, Perry picking up the copy of *The Washington Tribune* the paperboy had pushed through the brass mail slot. The alarm was on, just as I'd set it last night. The house was quiet, settled. If someone had been here, I would have known immediately. Felt it.

'I'm good from here,' I said to Perry. 'You don't want to keep that nice driver waiting. He already doesn't know what to make of us.'

'I'll get you all the way inside. I want to kiss you goodbye without an audience. That nice driver is watching us.'

I glanced out at the cab. 'So he is.'

His kiss was long and deep. 'I'm going to miss you,' he said. 'I really am.'

'I'll miss you, too.'

'Come to London.'

I placed my hands on his chest and gently pushed him away. 'Maybe for a visit. Maybe during the holidays.'

'I'll buy your plane ticket.'

'Whoa, whoa. Hold on, OK?'

'What?'

I took a deep breath. 'Perry, you know I love you like a friend and you know how much you mean to me . . .'

'Don't finish that sentence. Especially if the next word is "but."'

'I don't want anything to ruin what we have . . . what we've had for so many years.'

'Are you saying having sex ruined our relationship? It's not supposed to work that way, you know.'

I smiled. 'I know. And I'm not saying that. But can you please give me some time? I'm still working through a lot of things.'

'Is it Nick?'

'Not in the way you might think it is, but yes.'

He smiled a heartbreak smile and kissed me on the forehead. 'OK, Medina. Have it your way. I'll wait to hear from you.'

He left so quickly that I didn't think he heard me say goodbye. Or tell him that I still loved him.


After he was gone, I went upstairs to my bedroom and took off my dress for the last time. I wasn't going to wear it ever again, not with all the memories that were associated with it now. I pulled on a loose-fitting pair of yoga pants and a sweatshirt and went down to the kitchen to make coffee. Any other day, I would have gone for a run to clear my head and try to work through my confused, mixed-up emotions, but I needed a few days off so my leg could heal before I was ready for exercise. I poured coffee into my to-go mug to take over to the studio. In spite of what Perry had said to me, I still intended to look through my homeless photos to see if I could locate a photo of the Professor. And if I found one, I'd join Tessa and the crowd that was looking for him.

On my way out, I set the house alarm. Normally, it wasn't something I did since I was just going to be across the alley in the carriage house and it was broad daylight. But after last night, I was spooked. I hadn't taken five steps across the alley when I realized that the door to the carriage house was ajar and the padlock was swinging from the hasp where someone had cut through it with bolt cutters.

Perry had insisted on checking my apartment when he brought me home, and we'd both been reassured that no one had tried to break into my house last night. It never occurred to me to check the studio.

Someone had gone in and torn up every single homeless photo I'd taped to my wall. The pieces were all over the floor, a blizzard of black-and-white scraps. The destruction had been deliberate and savage; it felt like the worst kind of violation. When I could finally catch my breath, I read what they'd written on the whitewashed wall where the photos used to be, using an indelible Sharpie that had been taken from my desk and thrown on the floor: STAY AWAY OR YOUR NEXT.

An intruder who couldn't spell, but the message was unmistakably clear. Last night's drive-by shooting and this vandalism to my studio were meant to scare me off, warn me away.

The next time someone would play for keeps. I'd end up like Javi.

Dead.

# NINETEEN

The first thing I did was gather up all the torn fragments of my photos and throw them in the trash. I'd made a folder on my computer with copies of each one, so replacing them would be easy enough. Still, I was livid.

The second thing I did was find a leftover can of Kilz in the storage closet and paint over that threatening message. Twice.

There was no point calling the police over a busted lock, torn-up photos, and some graffiti. If there were a dead body lying in the middle of my studio, I'd probably get their attention, but not for a minor crime like this. Especially if I didn't intend to tell them about everything else: Townsend, Javi, what had happened outside the restaurant last night.

And I didn't.

Instead, I called a locksmith who showed up while I was going through more homeless photos, continuing the search for a picture of the Professor. One hour and $323 later, I had a new lock installed – no more padlock and key – and an imposing-looking deadbolt.

I also knew something with absolute certainty thanks to that break-in: there *was* a connection between Everett Townsend and the Professor. Javi had been right.

Diana Townsend had lied.

Grace called in the middle of the afternoon after I'd taken a break from looking through photos and decided to start reprinting the pictures that had been destroyed instead.

'Hey,' she said, and there was a thrumming excitement in her voice so I knew she had something to tell me. 'What's new?'

'Nothing much.' There was no way I was going to tell her about Perry, the attempted shooting last night, or the vandalism to my studio. At least not right now. She'd totally flip out. 'What's new with you?'

'Guess what story just showed up on my computer? And you guys broke it. IPS.'

I'd left IPS three years ago, but Grace still acted as if I was on temporary sabbatical. Sort of like Perry did. They both expected me to go back to journalism.

'Gracie, are you at work? On a Saturday afternoon?'

'Something came up so I had to come in for a few hours.'

I loved Grace, but she was terrible at delegating responsibility. 'Uh-huh.'

She bristled. 'I know that tone of voice. It was *important* or I wouldn't be here. Anyway, I'm done and on my way home.'

'That's good. So what's the story?'

'Guess who was just named as a new assistant to the Papal Nuncio?'

I didn't need to guess. 'Are you serious?'

'He didn't breathe a word about it. I had no clue.'

'Me, neither. Maybe it came up all of a sudden, and he didn't have a chance to say anything.' Maybe Diana Townsend had called in a favor and arranged this plum appointment for Jack as thanks for everything he'd done in helping her organize the funeral for her late husband.

Who wasn't actually dead.

Maybe it was her way of buying his silence.

'Sophie?'

'What?'

'It's great news, don't you think? Jack will definitely get noticed in Rome now. A job like that is going to fast-track him up the ecclesiastical food chain.'

'Yeah,' I said, 'it will.'

'You don't sound excited.'

'It's not that,' I said. 'I'm just surprised.'

Or maybe I wasn't.

'Come on, you can't be too surprised. We both know how ambitious he is. This is a dream come true for him,' she said. 'Did you watch Everett Townsend's memorial Mass yesterday? Jack and the Papal Nuncio were on the altar together, along with the Cardinal. So they're probably already pals.'

'I know. I saw them.'

'I called him,' she said, 'but his phone went to voicemail, so I left a message saying congrats. We need to get together, the three of us, to celebrate.'

'That would be great,' I said. 'We should do that.'

'Soph?'

'Yes?'

'What's up? What's going on?'

'Nothing.'

'Sorry, not buying it. You've been answering everything I've said in monosyllables. You're pissed off about something. What is it?'

I couldn't tell her that I thought Jack might be covering for Diana Townsend's lies about her husband and that the position at the Papal Nuncio's office had been the payoff for his silence. I just couldn't. I said the first thing that came into my head. Which wasn't a lie.

'Nothing. Just some stuff going on with my grandfather's estate and my mother. It's kind of a mess. Sorry. I didn't mean to take it out on you.'

'Want to talk about it?'

'I will. Just not right now.'

'OK,' she said. 'Whenever you're ready. Sorry to hear about it.'

We disconnected and I looked at my watch. It was four fifteen. Grace might not have been able to reach Jack earlier today, but I knew for sure where he'd be in forty-five minutes. On Saturday night, he always said the five p.m. Mass in the chapel at Gloria House for the seminarians as well as for folks in the neighborhood who were welcome to attend.

After what had happened last night outside the Iron Gate and today in my studio, I needed to talk to him about Diana Townsend. Again.

I decided to go to five o'clock Mass at Gloria House.

I changed out of my yoga pants and sweatshirt into a pair of black trousers and a cream-colored sweater and drove the Mini over to Stanton Park. The parking lot was crowded with cars belonging to local folks who had come for Mass, but I managed to tuck into a tiny space where no other car could possibly fit. The benefits of a toy-sized car in the city.

It was after five, so I was late when I walked into the chapel and slipped into a pew before one of the seminarians began the first reading from the Old Testament. I caught Jack's barely raised eyebrow when he spotted me as I made a guilty half-genuflection and blessed myself. I mouthed *Sorry* and picked up the prayer book to follow along with the readings. The Gospel, from Luke, was a familiar one: ask and you will receive; seek and you will find; knock and the door will be opened to you. Jack's homily was all about being receptive to what came at you in life – 'man plans and God laughs' – but ultimately having faith that if you knocked, the right door would be opened to you, even when you thought you'd ended up at the wrong house.

I hoped what he said was true because I had questions for him once Mass was over and I hoped he would answer them.

And that he would tell me the truth.

*Seek and you will find.*

I waited while Jack greeted all the visitors from the community as they left the chapel, watching as he charmed the women and glad-handed the men, and saw the compassion in his eyes when someone leaned in to tell him something in confidence – a sick child, an unemployed relative, an unexpected death. He was a good man. He cared about these people and their problems, and it was genuine.

But he was also human. And he was ambitious.

After everyone was gone and the seminarians had filed into the dining room for dinner, he said, 'Do you want to stay for dinner, or do we need to have a drink?'

'I don't want you to miss dinner, but I wouldn't mind a drink.'

'Let's go upstairs to my suite,' he said.

He knew.

We walked into his living room and he said, 'Gin and tonic?'

'I'd love one. Could you make mine light, though? I'm driving.'

'Sure. Have a seat while I make our drinks. I think it's gotten too cold to sit outside.'

'It has,' I said and took the sofa. 'Summer vanished overnight.'

My gin and tonic was light, as requested. His was not. Heavy on the gin. He handed me my glass and excused himself to change out of his blacks. When he returned wearing jeans and a Georgetown sweatshirt, he took the recliner opposite me.

He raised his glass. 'Cheers.'

I raised mine and we drank. By now the tension between us was palpable.

'What's up?' he said. 'I was surprised to see you here tonight. Usually, you call or text to let me know you're coming.'

'I know. Sorry. Gracie called me a while ago. I understand congratulations are in order. Assistant to the Papal Nuncio. You must be thrilled.'

I'd caught him off guard. 'The news is out already? I only just found out myself. How did she know?'

'Grace is a journalist, remember? She knows things *before* they happen.'

He gave me an ironic smile and said, 'Yeah, that sixth sense of hers.'

'So, *are* you thrilled?'

'I am. It's part-time, so I can keep teaching. That was one of my conditions. Basically, I get to be a glorified secretary. My boss is not only an archbishop but also has the rank of ambassador. So there's the diplomatic side of the job, plus the Nuncio is also very involved with the American bishops and the American Church. He's the conduit between them and the Pope. Which was part of the reason I said yes.'

Of course it was. If not *all* of the reason.

'Did Diana Townsend recommend you for the position?'

He reddened slightly. 'She did.'

I nodded and he said, 'And if your next question is whether I asked her if the man she just buried was really her husband, the answer is no. I couldn't do that to her. I think you're flat-out wrong on this, Soph.'

'Jack, you *saw* him in that alley. We both did, but you knew him. You never thought for one minute that he *wasn't* Everett Townsend?'

'No, I did not.' He ticked off reasons on his fingers. 'We found him next to his car. Behind his townhouse. Wearing his clothes. His watch. With his wallet. His phone. His briefcase was next to him. Jesus, Sophie, what more do you want?'

'Someone took a shot at me last night when Perry DiNardo and I were leaving the Iron Gate after dinner. Then today I discovered that someone had broken into my studio and ripped all my homeless pictures off the wall and wrote "stay away or your next" in bad English where the photos used to be.'

'My God.' He looked shaken. 'Are you OK?'

'My right leg looks like it went through a meat grinder because Perry dragged me down on to the sidewalk, and my ribs hurt like hell; fortunately, they're only bruised, not cracked or broken. Otherwise, yes, I'm doing just great, thanks.'

'I'm . . . so sorry.'

'Jack,' I said, 'Diana's lying. For reasons I don't totally understand, Everett Townsend managed to fake his death by substituting the body of a homeless man with Alzheimer's who was his double. His doppelganger. He could have fooled most people – and he did. But surely not his wife. *Come on.*'

'Do you realize what *you're* saying?' he asked. 'That an Associate Justice of the Supreme Court is still alive and well and . . . out there somewhere. Hiding out. Do you realize how crazy that sounds? Why would he do that?'

'Because he's in some kind of trouble – what it is, I don't know – and as improbable as it seems, faking his death and trying to start over somewhere else was the better option.'

He snorted. 'Who is going to believe you? Can you prove it?'

'No. The only one who really knows the truth is Diana Townsend.'

'*I'm not going to ask her*. Leave it alone, Sophie. Drop it.'

'OK, if you tell me why someone murdered Javi, shot at me last night, and broke into my studio and left a message to stop looking for the Professor, Everett Townsend's double, or I'm next.'

'I don't know.'

'You don't *want* to know.'

He banged down his glass. 'I'm hungry. Are you staying for dinner?'

'No . . . I'm going home. Thanks for the drink.'

'I'll walk you to your car.'

'You don't need to.'

He did, anyway. We didn't say a word to each other until we got to the parking lot. I didn't remember ever being this angry at him, and I know he was furious with me.

He pulled me to him and whispered into my hair. 'Don't do this. Please.'

I stepped away and turned to get in my car. 'I should go.'

He was still standing there when I looked in my rearview mirror before I pulled out on to the street.

Trying to prove Everett Townsend was still alive could very well get me killed. And as I told Jack, I had no way of doing that anyway. Perry had told me to drop this and so had Jack – each for their own reasons. For that matter, so had Leo Duval.

But whether any of them liked it or not, I *was* involved. I couldn't walk away. It was time to leave another message for Napoleon Duval and ask if we could meet.

Because there were a few updates he needed to know about.

I ordered a pizza from DC Pizza on 19th Street and opened a really good bottle of Bordeaux that Max had given me the last time I had him over for dinner. I ate a mushroom, black olive, and feta cheese pizza tucked up in my favorite chair with its bay-window view of S Street, which was quiet for a Saturday night. Max's outstanding wine made it a gourmet meal.

Halfway through dinner, my phone buzzed with a text. Perry. He'd just landed at Heathrow and wanted me to know. I texted back that I was glad he was back in London and that it had been good to see him.

He wrote: *Good to see you, too. Be in touch.* Little flickering dots appeared on my screen. He was writing something else, so I waited.

*I miss you.*

I picked up my phone and tried to think of how to reply, my thumb hovering over the screen. The longer it took me to write something, the more obvious it was I probably wasn't going to write, *I miss you, too.* Finally, I typed: *Take care of yourself.* And hit send.

Silence from him, then the flickering dots again. They went on for a few seconds and then stopped. He had changed his mind and wasn't going to write anything else after the text I'd just sent.

I didn't want to hurt him, but I didn't want to lead him on, either. Right now, my relationships with two men I cared about a lot were at an all-time low.

And I didn't know what to do to fix them.

*    *    *

I wrapped up the leftover half of my pizza and put it in the refrigerator for tomorrow's lunch. Or maybe dinner, depending on how the day went. Then I poured another glass of wine and went into the dining room. Going through Chappy's box would distract me from things I didn't want to think about right now.

An hour and another glass of wine later, I'd dug through most of the box, learning more about my grandfather than I ever expected – or wanted – to know. That he was frequently late on his rent for the rooms he had taken in Greenwich Village because he was so broke. That he was a regular at McSorley's Ale House, based on the number of beer coasters and napkins he'd collected with notes he'd written on them. That he had his wisdom teeth out. Where he got his haircut. And on and on.

I was about to call it a night when I saw the edge of a blue-and-white envelope that reminded me of the ones my mother used to get years ago when she had her pictures developed at a drugstore before everything went digital. I pulled it out from under a pile of papers: it *was* filled with photographs, black-and-white snaps that looked as if they'd been taken with someone's inexpensive camera – a Kodak Brownie, perhaps. I flipped through the pictures and smiled. Chappy had written *Coney Island Beach Party with the Gang, Aug 58* on the envelope. There was a date stamp on the back of each photo: August 12, 1958. The pictures were sweet, a carefree day spent with friends: one of the guys being buried up to his neck in the sand, the girls vamping for the camera in fifties bikinis – boy shorts and G-rated brassiere tops – a human pyramid with a backdrop of the ocean, a couple of guys pointing to an enormous sand fortress they'd built. Everyone tanned and fit and lean and happy. I stopped when I got to the last photo because it was my grandfather as I'd never seen him – bronzed and well muscled, and, frankly, gorgeous, smiling at the camera as if he were flirting with the photographer.

And there was something else. He looked *nothing* like the man in Oriana's photos. I was sure of it. If I blew up this picture and the ones she had, there would be no doubt. The grandfather clock chimed eleven. I got my jacket, locked up the apartment, set the alarm, and headed over to my studio.

Half an hour later, after I'd enlarged Chappy and Oriana's

photos enough so they weren't too pixilated and printed them out, it was totally obvious that Chappy wasn't the man in the photographs with Oriana. But it was also true that whoever he was, he did look a lot like him. Enough so that if I hadn't found that other photo, Oriana might have been able to fool me. Fool my mother.

I reached for my phone. Tommy was working the overnight shift at the hospital. I sent him a text and asked if he could call me when he got his next break, even if it was three a.m.

I got lucky. He called at midnight.

'What's up?' he said. 'Is everything all right?'

'Yes, fine,' I said. 'I have a huge favor to ask.'

'What do you need and why do I have a feeling I'm not going to like it?'

'You're not, but it's really important, Tom. I mean it.'

'OK,' he said. 'What is it?'

'I promise I'll explain my reason for asking when I see you, but for now, could you get a copy of any photographs that were taken of Everett Townsend when he was in your morgue? Your medical examiner does take photos, doesn't he? I mean, of someone who dies in the hospital?'

'Uh, yeah.' His voice dropped to a whisper. 'But the photos are in the medical examiner's office – not here – because the ME's not a hospital employee, Soph. He works for the local government. If we had photos of Townsend – or any patient – and someone found out, do you know how much trouble the hospital would be in? It's a major HIPPA violation and we'd be fined, like, ten thousand dollars. Plus, the next of kin or the person, if they were still alive, could sue our asses off. It's a big deal. A very big deal.'

'I guess that's a no.'

'It's a hard no,' he said. 'Why do you want photos of Townsend?'

There was no way I was going to get his help now unless I told him the truth.

'Because he wasn't Everett Townsend. The man who was in your ER that night was somebody else. A homeless man named Paul Smith who looked just like Townsend. He also happens to be missing.'

'You can't be serious.'

When I didn't reply, he said, 'Jesus. You are.'

'I am. Tommy, you can't repeat this to anyone, OK? Another homeless man was already killed because he was in your ER that night and recognized Smith. He told some of the hospital staff that it wasn't Everett Townsend. He was adamant and a bit loud, too. Someone must have overheard him.'

'Sophie, Townsend's *wife* identified him.'

'I know she did. Look, I'm sorry I asked,' I said. 'I sign those HIPPA forms year after year every time I see a doctor or dentist or whoever, but I never thought much about them or what the consequences might be for you guys.'

'Well, now you know. I'm sorry. There aren't any pictures that I can get my hands on. You gotta go through channels to get them from the ME – and that probably involves a criminal investigation.'

Which wasn't going to happen.

'I'll just have to try to find another way to prove it wasn't Everett Townsend.'

'How are you going to do that?'

'Keep looking through the photos I've been taking at the homeless camps. Paul Smith might be in one of them, but so far I haven't had much luck.'

'Will you let me know if you do?'

'Sure. Thanks, sweetie. I'd better let you get back to work.'

'Right,' he said. 'I'll call you tomorrow to check in. Oops, I gotta go. Someone's paging me. Bye.'

He hung up.

Damn, damn, damn. I should have realized there wouldn't – couldn't – be any hospital photos. But what were the odds there was some physical distinction, however slight, between the Professor and Everett Townsend – just as there had been between Chappy and the man Oriana tried to pass off as his double?

Probably pretty damn good.

And there had to be a photo of Paul Smith somewhere. Maybe I could track down a family member. A relative. Someone.

Anyone.

Then I could compare the two men.

Because photographs – unlike people – don't lie.

# TWENTY

I was up early Sunday morning and back in the studio. I still needed a picture of Paul Smith. My phone rang just after seven a.m.

Harry.

'Morning, sweetheart,' he said. 'Did I wake you?'

'No, I'm up. What's going on? Is everything OK?'

'Actually,' he said, 'it's not. I've got the phone on speaker. Your mother's here, too.'

One of those calls. Which meant it was something serious.

'Hi, Mom. Are you OK?'

'Yes, yes. I'm fine, Sophie. It's your grandfather. I'll let Harry explain.'

I closed my eyes and wondered if whatever *it* was trumped my discovery last night that Oriana's photos were of someone who was not Chappy.

'We got a call from Knox Porter in Connecticut yesterday morning,' Harry said. 'It seems your grandfather is being sued by the IRS for non-payment of taxes. They're taking Chap – or rather the estate of Charles Lord – to court. In Connecticut.'

'What taxes didn't he pay?'

'The whole thing is ridiculous.' My mother jumped in, obviously forgetting she'd just said Harry was supposed to tell the story. 'It has to do with photographs your grandfather donated to a charity in Danbury that helps children with special needs. The photos were sold at a fundraising auction and raised quite a lot of money. Chappy turned all of it over to the charity, of course, but according to the IRS, that money was also income to him. You know your grandfather. He ignored their letters and requests, claiming he'd never taken a dime of the money so he owed nothing. And, of course, he never said a word about it to me. Or Harry. We had no idea until Knox called.'

'That sounds like Chappy. Donating photos to a charity for special kids *and* ignoring the IRS,' I said.

'Except the IRS has this thing about being ignored,' Harry said. 'They don't like it and now they're going to court to get their money.'

'Isn't this Knox Porter's headache and not yours?' I asked. 'CIFA inherited Chappy's estate – all of it. So they have to settle or pay the taxes, right? Maybe they'll need to sell a few more photographs to cover what he owes, but at least they have the money and the assets to do it.'

'Well, that's the thing,' Harry said. 'I called Sam after our conversation with Knox, just to run this by him. He made a few phone calls and dropped by the house yesterday afternoon to talk about it.'

OK, definitely serious if Sam showed up in person.

'And?'

'It seems that even though Chap had moved to Virginia last year, he was still legally domiciled in Connecticut. Virginia was his residence but not his domicile. He owned a house in Connecticut. He paid taxes in Connecticut. His car was still registered there.'

'OK.'

'Holographic wills are legal in Virginia,' Harry said. 'They are *not* legal in Connecticut. And that's where Chap lived – officially. And why the IRS is suing him there instead of in Virginia.'

'That doesn't sound good.' A will that was already sketchy and now was no longer legal because of a technicality. And the IRS was involved.

'Unless we can find another will somewhere – anywhere – then Chappy died intestate.'

'Isabella might not have gone through Chap's papers document by document,' I said, 'but if there had been another will, I think she might have mentioned it.'

'Which she didn't,' my mother said. 'So there's very likely *not* another will.'

'If Chap died intestate,' I said, 'what does *that* mean?'

Though I was starting to have a pretty good idea.

'His estate goes to his next of kin,' Harry said, leaving the rest of the sentence unfinished.

'Chappy's next of kin . . . might be Oriana Neri?' I asked. 'His first wife for all of about two minutes?'

'It might,' my mother said, 'although that would happen over my dead body.'

'What does Sam say?' I asked.

Harry let out a long, defeated breath. 'The marriage is legal. There is no record of a divorce decree anywhere that Sam could find. He's still going to turn over every rock he can locate in Las Vegas, look underneath, and see if he can find something. Anything.'

'I have some news as well – it's also about Chappy and Oriana,' I said. 'I was going to call you this morning, but you called first.'

My mother groaned. 'I don't think I can take any more news about those two.'

'It's good news, Mom. Well, sort of good – though after what you just told me, I'm not sure it matters as much.'

'What is it?' Harry said. '"Sort of good news" has got to be better than what we just found out.'

'When I picked up the photos for the Dupont Underground exhibition the other day, I also went by the barn and borrowed a box that Isabella had labeled with Chap's papers and documents from 1958, the year he married Oriana,' I said. 'Last night, I found an envelope with photos of a beach party Chappy went to with some friends on Coney Island that year. There's a picture of him in a bathing suit.'

'And?' my mother said.

'I blew it up and blew up Oriana's photos that she said were of her and Chap. They're not.'

'Not . . . what?' Harry asked.

'Chappy's not the guy in her photos. It's someone else.'

My mother sucked in an angry breath. 'She lied. That scheming little bitch.'

'*Mom.*'

'*Caroline.*'

'I don't care. It's true.'

'Are you sure about that?' Harry asked me.

'One hundred percent. Look, I'll drive out to see you tomorrow and bring the photographs. Maybe we can talk to Sam and figure out what to do next. We don't have to tell Oriana about this new situation right away, do we?'

'Even if it's true that the marriage is legal,' my mother said, 'Harry and I already talked about challenging this, fighting it.'

'Does Knox know that the will's invalid?'

'He knows about the lawsuit, of course, since he's the one who called us. But he didn't say anything to indicate he realized it changed the legality of the will. The only reason your mother and I know is because we talked to Sam – and Sam's a damned good lawyer,' Harry said. 'Not every lawyer is up to speed on holographic wills.'

'If Knox understood what this meant, you can be very sure we would have heard from him by now,' my mother said.

So not only did Harry and my mother not want to tell Knox that CIFA was suddenly no longer the beneficiary of Charles Lord's estate, they also didn't want Oriana Neri to know that just as suddenly she might be its sole beneficiary.

Jesus.

What a mess.


After we hung up, I switched gears and instead looked for photos of Everett Townsend. I found a few that I blew up and printed out. He was, of course, fully clothed, which was going to make this harder. Still, it was uncanny how much he looked exactly like the man Jack and I found unconscious in the alley. Almost an identical twin, but most definitely a doppelganger.

It wasn't impossible.

Because I photograph people for a living, I'm always reading anything I come across about our anthropological history – who our ancestors were – as well as anything about the discoveries scientists were making as they learned more about DNA and genetics. That each of us shares 99.5 percent of our DNA with every other human being on the planet, meaning a tiny one-half of one percent was all that made us different from each other. Which was also why it was possible – and even likely – that somewhere in the world there was at least one other person who looked almost exactly like each of us, even though they were unrelated by blood. What was even weirder was that our doppelganger could be a total stranger who lived thousands of miles away and was someone we might never know.

A car pulled up in the alley and my heart started rabbiting in my rib cage. Who would show up this early on a Sunday morning? At least I had locked the door. I was about to open the drawer with the revolver in it when Tommy knocked on the door and yelled, 'It's me.'

'Coming.'

He was dressed in blue scrubs, sneakers, and a hoodie; his face was lined and tired.

'I made coffee,' I said. 'Can I pour you a cup? Or we can go back to my place and I can fix something for breakfast. I didn't find any photos of Paul Smith by the way, or I would have let you know.'

'I did. And I will take a cup of coffee, please.'

'You did what?'

'Find a photo of Paul Smith.' He gave me a triumphant grin, pulling his phone out of his pocket and turning it on.

'*How?* You said it was illegal.' I poured his coffee and handed him the mug.

'It is. And I could get in serious trouble just for having it on my phone. But when you told me the reason you wanted it, I started asking around, talking to people who were in the ER that night.'

He turned the phone around and handed it to me. 'Here,' he said. 'Have a look.'

It was a picture of Paul Smith in the ambulance with his shirt open and electrodes strapped to his chest. An IV in his arm. Oxygen mask over his face. Hands resting on his chest and a little device clipped to the index finger of his right hand to check his oxygen level.

'Where did you get this?'

'From one of the nurses who was on duty when they brought him in,' he said. 'She was in last night. One of the EMTs texted the picture to her, sort of a "Hey, guess what VIP is in my ambulance and on the way to the ER?" She kept it, never deleted the text, and when I asked her if she remembered anything about the night Townsend came in, she showed me the photo. I asked her to send it to me and then told her to delete it and told her why.'

I heard a whoosh as he said, 'I just sent it to you.'

I imported it on to my computer and zoomed in on the photo.

And found the proof I needed.

'Take a look,' I said to Tommy, pointing to the man's right hand. 'Do you see that birthmark, how unusual it is? I noticed it when I was with him in the alley. I held his hand and told him that help was coming.'

He leaned in. 'Yup. I see it.'

I switched screens to a photo of Townsend, in the black robe he wore when the Court was in session, standing in front of an American flag and the Seal of the Supreme Court. Hands folded and, fortunately, his right hand covering his left. I zoomed in on his right hand.

'Look at that.'

'No birthmark.' He whistled.

'That wasn't Everett Townsend lying in your morgue.'

'No,' my brother said, 'I guess it was not.' He looked at me. 'Now what?'

'Now I have to find a photo of the Professor or I don't have irrefutable proof.'

'What are you going to do with the photo I just gave you?'

'Give it to Grace,' I said. 'But she has to protect you and that nurse and the EMT and now me. She can't use it.'

He turned pale. 'No, she cannot.'

'She won't. Because you know what this means.'

'What?'

'Everett Townsend is alive and well . . . somewhere. If someone – say, the FBI – starts looking for him, they'll find him. Then he can explain everything himself. That photo will be a moot point.'

'What are you going to do now?'

'Look for a photo of Paul Smith – and if I don't find one, go over to the Streetwise offices tomorrow morning and see if someone there has a photo of him.'

'Be careful.'

'I will. You be careful, too. I've dragged you into this,' I said. 'And there's something I probably should tell you. Someone took a shot at me last night when I was leaving a restaurant. Also, the studio was broken into and there was some vandalism.'

'Jesus Christ, Sophie.' His head swiveled and he looked around the room.

'I cleaned everything up, and other than a bad scrape on my leg when Perry DiNardo dragged me to the ground and some sore ribs, I'm OK.'

'What if they try again?'

I opened the top drawer of my desk and showed him the revolver. 'They'd better not.'

I finally persuaded Tommy – who was now completely wound up – to go home and get some sleep. I swore I'd let him know if I found a photo of the Professor.

And if I did, then I was turning everything over to Grace.

Who, hopefully, would make it rain.

I found the photo not long after Tommy left, when I had all but given up hope. It was one of the first of the series of homeless photos I'd taken – the day I met the kid who was begging near the off-ramp from the Teddy Roosevelt Bridge at the entrance to Rock Creek Parkway. Paul Smith was one of the people who had been living under the bridge. He had on a shabby-looking dress coat over a worn suit and tie, but there was an air of elegance and refinement about him that I had forgotten until I saw that photo. His left hand was by his side and his right hand lay across his heart as he stared directly into the camera lens. I blew up the photo.

And had all the proof I needed that Javi was right.

My first thought was that I needed to take this to Leo Duval. My second thought was that after I spoke to him the other day, someone shot at me and then broke into my studio, trashing the place and leaving that warning message. As Perry and I had discussed over dinner, that meant someone I had confided in had very likely said something to someone else who didn't want me poking my nose into whether Townsend had faked his death. Duval was on that list.

I would call Duval, but first I wanted to talk to Grace. Once this bombshell news made it into the press and was out in the open, there would be no turning back. No more reason for anyone to shut me up or warn me off.

I called Grace.

We met at the eleven-thirty Mass at St Matthew's. She planned to go anyway, and I figured it was the perfect place to hand off

a thumb drive with an incriminating photo that could get anyone
who had it in serious legal trouble. And tell her a story she probably wouldn't believe until she saw that photo: Everett Townsend
had faked his death; the man who died in his place was a homeless man who was his doppelganger. I also planned to tell her
about Javi, which I knew would devastate her, but I knew it
would fuel her anger, too. She would make damn sure the truth
got out once she knew what had happened to Javi and why. I
asked her to sit in a pew where there wouldn't be many people
around us – though the eleven-thirty is always a crowded Mass
– and said I'd explain when I saw her.

She was there when I arrived as the bells tolled that Mass was
about to begin. I knelt next to her. 'It's Luke's Gospel. "Seek
and ye shall find. Knock and the door will be opened to you,"'
I said.

'How do you know?'

I tapped my temple with a finger. 'Psychic.'

She kept her voice low. 'What's going on, Soph? What's this
about? You were pretty evasive on the phone.'

There weren't many people sitting around us, but I still didn't
want to be shushed – or glowered at – so I told her in bits and
pieces as unobtrusively as I could during Mass. I shut up during
the homily because of an overwhelming sense of Catholic guilt
that the white-haired priest saying Mass was looking directly at
me and was going to call me out from the pulpit if I didn't quit
whispering.

I passed Grace the thumb drive with the photos after we came
back from communion as the cantor was finishing the second
hymn. She slipped it into the pocket of her jacket.

'You can't say where you got this,' I said.

'I know. But I'm going to have an uphill battle to get our
managing editor to run a story like this with no attributable
source.'

'What if you made some calls and shake some tree branches?'
I asked. 'You could light a fire under a few people – say, at the
FBI or even the Supreme Court – people who would at least start
asking questions. Then you'd have some more meat on the bones
of the story.'

She gave me the dumb-question look and said, 'Thank you,

Captain Obvious, for all those cliched idioms explaining what I need to do

'I'm sorry. But you're not going to bury this, are you?'

Grace stuck her hand in the pocket with the thumb drive as if making sure it was still there. 'No, I most definitely am not. But that photo could get us sued to hell and back if we used it, not to mention what they'd do to anyone else who had a copy. Including you and Tommy. But, yeah, I'll talk to my boss and make some phone calls.'

I got a text from Grace at midnight.

*It'll be in tomorrow's paper. Front page. Above the fold. Thx.*

# TWENTY-ONE

*FBI Investigating Possibility that Associate Supreme Court Justice Everett Townsend Is Still Alive.*

As Grace had promised, it was the front-page banner headline in *The Washington Tribune* on Monday morning. There was no mention of the photograph Tommy had gotten from the ER nurse. The article cited 'an anonymous tip' that had led to further inquiries.

I turned on CNN while I was eating breakfast. The Townsend story was the lead story. I surfed channels. It was the lead story everywhere. If the FBI didn't track Everett Townsend down first, every journalist in America would be looking for him now as well. It would only be a matter of time.

Grace called just before nine. 'I owe you lunch. At the very least. How about Bistrot du Coin at noon?'

'Do I get to hear about all the stuff you couldn't print?'

'You do.'

'Did you call Diana Townsend?'

'I did.'

'What did she say?'

'I caught her off guard. She wanted to know where I got my information and then she got angry. "How dare you?" and all that grieving-widow stuff. I pushed her a little harder about Paul Smith and her work in the homeless community, and she got very quiet. The next thing she said was to stop harassing her or her lawyer would be in touch. Then she hung up.'

'You hit a nerve.'

'I hit them all,' she said. 'I wonder what Jack knows. You said they're really tight.'

I closed my eyes. Jack. What *did* he know? Grace didn't know I'd pushed him to talk to Diana and that he'd refused. She also hadn't connected the new assignment to work for the Papal Nuncio with Diana possibly buying his silence and complicity by wangling the job for him.

'I don't know,' I said.

'Are you going to call him?'

'No, I think not. Are you?'

'Yes. He's a source.'

'Let me know?'

'I'll tell you at lunch.'

Grace didn't need to tell me anything. Jack called me half an hour later.

'I saw Grace's byline on the Townsend story,' he said.

He wasn't going to make this easy. 'Yes. Has she called you yet?'

'No.' He sounded startled. 'She's going to call me? Why?'

'Come on, Jack.'

'I can't tell her anything.'

'She's still going to call, and you can tell her that.'

'Did you have anything to do with this?'

'I did.'

His silence went on for so long that I thought he might have disconnected. Finally, he said, 'I couldn't push her, Sophie. I just couldn't. She was really upset when I went over there that night after she left the hospital. She kept asking me all kinds of questions about you and me finding him – and, Jesus, I didn't have any reason to believe it *wasn't* Rhett lying there in that alley.'

'Did she ever tell you the truth? That she *did* know?'

'I can't answer that. And you know why, too.'

'I do.'

'How did you find out?'

I wasn't going to breathe a word about the ambulance photo Tommy got from the ER nurse, not even to Jack who would keep it a secret.

'From Javi. After that, it was easy finding a photo of Townsend, and it happened that I'd taken a photo of Paul Smith the very first day I began taking photos for what turned into my homeless series. So I blew them both up and took a look. Paul Smith has an unusual birthmark on his right hand. I noticed it when I was holding his hand in the alley. And Townsend . . .'

He finished the sentence. 'Doesn't have a birthmark on his right hand.'

'No, he doesn't. I figure Everett Townsend met him through Diana's charity work with the homeless. So he knew Smith, realized how they looked almost exactly alike – that they were doppelgangers.'

'And then he had him killed, somehow got Paul Smith dressed in his clothing with his watch, his phone, all of it.' Jack's voice had so much oppressive heaviness and weight in it that he could have been standing on Jupiter.

'Yes.'

'My God.'

'Have you called Diana since the story got out?'

'She called me. I'm on my way to see her now.'

'Then I'd better let you go. I'm sure she's anxious to talk to you.'

'She is,' he said. 'Goodbye, Sophie.'

He hung up, and I wondered what in the world he could say to Diana Townsend that might comfort her or make this situation better, because there was no way she wasn't complicit. Sure, her husband was alive, but two people were dead so that Everett Townsend could carry out his charade.

What about *them*?

I also wondered what questions Jack would ask himself when he sat down to do some serious soul-searching about why he had kept quiet in spite of my insistence that something was wrong.

Why he had *really* kept quiet.

Last of all, I wanted to know what Everett Townsend had done, what crime he must have committed, that made him decide to fake his death and go into hiding. For the rest of his life.

I had decided to drive out to Mayfield after lunch with Grace to show Mom and Harry the photos of Chappy at the beach and the man who was *not* Chappy, posing with Oriana. As long as I was making the trip, I figured I'd bring the box of his memora- bilia with me and put it back where Isabella had left it in the barn.

Most of the contents were strewn across my dining-room table or in piles on the floor. I picked up his 1958 calendar one more time and looked at May 3rd, the day Chappy and Oriana got married. Nothing – really *nothing* – to indicate their wedding, which Oriana said had been a drunken impulse decision that they barely remembered the next morning. I flipped pages for the rest of May and June until there were no more mentions of 'O.' The beach photos had been taken in August. Chappy must have left LA and moved back to New York sometime in July after Oriana moved out. Before long, he'd gotten together with old friends and spent that day at the beach with 'the gang' as he called them on Coney Island.

I pulled out the last few papers and documents in the box, just in case there was something I'd missed. The letter from Ward Evans, Annulment Attorney, who was a Las Vegas lawyer, was tucked among papers terminating the rental agreement on Chappy's apartment in LA and requesting a forwarding address where the security deposit could be mailed. The letter, dated September 27th, 1958, informed my grandfather that he would almost certainly be granted an uncontested annulment *ab initio* for his marriage to Oriana Neri, despite the fact that a process server had been unable to locate the defendant who also did not respond to a summons publicized in the *Los Angeles Times* within the required twenty-one day period. Evans also wrote that 'want of understanding' – both parties were intoxicated when the marriage ceremony was performed – was more than adequate grounds for the judge to grant Chap's petition. A *civil* annulment, not a religious one. Finally, Evans stated that in cases of a one-signature annulment, the process usually took longer – probably between sixteen and twenty weeks until it was finalized – and that Mr Evans would mail Chappy the decree as soon as the family court judge issued it.

I looked up *ab initio*, though I was pretty sure what it meant: from the beginning. As in *the marriage never happened*. Even if the annulment decree wasn't somewhere among Chap's papers, this letter was still something concrete for Sam to go on – dates, the name of his attorney, a family court in Las Vegas.

Had Oriana known about this? Ward Evans wrote that a process server was unable to locate her and serve her with a complaint, nor had she replied to a summons in the *LA Times* – which she might not have seen. Oriana said they'd gone their separate ways and lost touch almost immediately; she moved in with a director who promised to make her a Hollywood star. He went back to

New York. Whether she knew about it or not, I was ninety-nine percent sure the civil annulment had been granted.

I called Mom and Harry and told them the news.

My mother was elated. Harry, who sounded relieved and happy, said he would call Sam so he could get to work tracking down the annulment decree from the court in Las Vegas.

'There's one more thing,' I said.

'What is it?' my mother asked.

'I know you said we should let Sam communicate with Oriana from now on, but I'd like to talk to her. Show her the photos and the letter from Chap's attorney,' I said.

'I still think we should let Sam handle it,' my mother said. 'You don't have to see her again, sweetie. It's not necessary.'

'Caroline,' Harry said, 'Sophie can handle Oriana just fine. Let her do it.'

'I want to finish this,' I said. 'In person.'

'All right,' she said. 'If you want to.'

'I do. And, Mom, doesn't this mean that because you're Chap's next of kin, now you inherit his estate?'

I heard her sharp intake of breath. 'I suppose it does. Right, Harry?'

'We'll talk to Sam, of course, but . . . yes, I would say so.'

'Have you spoken to Knox?' I asked.

'Not yet,' my mother said. 'Everything is changing so fast. It's going to be a difficult conversation when he finds out the will is no longer valid.'

Right. Cue the lawyers. Thank God for Sam.

'Let me know?'

'Of course,' Harry said. 'By the way, we saw Grace's byline in the paper this morning, and we've been watching the news. That's quite an incredible story she's uncovered.'

'Isn't it?'

'My God, what an awful thing to do,' he said. 'If it's true, Everett Townsend had another man killed in his place so he could take off and go into hiding somewhere. Why would he do that? What is he running from? A drug dealer? The mafia?'

'I don't know. It's crazy.'

'Take care of yourself, honey. We'll talk soon,' Harry said. 'And thank you for the call – and especially for the news.'

After he disconnected, I got dressed and went over to my studio where I made copies of Ward Evans's letter along with the photos I had blown up of my grandfather at Coney Island and the enlargement of Oriana's photos of her with another man.

Then I called Oriana and told her I'd like to stop by this afternoon to continue our conversation.

'You're being rather mysterious, Sophie,' she said. 'I trust it's good news.'

'It is,' I said.

'Excellent.' If she were a cat, she would have been purring. 'I'll see you later then.'

I probably should have felt more guilty than I did for leading her on. I *did* have good news. Just not for her. She'd lied and I'd caught her. My grandfather wasn't the man in bed with her in the erotic photos. As for the marriage, maybe she hadn't known that Chappy sought an annulment. Or maybe she had. Right now, I was inclined to believe she'd lied about that as well.

Once someone lies to you and squanders your trust, you can never again fully believe what they tell you.

Which was why I didn't believe Oriana Neri.

About anything.

I had already gotten a table next to the window at Bistrot du Coin when I saw Grace get out of a cab, clutching her phone as if she were going to strangle it. I rapped on the window and she saw me, nodding and holding up a finger. She pointed to her phone and then clamped it to her ear. By the time she sat down across from me ten minutes later, her cheeks were flushed and she looked elated.

'Sorry about that. My phone has been ringing all morning.'

'I'm not surprised. I already ordered for both of us,' I said. 'Steak-frites and a glass of red wine each. I figured you needed the wine. So before you have to blast out of here with a to-go box, tell me everything.'

A waiter set down our wine along with a basket filled with slices of warm baguette and a small dish of whipped butter, and promised our food would be here soon. The restaurant was packed and noisy as it always was, the sound amplifying as it bounced off the high ceiling. Grace had to lean in close so I could hear what she was saying.

We clinked glasses and she said, 'I can't thank you enough for that story. When I saw those photos side by side, I couldn't believe how much Townsend and Paul Smith looked alike. More than doppelgangers. Practically identical twins. It was uncanny. If you hadn't spotted the birthmark on Smith's hand, I don't think there would have been a snowball's chance in hell of anybody ever realizing it wasn't Everett Townsend.'

'I know. I got lucky. Plus, there was Tommy's illegal photo. Which was the final proof that it was Smith, not Townsend. Except that photo could get everyone who has a copy of it in a boatload of legal trouble, not to mention a huge fine.'

She nodded. 'Including – and maybe especially – the *Trib*. Don't worry. It's never going to see the light of day.' She picked up her knife and pantomimed drawing an X over her heart with the sharp tip. 'I swear.'

'Good. It can't. So tell me everything.'

She reached for a slice of baguette and slathered it with butter. 'I talked to my editor right off the bat and told him what I had. He told me to come back with something substantial that we could print without getting our asses sued off, because what I had wasn't enough.'

She chewed on a piece of baguette. 'So the first thing I did was go down to that homeless camp where you took Paul Smith's picture. Since it was a Sunday, everyone was there instead of out and about or at their day jobs. One of the women told me she saw the Professor, as they call him, getting into a car a few days ago. She couldn't remember which day, unfortunately, but she did say he hasn't been back to the camp since then. All his stuff is still in his tent. They've been looking for him, but no one has seen him at his usual hangouts.'

'Any information on the car?'

'It was blue.'

'Oh. Did it look like anyone forced him to get in?'

'She said no.'

'So he wasn't abducted.'

'Nope.'

'He also had Alzheimer's. Or dementia,' I said. 'He could have been confused.'

Our steak-frites arrived and Grace reached for the ketchup. 'I'm famished.' Her phone buzzed and she glanced at the screen before silencing it. 'Sorry.'

'It's OK. Go on.'

'I asked if I could see his tent. The woman said the Professor was really private and wouldn't like a stranger going through his things. I didn't push it,' she said. 'I asked her if there was anything else and she said, "Yeah, he leaves a lot of stuff in his car – clothes and things – even though it doesn't run anymore."'

'He has a car? He drives?'

'Not since the car died. The others at the camp were worried about him getting behind the wheel with his memory problems,' she said. 'So they weren't sorry when his car conked out.'

'If he drives, or drove, a car, then he must have a driver's license,' I said.

'You'd think,' Grace said, her eyes widening.

'I wonder where it is.'

'I don't know. I didn't even think to ask.' Her phone buzzed again and she silenced it, this time without looking.

'When Jack and I found him, he had Townsend's wallet,' I said. 'What do you bet whoever killed him took Paul Smith's driver's license and any ID he had – if he was carrying it at the time – and gave it to Townsend? Because if Paul Smith could pass as Everett Townsend, why couldn't Everett Townsend pass himself off as Paul Smith? He'd have a ready-made life, including a license, a social security number somewhere – a past.'

'Damn,' she said. 'You're right and I'm an idiot. I didn't even think about the license.'

'All he'd need was a fake passport and he could go anywhere. No one would be looking for him or Paul Smith. He could get out of the country relatively quickly.'

Grace drummed her fingers on the red-and-white checked table-cloth. 'When I got back to my office yesterday, I called a friend who is an agent in the local FBI office,' she said. 'And told him what I had. At first, he was, like, *Nah, no way*. That's crazy. Maybe Paul Smith just wandered off, especially if the guy's got Alzheimer's or dementia. But then I sent him the pictures and told him about Javi. I could hear his computer keys clicking, so I knew he was looking into it. A moment later, he asked how I knew about the birthmark, and I told him my source had taken the photo of Paul Smith at the camp. And then had also found "Townsend" in the alley and noticed the birthmark.'

'What did he say?'

'He said, "I need to talk to your source." I told him "nice try." I promised to protect you and that you'd already been shot at and had your studio vandalized. So no go. He said, sort of joking, "Well, you can't blame me for trying, can you?" He called me later and thanked me and said the FBI *was* looking into it. Also, that I could print that information, but that was all he could give me.'

'By now, the FBI probably knows about the driver's license and has put two and two together. They'll be looking for "Paul Smith" at every car rental place, train station, bus station, port, and airport,' I said. 'They don't need to talk to me anymore. Besides, they could get my name and Jack's from the EMT team that showed up in the alley, or even someone at GW who was in the ER that night. That's how Javi knew to get in touch with me.'

Our waiter came by and asked if we were finished with our meal. We said yes, so he took our plates.

'Dessert, ladies?'

'No, thanks,' I said. 'The meal was wonderful, but I think we're both stuffed.'

'But we will have two espressos,' Grace said. 'And could you also bring the bill?'

He nodded and left.

'Sorry to rush you, Soph, but I'd better get back to the office,' she said to me. 'I'm following up with MPD about Javi, now that it's likely his death is related to Townsend. I also have a call in to the director of the funeral home that cremated Paul Smith. They won't have photos either, but maybe someone remembers the unusual birthmark.'

'How'd you find the funeral home?'

'Looked in the back of the St Matthew's bulletin at all the advertisements and figured one of the funeral homes that advertise there was the place Diana Townsend used.'

'And was it?'

She gave me a triumphant look. 'First one I called.'

'Grace Lowe, girl detective.'

She laughed and I said, as casually as I could, 'What did Jack say?'

She looked pained. 'He was pretty short with me. Told me he couldn't possibly discuss anything concerning someone who had come to him in confidence and that I should know better than to ask.'

I took a big gulp of wine and set my glass down. 'I think the Papal Nuncio appointment was Diana's way of paying him back for his support during this whole thing. She recommended him for that position. She bought his silence.'

Grace picked up her glass. 'My God. I didn't think of that. Either.'

'I know.'

'You did.'

'Yes. I told him, too.'

'And?'

'I'm not sure what the status of our relationship is at the moment. I wouldn't say it's particularly good.'

'Oh, Soph. I'm so sorry.'

We finished our espressos and Grace paid the bill. When we were outside on Connecticut Avenue, we made reservations for Ubers.

'Where are you off to?' she said. 'Not going back to the studio?'

'No. Georgetown.'

She gave me a quizzical look because I wasn't usually so opaque. Especially with her. 'OK.'

'It's something to do with my grandfather's estate.'

'You were talking about that the other day. I hope everything's OK.'

'It will be a lot more OK after this meeting. At least I hope it will.'

'That's good. Anything you want to talk about?'

'Yes, but it's a long, complicated story.'

'Come for dinner this Friday. Ben has a poker night with the boys. We can have a girls' night in.'

'All right,' I said. 'And in the meantime, you'll keep me informed of any progress you make on the Townsend story, right?'

She nodded and we exchanged air kisses. My Uber arrived first. As it pulled away from the curb, I looked out the back window. Her phone was clamped to her ear again. Then her car drove up and she got in. I wondered how long it would take for the FBI to track down Associate Justice Everett Townsend. And what would happen next.

On my way to Georgetown, I texted Perry a link to Grace's story and wrote, *Thanks for listening to me the other night.* I hesitated and then added, *We make a good team.* Before I hit send, I added a heart emoji.

He wrote back immediately. *We do.*

I replied. *We always have.*

And got a smiley face in return.


Oriana Neri met me at the front door after my Uber deposited me in front of her Georgetown home. This time, she was wearing a white cashmere boatneck sweater and caramel-colored wool trousers. She took one look at my face and her eyes hardened.

She opened the door wider and said, with the slightest chill in her voice, 'Won't you come in?'

She led me into her sunny, cheerful living room and said, 'Please have a seat.'

I took the sofa and pulled a large envelope out of my purse, placing it on the coffee table. Oriana sat in a wing chair across from me.

'I want to show you something,' I said. 'Actually, several things.'

She steepled her fingers and nodded, still cool. 'All right.'

I took out the prints I'd made of her and the man she said was my grandfather in bed together.

'These are yours,' I said, sliding them over to her.

'I know that,' she said. 'I showed them to you.'

Then I took out the print of Chap in his bathing suit at Coney Island. 'And that is my grandfather. This photo was taken after he left Los Angeles and moved back to New York City. The date stamp on the back, as you can see, is August 12, 1958. A few months after you were married.'

She looked at the photo as if it were toxic and didn't touch it. So I took out the enlarged versions of both photos, laid them on the coffee table facing her, and slid them over. I didn't say anything. Neither did she.

Finally, I pulled out the letter from Ward Evans, the Las Vegas annulment attorney Chappy had contacted, and handed it to her. 'And then there's this.'

She stood up and got her glasses, which were on the fireplace mantel, and sat down again to read the letter. When she was done, she picked up the two photos so she could study them more carefully. I felt as if I were watching the life drain out of her.

After a moment, she took off her glasses, folded them, and set them on her lap. 'Well,' she said. There was an ocean of sadness and regret in her voice. 'Well.'

'The marriage was annulled,' I said, 'whether you knew it or not. And you lied about these photos.'

'Don't judge me harshly.'

'How else am I going to judge you? Look what you tried to do to my family.'

'I had my reasons.'

'Of course you did,' I said, and she flinched at the sarcasm.

'*I am going to lose my home.*' She looked at me, anguished and outraged. 'This house belongs to Gianni's children – his next of kin – since he and I were never legally married. He didn't leave a will, so they inherited everything. They let me stay here for a while, but now they've decided to sell, and I haven't got enough money to buy them out.' There were tears in her eyes.

Wow. What goes around comes around. Her kids were kicking her out of her home because they wanted the money from the sale of the house.

Sam was right. Estate settlements were brutal because they brought out the worst in people – arguments and fights over trivial items and perceived slights. Siblings who never spoke to each other again. Especially if money was involved.

'I'm sorry,' I said. 'My grandfather made out his will without telling my mother he intended to leave his estate to a small arts school in Connecticut with a degree program in photography and photojournalism.'

I didn't see the point in telling her we had just discovered the will was invalid and that Chappy, too, had died intestate, so now everything went to Mom.

'I think you should leave,' she said.

I stood up. 'If you'd managed to sell those photos that you said my grandfather took – fakes – you'd be committing fraud. My family would be caught up in that as well. It's a federal offense, and there are consequences. At least that's not going to happen now. Which I think is a good thing for everyone.'

She was no longer looking at me. I left the room, but as I opened the front door, I heard her start to sob. And in spite of everything she'd tried to do, my heart went out to her.

# TWENTY-TWO

My phone rang as I was in the middle of requesting another Uber. I almost didn't answer until I saw the caller ID. *Russell, Victoria.*

I closed the Uber app and answered the phone. 'Vicki?'

'Sophie. Yes, it's me. How are you?'

'Fine.' She hadn't called just to ask about my health. 'Is everything OK? Is Quill OK . . . the kids?'

'Quill is . . . fine,' she said after a moment. 'The kids are fine. I was wondering if you might have some time to come by for a chat.'

I wanted to say, *About what?* Instead, I said, 'Sure. The next time I'm out at Mayfield visiting Mom and Harry—'

'I'm not at Fernway.' She cut me off. 'I'm at the Georgetown house. I won't be going out there for a while.'

The Russells' Georgetown house was a couple of blocks from where I was right now. I could walk there.

'I could be at your house in ten minutes,' I said. 'I'm in Georgetown.'

'Oh.' I'd caught her off guard. 'Well . . . yes. Ten minutes. See you then.'

She must have found out that I'd been at Fernway the day she was there with Rhett Townsend. Why else would she want to see me?

Had Quill found out as well?

In ten minutes, I'd know.

The Russells' Georgetown home was a gorgeous three-story redbrick Federal mansion that dated from the late 1700s and was on the National Register of Historic Places. I climbed the steps and rang the doorbell.

Vicki opened the door and I almost didn't recognize her. No makeup, haggard face, and utterly, utterly drained. Untucked black silk blouse. Black jeans. Black ballet flats.

I blurted out before she could say anything, 'Are you all right? Has something happened?'

'Please come in,' she said. 'Would you like a drink?'

'No, thank you.'

'I'm having one.'

She hadn't answered my question about whether she was all right. Or maybe she had.

The answer was no.

I followed her into the library, which was just off the foyer. They'd redone it since the last time I was here, years ago. Two book-filled bookcases that flanked the carved wooden fireplace surround and mantel were painted crimson; the rest of the walls were covered with an elaborate red-and-gold paisley wallpaper that made me think of fabrics I'd seen in India. Matching paisley curtains hung in the oversized windows. An oil painting of a fox hunter dressed in his pinks, his horse leaping over a thicket of brush, hung over the fireplace. There were books piled on every table in the room, including the large desk, and, in a corner, an antique wooden trolley table was filled with an impressive assortment of bottles of alcohol.

'Please have a seat,' she said. 'Are you sure you won't have a drink?'

'I'm sure. Thanks, anyway.' I sat in a red leather chair that matched the walls and pulled out a needlepoint pillow that I had just sat on – a sly-looking fox – placing it on the book-filled table next to me.

Vicki topped off her Scotch on the rocks. She took the sofa across from me, kicking off the ballet flats and sitting cross-legged like a kid in front of a campfire.

She drank some Scotch and said, 'I saw you.'

We weren't playing games. 'When?'

'I saw your car leave. Actually, I heard it, so I went out and looked over the gate to the back garden. Not too many people drive a red-and-white Mini.'

'Do you know why I was there?'

'I do now.'

'Quill tried so hard to keep his project a secret. You were never supposed to know.'

'I did, though. At least, I knew *something* was going on. A couple of times when I came home, I smelled your perfume. Just a faint, lingering scent, but I realized a woman had been there while I was gone.' She gave a brittle laugh. 'Do you know what I thought?'

'Oh, God. That Quill was . . .?' I couldn't finish.

'Exactly. That he was having an affair. Which made it so much easier when Rhett came on to me.'

'I see,' I said. 'Quill adores you, Vicki. He'd hang the moon someplace different if you wanted him to.'

She took another deep drink. 'Not right now he wouldn't.' She brushed at her eyes with the palm of her hand.

'I'm so, so sorry. How did he find out about you and Everett Townsend, if you don't mind me asking?'

'He found a used condom under the bed.'

It didn't get more in-your-face explicit than that, short of walking in on them having sex. 'Oh. Are you two going to be able to . . . fix . . . this?'

'I want to,' she said. 'I hope he does.'

'Give him time.'

She nodded and swiped at her eyes again.

'Jack O'Hara and I found Townsend's lookalike, his doppelganger, collapsed on the ground behind his townhouse on Capitol Hill,' I said. 'We were out for a run and took a detour through an alley.'

Her eyes were huge. '*You* found him?'

'His name was Paul Smith. He was an absolute double for Everett Townsend. And he was homeless.'

She folded her lips together and nodded, a look of horror – and some shame – on her face.

'Did you know anything about his plans? What he intended to do?' I asked. 'Did he confide in you, say anything, drop a hint? *Anything?* You were with him that last day.'

'No,' she said. 'Nothing. He didn't tell me a thing. Though he did seem more . . . intense . . . that last night.'

I closed my eyes, not wanting to imagine writhing bodies, tangled sheets, and a marathon session of torrid sex.

'Sophie,' Vicki said. She set her glass down on the coffee table in front of her and leaned forward, hands clasped together and resting on her knees. 'Nobody except you, Quill, and I know that I was with Rhett that day.'

'Well, presumably Rhett knows about me, too.' Talking about him in the present tense because he was still *alive*.

'No. I told him I thought I heard something, but I was mistaken.'

I waited because I knew exactly what was coming next. And she knew I knew it, too.

'No one else needs to know,' she said. 'There's no reason to drag us . . . to drag *Quill* into any of this. We had nothing to do with Rhett's decision to flee. *I* had nothing to do with his decision to flee. So we – *I* – would appreciate it if you didn't say anything to anyone. Keep it our secret. And, hopefully – eventually – we'll all forget about it.'

She was making this about Quill. Please do this for *him*. When it was really about *her*. 'Did Quill ask you to do this? Did he want you to ask me to keep quiet?'

She heard the reproach in my voice and said, subdued, 'No. He did not.'

I nodded. Now I wished I'd asked for a drink.

'So . . . will you?' She was pleading. She was scared.

She didn't want to get dragged into a murder investigation. *Two* murders.

'If your name comes up in some way when the FBI starts looking into this, when they find Everett Townsend – and they will – and you were to be questioned, what are you going to say? You're not going to lie, are you?'

Vicki picked up her glass and shook it so the ice cubes made a tinkling sound. As if something had shattered into pieces. 'No,' she said, 'I am not.'

'Good,' I said. 'I'm not, either.'

'And if they don't ask?'

She was pushing. So many people had secrets they wanted – *needed* – to keep because of what Everett Townsend had done. Including me. The photo Tommy got from the ER nurse.

'If they don't ask, I suspect it's because what happened between the two of you isn't relevant to what he did. In what's going to be a murder investigation.'

Grace's story in the *Trib* had focused strictly on Townsend. There was no mention of Javi's death. Yet. So Vicki wouldn't know about a second murder, and I wasn't about to enlighten her.

'I should go. And I can see myself out.' I stood up. 'I really, really hope you and Quill can work this out, Vicki.'

'Me, too,' she said, and now the tears were rolling down her face.

I booked an Uber to take me home to S Street. On the drive through Georgetown and Dupont Circle, I thought about Oriana and Vicki. Oriana sobbing and Vicki in floods of tears. I thought about Jack and what had happened to our relationship because he'd tried to protect Diana Townsend. And Nick, who had gone to Vienna to meet a woman he loved, another spy, and paid for it with his life.

When I got home, I stripped off my clothes and climbed into bed even though it was only four o'clock in the afternoon.

I slept until the next morning.

The search for Everett Townsend went on for four drama-filled days. It was ended by Townsend himself: he calmly walked into the office of the American Consulate in Halifax, Nova Scotia, and said, 'I'm Justice Everett Townsend. Could you please tell the consul general that I'm here because I believe a few people are looking for me?' to an utterly flabbergasted security guard.

In the meantime, I'd had nonstop calls from Harry and my mother, updating me on the latest developments concerning Chappy's estate. Knox Porter had, of course, been devastated by the news that the will was no longer valid and had immediately driven to Middleburg to talk to Mom, Harry, and Sam. With his lawyer.

To her everlasting credit, my mother told Knox that she intended to honor her father's wishes and that the Connecticut Institute for Fine Arts would be the recipient of the majority of the estate of Charles Lord – with some caveats. First, the IRS lawsuit had to be settled. Then she wanted to establish the Charles T. Lord Foundation, which would oversee the bequests to CIFA. The foundation office would be located in Chap's home – which would also become a museum, a study center, and a gallery where photography by CIFA students as well as professional photographers would be displayed, as my grandfather had intended.

My mother would be the honorary director of the foundation.

I would be the honorary deputy director; when Mom stepped down or retired, I would become the director. We would be involved in the activities of the foundation, but we would also have veto power over any decision or project we believed didn't align with what Chap would have wished. Otherwise, Knox would run things.

Mom had smiled sweetly and said, 'Take it or leave it, but it's a good deal, Knox. You'll still get everything that was stipulated in the handwritten will. I just want some input – and for Sophie to have some as well because of her profession – into matters involving my father. Her grandfather. Our family. I don't imagine the clause giving us veto power will be exercised very often, if at all.'

In the middle of all of this, Darius had called and said, 'What the hell happened? You promised to have dinner with me, and now I think we definitely need to sit down and talk. Knox stopped by when he was in town to see your mother and her lawyer, and we had lunch. He filled me in. The Charles Lord exhibition is still on, of course – right?'

'Of course,' I said. 'Nothing has changed.'

'Good. So when are you free for dinner?'

After everything that had happened, I wasn't ready for a date with Darius. Not now. Besides, my track record with men over the last few weeks was pretty abysmal.

'Would you mind if we just made it coffee and pastries? Our usual?' I asked. 'My life has been kind of upended since I saw you.'

Silence from him and then he said, 'Sure. Coffee and pastries at Tatte. I'm buying. When?'

'I don't know. Can I let you know'

'All right. Call me.'

He hung up, and I had a feeling he was irritated with me. Which was about par for the course these days.

The day Everett Townsend turned himself in at the American Consulate in Halifax, I came home from a run to find a black Ford SUV idling in the alley that led to my studio. A tinted window powered down and Leo Duval said, 'Hop in.'

'I'm all sweaty.'

'Hop in anyway. Townsend turned himself in, as I'm sure you heard.'

I hopped in and said, 'What's going to happen to him now?'

'He's going to jail. There's a laundry list of charges he's facing. Two people are dead, and he's responsible. For openers. Then there's the rest of it.'

'What happened? Why did he do this?'

He drummed his fingers on the steering wheel and stared straight ahead.

'You know but you can't tell me, right?' I reached for the door handle. He could keep his damn secrets. 'I need a shower. Thanks for what you did tell me. I should go.'

'Stay,' he said. 'Don't go.'

I removed my hand, put it in my lap, and waited.

'If it hadn't been for you, we wouldn't have checked into the relationship between Ozupov and Townsend. What I'm going to tell you doesn't leave this car.'

'OK.'

The story was uglier than I could have imagined. Townsend, when he was still a District judge, was on Ozupov's superyacht – not the one he owned now, but still a small ocean liner – for a long weekend free-for-all. Booze, women, drugs, no limits. Townsend fell hard for a young Russian beauty, who was also Ozupov's seventeen-year-old goddaughter, and they had sex. Something happened and the girl told Townsend she was done with him, she was interested in someone younger than he was, and she wanted to walk out. They argued late one night; during their fight, she slipped and fell overboard. Townsend panicked because the girl was gone and it was midnight. He looked down and couldn't see her, didn't hear her. So he decided to keep quiet about what had happened.

'He didn't call anyone? Throw a life ring overboard?' I said. 'He did *nothing*?'

Duval shook his head. 'The next morning, when everyone started looking for her – and couldn't find her – the presumption was there had been an accident. She fell, she was drunk . . . she was high. Ozupov was beside himself with grief.'

'You wouldn't be telling me this story if Townsend had gotten away with what he did.'

'There was a witness,' he said. 'Another girl. One of the stewards on board. She had photographs of the two of them together. She wanted money in return for her silence. So Townsend paid her off and got the photos.'

'But?'

'She showed up. Recently. Older. Broke. In debt. And she still had a few more photos she had held on to. This time, she wanted more than Townsend could afford. So he went to Ozupov and told him the truth,' he said.

'He told a Russian oligarch he was being blackmailed by a former crew member on his yacht. Over the death of his goddaughter. Oh my God.'

'Townsend insisted it was accidental, but Ozupov was furious. Why had Townsend waited so long to tell him about his goddaughter? Why had he allowed this "problem" to fester all these years? Ozupov said he'd "take care of it," and you can guess what that meant.'

'Bye-bye former crew member.'

'No one will ever find her. She's gone.'

*The Russians play for keeps.*

'Ozupov made Townsend change his vote on the Supreme Court case on soft campaign money,' I said. 'Didn't he?'

'Ozupov told Townsend he *owned* him, and Townsend would do whatever he wanted him to do.'

'Which is why he decided to fake his own death and disappear.'

'Yup.'

'You must have someone in Ozupov's inner circle talking to you, or you would never have found out about any of this,' I said.

He didn't answer.

'Will it come out when Townsend is brought back here and starts facing murder charges?'

'I rather doubt it,' he said. 'There's enough to send him to jail for a very long time as it is.'

'No point muddying the waters with two more deaths that would incriminate a philanthropic Russian oligarch?'

He heard my sarcasm. 'We've got bigger fish to fry, and Ozupov is Teflon. Nothing sticks to him. You allocate your resources where you can actually get something done. We haven't got unlimited resources and deep, deep pockets for something like that involving foreign nationals.'

I put my hand on the door handle once again and this time he didn't try to stop me. 'Thank you for telling me this. Maybe we'll see each other again?'

'We might.'

'Goodbye, Leo.' I got out of the car.

'Goodbye, Sophie.'

His car was gone before I even got up the steps to the front door.

# TWENTY-THREE

And then there was one.

I showed up at Gloria House just after five thirty on Saturday because I knew Jack would be saying Mass as usual and I wanted to be there as it let out. He stopped mid-stride when he saw me sitting on one of the benches in the foyer as he walked out of the chapel and prepared to greet the congregation as they left.

I lifted the large fragrant-smelling white paper bag I was carrying and mouthed, '*Chinese.*'

I'd also brought a bottle of red.

He gave me a half-nod and a grave smile. Then he turned his attention to an elderly woman with a walker, leaning down so she could share a confidence with him. When he had finally finished speaking to the last couple in line, he came over to me and held out his hand for the bag. I gave it to him.

'I didn't know you were coming.'

'I didn't know myself. It was sort of spontaneous.'

We walked up the flight of stairs together to his suite. When we were in his sitting room, I said, 'If you open the wine, I'll get our dinner ready. Chopsticks OK?'

'Sure. You know where they are. Top drawer of the cabinet with the booze on it.' He took a look inside the bag and said, 'How many people were you planning to feed?'

'You'll have leftovers for tomorrow night,' I said, 'since the cook takes weekends off. Besides, you'll be hungry in an hour anyway.'

That made him smile. 'Thanks.'

We sat across from each other cross-legged on the floor, using his coffee table as a dinner table. He said grace and then raised his wine glass.

'To what?' he asked.

'I don't know. Let's just drink.' We did and then I said, 'We need to talk about . . . everything, Jack. I don't want this to destroy our friendship.'

He gave me a long, steady look and said, 'Diana is probably going to go to jail.' He started ticking things off on his fingers. 'Felony murder. Obstruction of justice. Accessory after the fact. Destroying evidence. I forget what else there is, but that's enough right there to make sure she goes behind bars. For a long time.'

'How's she doing?'

'Not well.'

'What happened – that you can tell me about? Was she involved from the beginning?'

He shook his head. 'Lord, no. She had no clue what Rhett was planning – until she got to the hospital.'

'But she knew the man in the hospital wasn't her husband, didn't she?'

'She did.'

'So why did she identify Paul Smith as Everett Townsend? And demand that his body be taken to the funeral home immediately? She got a doctor to sign the death certificate and the ME to say he could be cremated. No autopsy. She pitched a fit and got her way.'

'She panicked, Soph. She didn't know what to do, but it was clear the guy lying there on life support was *supposed* to be Rhett. Wearing his clothes, his wedding ring, his watch. He even had his business mobile,' he said. 'Then she heard someone – Javi, obviously – telling a couple of the doctors and the nurses that it wasn't Townsend, that it was someone known as "the Professor."'

'She overheard Javi? Oh God, Jack.' Which meant Diana was probably somehow responsible for his death. 'She told somebody. Right away, too. Because whoever she told followed Javi home from the hospital.'

He laughed, but it was bitter. 'You know who she told? She told *Rhett*.'

'What?'

'I told you she panicked,' he said. 'So she went outside where she had some privacy and called his other phone. His private mobile. It went to voicemail, but she left a message asking him what the hell was going on and telling him it wasn't going to work because there was already someone at the hospital – a young biracial kid – who recognized Paul Smith from the homeless camp.'

'And then Townsend picked up the voicemail – so *he* knew. Rhett Townsend knew what was going on at the hospital,' I said. 'Whoever took care of Paul Smith also took care of Javi? And tried to scare me?'

'Rhett put a lot of criminals behind bars during his years as a judge before he was named to the Supreme Court. You pay someone enough money and they'll whack anyone you want whacked.'

'So Diana ended up being complicit in everything,' I said.

'Look.' He placed both hands on the coffee table and leaned in toward me. 'There but for the grace of God go any of us. One stupid decision, a moment of panic, and good, decent people do things they'd swear on a stack of Bibles they'd never do.'

'It wasn't just one stupid decision. She compounded it with everything she did after that.'

'She felt like she was sinking in quicksand. She didn't know how to get out of it.'

'The truth might have worked. Even if it got her in trouble then, it's nothing compared to the trouble she's in now,' I said. 'Jack, you teach *ethics*. Come on.'

He buried his face in his hands. 'I know,' he said. 'I know.'

'You didn't ask her if she lied, did you?'

He looked up and his eyes were full of heartache and self-recrimination. 'No.'

'You didn't want to know.'

'No.'

'And then she pulled some strings and got you the position at the Papal Nuncio's office.'

'Yes.' He began shredding one of the paper napkins. 'I called a few days ago and said I'd reconsidered and that I needed to concentrate full-time on my teaching.'

I looked him in the eye and said, 'That must have been hard.'

'Not taking the thirty pieces of silver? Even Judas threw them away.'

'Wow. That's harsh.'

'But true. You were right, Soph. I wanted that job. I knew why I probably got it, why she recommended me.'

'You've always been ambitious. Grace has been saying so since high school. I guess I didn't want to see it, but I knew it, too. She says you want it all. Not just a bishop's beanie. A cardinal's beanie. And maybe a position in Rome.'

He finished shredding and focused on shaping the bits of paper into a small white mountain, a sad smile on his face. 'Yeah. Gracie. She saw right through me, even then. That keen journalistic sixth sense.'

'I know. She's good.'

'She is.'

'I'm going away for a while, Soph. I've asked for a leave of absence.'

I sat up. 'Where? For how long? When?'

'A semester. I'll leave in mid-December after I finish teaching for this term.'

'Where are you going? What are you going to do?'

'I don't know where just yet. A retreat somewhere. As for what, I need to do some soul-searching after all this.'

'You are coming back, aren't you?'

'I don't know.'

I caught my breath. If I lost Jack, too . . . 'I would miss you a lot if you don't.'

'You'd be fine, Soph. You're strong.'

I said, with a laugh that nearly turned into a sob, 'Nick went to Vienna to meet with a Russian spy who was his lover because she had some information the CIA wanted. The Russians found out about her, tortured her until she gave up the details of her meeting with him, then assassinated him. And probably her as well.'

I didn't think anything could shock Jack, but I was wrong. His face turned pale. 'I am so, so sorry, Sophie.'

'Please come back from wherever you're going. You were right that I would have been better off if I'd stopped looking for answers about what happened to Nick. You told me that just before we found Paul Smith in the alley. Now I've got closure, but I hate it.'

'What are you going to do about it?' he asked in a gentle voice.

'I guess it's my turn to say I don't know.' I picked up a small white bag and opened it, shaking out the contents. Three fortune cookies. 'We got an extra one. Choose yours. Maybe we'll find some answers.'

'Come on, you don't believe those fortunes, do you? The last one I got said, "If at first you don't succeed, don't take up skydiving."'

I laughed and said, 'These are *quality* fortune cookies.'

He picked up a cookie, broke it open, and pulled out the piece of paper. '"If you look back, you will soon be going that way." Hmm. OK. What's yours?'

I cracked mine open. '"Some things are just too heavy to haul around."'

Our eyes met and we held out our fortunes at the same time. 'We got each other's,' I said.

'We did,' he said and picked up the third fortune cookie. 'I get another turn.'

'You're being greedy, but OK.'

He pulled out the slip of paper. '"He who is not getting better is getting worse."'

'That sounds really profound. I told you those were good fortune cookies.'

'Actually, this one says, "Change is inevitable except for vending machines." What I just said is something Ignatius Loyola said.'

Of course. The saint who founded the Jesuits.

I smiled and said, 'So we both need to work on getting better to avoid getting worse?'

'After these last few days, I've got a lot more work to do than you do. But yes, that's what we need to do.'

'OK,' I said, 'then let's do it.'

# Acknowledgments

I owe thanks to many people who patiently and generously shared their knowledge and expertise in answering all my research questions – often on more than one occasion – as I wrote this book. As always, if it's right they said it; if it's wrong, it's on me.

Grateful thanks to: Hossein Amirsadeghi, Reverend Doctor Peter Barlow, George H. Bosse, III, Jennifer A. Crane, Esq., Dr Alexander de Nesnera, André de Nesnera, Claudia de Nesnera, Rosemarie Forsythe, Daniel J. Hale, Alma Katsu, Lori McLean, Sandi McLean, Scott McLean, Shari Mesh, Peggy O'Neil, Jim Schlett, MPO Jim Smith, Fairfax County Police Department and David Swinson. And thanks once again to Max Katzer for letting me borrow his name.

Special thanks to Doris Warrell, Director of Development and Communications at Street Sense Media in Washington, D.C., for introducing me to Street Sense, the terrific multi-media non-profit that publishes D.C.'s weekly homeless newspaper on which I heavily based Streetwise, my fictitious organization. Street Sense Media is located behind the beautiful Church of the Epiphany on G Street, and I am grateful to Doris for letting me "borrow" their offices. It should also be apparent that the programs Streetwise offers – the newspaper vendor program, case management services and workshops in the creative arts – are not my creation but based on programs and outreach Street Sense offers to the homeless, or to be precise, the unhoused of Washington, D.C.

Thanks as always to Donna Andrews, John Gilstrap, Alan Orloff and Art Taylor, my critique group buddies these last twelve years for insight, comments and other help as I wrote early drafts of this book.

An article from the July 25, 2022 issue of *The New Yorker*, *The Floating World: Secrets of the Superyachts* by Evan Osnos, was particularly helpful in describing the incredible yacht owned by my fictitious billionaire Alexei Ozupov. Also helpful was *Steven Banks vs. Homelessness* by Alex Carp in the February 6, 2022 *New York Times Magazine*; although the piece focused on the homeless problem in New York City, there was much valuable information about the overall issue of homelessness in the U.S.

At Severn House I owe thanks to my terrific editor Rachel Slatter, not only for editing, advice and always being in my corner, but also for overseeing the reprinting of *Multiple Exposure* and *Ghost Image*, the first two Sophie Medina books. Huge thanks as well to Martin Brown, Senior Brand Manager, for unstinting and enthusiastic help and goodwill with publicity and advertising. Thank you to Tina Pietron for shepherding this book through the publication process.

Thanks and love to my indefatigable agent Dominick Abel for more than I can say for the last seventeen years we have been together. And finally, all love, gratitude and a full heart to André de Nesnera, my darling husband of forty years who makes it all worthwhile.